W9-ATF-325

Reading Between the Crimes

Reading Between the Crimes

A JANE DOE BOOK CLUB MYSTERY

Kate Young

CROOKED
LANE

NEW YORK

Published in the United States by Crooked Lane Books, an imprint of The Quick Brown Fox & Company LLC.

Crooked Lane Books and its logo are trademarks of The Quick Brown Fox & Company LLC.

Library of Congress Catalog-in-Publication data available upon request.

ISBN (hardcover): 978-1-64385-742-8
ISBN (ebook): 978-1-64385-743-5

Cover illustration by Mary Ann Lasher

Printed in the United States.

www.crookedlanebooks.com

Crooked Lane Books
34 West 27th St., 10th Floor
New York, NY 10001

First Edition: September 2021

10 9 8 7 6 5 4 3 2 1

To my little sleuth,
this one is for you, baby girl.

Chapter One

The sun was low in the clear blue sky as I locked up the office. I could tell when it set behind the mountain tops, it would be a sight to behold. The beautiful pink and blues blended together behind the shadowed hills made me want to take up photography. If I had the time. Wrapping my scarf around my neck, I stepped back to admire the newly installed sign above the door. The colors were perfect. "Cousins Investigative Services Inc." was displayed in a glossy bold gray-blue outlined in white. The design was tasteful and looked nice against the mixture of concrete and brick. I'd been working for my uncle as a receptionist/PI in training for almost two years now. My uncle had needed a receptionist/secretary after Harriet Wiseman took maternity leave to have baby number three. I'd leaped at the opportunity. Much to the chagrin of my mother. She thought working around her brother, who'd been a detective for sixteen years before retiring to open his own private investigation firm, would only further enhance my fascination with murder and true crime. Something she'd once blamed on the Jane Does, my mystery book club. She'd found the club to be abhorrent and a complete waste of my time. My mother had a difficult time understanding that true crime and unsolved cases got my blood pumping and fueled my desire to work in the investigative field.

And this past year I'd grown into my role. At least I believed I'd learned enough to be useful. Which was a significant win in my book. Mother tended to be more on the old-fashioned side, but recently, she had started to come around to a more modern way of thinking.

With an intake of crisp fall air, I glanced around, admiring the gorgeous hues, reds, golds, and burnt orange leaves as the trees swayed in the breeze in Sweet Mountain's square. Workers were busy stringing lights around the trees' bases and on the awnings of storefronts of our sleepy little town. In a few days, the town would be hosting our annual Octoberfest Pub Crawl, an event my friends and I looked forward to every year.

Strolling down the sidewalk, I took in the place I called home. I'd never wanted to live anywhere else. And a lot of those who did leave seemed to boomerang right back when it came time to settle down and start a family. Sweet Mountain, located forty-five minutes north of Atlanta, was the essence of small-town living, with a vibrant cultural arts community. Creativity flowed from our residents and was embraced by our well-known art museum. Today, local artists set up in the grassy area in the center of the square in our weekly oil painting workshop. They were positions around the covered, lighted, and recently elec-trified open amphitheater that could accommodate up to four hundred people. I wondered who the city had booked to play this year for the pub crawl.

"Hey, Lyla. How's your mom and them?"

I turned to spy a man I recognized as one of Calvin's friends, who had been instructing the crew stringing lights.

I lifted a hand as I groped for his name, which eluded me, and I came up empty. "Doing well. Thank you for asking. You're doing a great job! Everything looks great."

"Thank ya." The small, round man smiled. "Should be lots of fun this year. You're comin', aren't ya?"

"Wouldn't miss it for the world." We exchanged a smile, and as I rounded the corner, a low-sounding woof caused me to stop—a stalky bulldog who came strutting out of the pet store.

"Quiet, Bandit." His owner, sporting a UGA sweatshirt, said. "He isn't dangerous—just likes attention."

I let out a little chuckle as I bent and pet the little guy on the head. He rewarded me with a sloppy lick to the hand. I hadn't realized these dogs were so slobbery. Cute but slobbery. I held my hand away from my body as I rose. The gentleman laughed, and the two carried on toward his car. "Go, Dawgs!"

"Yeah, go Dawgs." I dug through my bag with my clean hand, extracted a couple of tissues and my hand sanitizer, and began cleaning up.

As I strolled toward the coffee shop to pick up an order I'd placed, I spied my friend, Rosa Landry, her arms laden with large boxes from Nobles Coffee Co., stacked atop each other. She spotted me at the exact same time. "Evening, Lyla."

"Hey. I'm surprised to see you. Are those—"

"Yes, they're yours. I was in the coffee shop, and the barista mentioned they had an order for the Jane Does Book Club, since I'm the one who usually picks them up."

"Ah." Tonight, my book club, would be having our monthly meeting. Our club had grown to a dozen consistent members since last year. Our core group of three hosted and scheduled the meetings. Some months, if we had a special speaker like a mystery writer or a Georgia Bureau of Investigation investigator, or we were watching a popular docuseries, we had close to twenty or more in attendance. Utilizing one of the libraries' conference rooms had become a necessity. After we hosted a retired special investigator from Atlanta, who discussed the ins and outs of investigations in reference to John and Jane Does, a special interest to our group, we'd been nameless, oscillating between a couple of ideas. True crime stories always intrigued the club. Because of our deep interest in such cases, it only seemed natural to our founding members that we should be dubbed The Jane Does.

And hosting special guests became infinitely easier when I started dating Special Agent Brad Jones. We met last year while working together on a Jane Doe case—my first case as a PI in training, and it had ignited something in me that solidified my desire to work in the field professionally.

Brad and I had been seeing each other casually for several months now. He was in his late thirties, with thick black hair cut close to his scalp, a sharp nose, and eyes a little closer together than average. He wasn't what you'd call traditionally handsome, but I found him immensely appealing.

"I was just on my way to pick it up." I adjusted my purse and briefcase strap to my other shoulder and took the top box from her.

"I figured." She smiled gratefully. The scent of pumpkin muffins wafted up from the box. My favorites. "But I knew you wouldn't be getting off work till about now, and I thought I'd save you the block walk."

"That was thoughtful, but"—I furrowed my brow, bothered I'd missed the schedule change—"I was under the impression you had to work tonight."

Rosa nodded. "I do. I've got my uniform in the car." Rosa was a Jane Doe club member who felt like she'd always been part of the group. Originally from Baton Rouge, she moved here after her Afghanistan tour and worked as the Sweet Mountain Police Department's desk sergeant. Unlike some of our other new recruits who were sporadic in attendance, she'd gone all-in on day one. Which we'd learned was her personality. She was an all-or-nothing type of gal.

"That was so kind of you. Thank you. I'm parked around the corner." We started for my car.

"No big. It was on my way. I had already put the freshly ground coffee beans and a mixture of tea bags in my car. I'm just across the street."

"Wow. You are on it."

Rosa grinned. "I try. Did you see the new brewery is having their grand opening during the pub crawl?" Rosa motioned over her shoulder with a head bob.

"No! That's excellent." A flurry of activity buzzed around the new microbrewery at the corner of East Cherokee and Bower. They were opening in the newly renovated historical building. Their craft beers are what was missing in our downtown district. We had a thriving retail and restaurant scene, but this would be Sweet Mountains' first brewery.

I put the box on top of the trunk and hit the key fob to unlock the car.

Rosa placed her box in the trunk next to mine. Her rolled-up sleeve exposed a new puffy tattoo on her forearm.

I winced. "That looks painful."

Rosa ran a hand through the shoulder-length dark hair that had fallen down over her left eye. Her thick brows rose as she inspected her new tat. "Nah, it's fine. I just wanted to finish the shading before I met up with friends from my old unit next month. Be right back."

I turned. "Wait a sec. I'll come help." I started to close the trunk.

"No worries. I'll be sitting most of the night; I need the exercise." Rosa trotted to the edge of the street and waited to cross. She called loudly over the street noise. "It's in a manageable crate. I got it."

"Okay." I laughed and watched Rosa trot down the sidewalk. When I turned back, I noticed a man standing in front of Smart Cookie, the shop located next to Cousins Investigative Services. He put his hand above his eyes and seemed to be staring right at me. I glanced behind me and around, thinking perhaps he was just waiting for a friend or partner. But as he pushed his square frames up on higher on his nose, he kept staring. He lifted a hand.

Out of habit and common politeness, I waved back. A grin broke out over the man's face. He kept waving. Weirdo. I decided to ignore him.

Rosa crossed the street with perfect timing, blocking his view of me.

"Something wrong?" She placed the crate of tea and coffee into my trunk.

"No. Some weird guy is over there wav—" The word died in my throat when I glanced back, and he'd gone. "Huh, guess I was wrong, and perhaps he thought I was someone else." I laughed at myself. Sometimes my overactive imagination got away from me.

"Maybe it was one of those dating app things, and he confused you for someone else. I tried once, and the picture of the person they matched me with was not a real likeness. I ran for the hills."

We both had a good laugh about that.

She glanced back down at her tattoo of a dog tag with "Landry" written on it and a number I assumed was her unit. The tag was draped over an American flag.

"I guess you're missing your friends a lot."

She gave me a sad smile. "Yeah, I do." Then she sighed and rolled her sleeve back down. "But I'm really happy with my new friends here too. Though I'm really bummed, I can't go to the meeting tonight. The book rocked. I can't believe I've never read *Crooked House* before." Rosa let out an exaggerated sigh.

It pleased me no end that we'd gained a new bibliophile friend—one who truly understood the love of great literature. Our motto in the Jane Does had always been, "It doesn't matter what you read, just read." Though I must admit, I'm a firm believer that you're missing out if you don't give mysteries a chance.

"It doesn't get any better than Agatha Christie, for sure. And we could have a mini club meeting just for you."

Her face lit up. "Could we?"

I nodded. "Definitely! I'm sure Mel, Amelia, and I could arrange something for you. The three of us never get enough of talking books."

"That'd be great! If everyone agrees, of course."

"Oh, they'll agree." Wine, food, and books on any night was a great time with my core Jane Doe Book Club.

"Terrific."

Speaking of which, my best friend, Melanie Smart, owner of Smart Cookie, popped her head out the door. The bell tinkled a faint sound as the wind blew the pink, blue, and white striped awning below the giant, glossy cookie sign. "Hey, y'all!"

I waved and Rosa said, "Hey, Mel. I'll catch you later, Lyla," before trotting over to her.

The sky began to grow dark, and I realized the time. It was close to six thirty, and we would be kicking off at seven o'clock sharp. "I'll see you at the library, Mel. Have a great day at work, Rosa." They both waved as I slid into the driver's seat.

I parked my car in front of the Sweet Mountain Library. The library was a gorgeous new, three-story, large brick facility located a few blocks from the town square. When it had gone up several years ago, I was pleased that the funding was available to expand the old, drab building we used for decades—and equally delighted that it kept to the style of our town square. The aesthetically pleasing mixture of stone and brick, and lovely large glass windows made it even more enjoyable to spend time in one of my favorite places.

Harper Richardson, one of our studious librarians, had her back turned to me when I entered. She appeared to be on the phone. I planned to sneak by the counter and not disturb her, when I froze, hearing the distress in her tone.

"No, please." Her voice came out strained. "You can't do this to me."

Now I felt like I was eavesdropping and hurried my steps.

"Don't you dare!" Her tone dropped into hostile territory. "I swear to God if you do, you'll be sor—" Harper turned mid-word and spied me just as I passed the counter. She disconnected the call and shoved her phone into the crochet bag she had in her hand.

I waved, my face flushing. "Evening, Harper."

"Evening." She looked downtrodden and shaken; her long strawberry-blonde hair, which was usually wound up in a tight chignon while she worked, appeared a bit messy today. She normally held herself in a reserved yet pleasant manner. She dressed simply, in attractive cuts that flattered her lean, slight frame. She had a penchant for earth-toned tunics, usually accented with long, decorative costume necklaces. Tonight, her sweater looked a little wrinkled, and her neck was absent of a chain.

Harper was a newcomer to Sweet Mountain. Arriving in our town a little over a year and a half ago—and shy as we soon discovered—she hadn't ventured out into the workforce or social clubs until a few months ago. Melanie had invited her to our book club after the two became friends. Harper frequented Smart Cookie weekly. Mel said it took a while to get her to open up, but when she managed to get her to talk, she liked Harper instantly. And after I got to know her, I did too. Harper was caring, helpful, and incredibly sweet-natured. I focused on her little, round face and smiled.

I didn't want to ask about her call, fearing it would be rude. I had no idea whom she'd gotten into such a horrific argument with, and though I was curious, it was clearly none of my business. But I also didn't want to rush away and give her the impression I didn't care to be a listening ear if she needed one. "Busy day?"

Harper's hands moved nervously over the stack of books on the desk. "Fairly usual for a Friday. I had to read to the children during story hour today, since our scheduled staff member didn't show. It's not that I mind, but when you commit to something, not sticking to it affects others, you know?"

I nodded.

She shook her head. "Oh, I did want to mention one thing to you." Her fingers went over the keyboard in front of the computer. "I hate to complain, and this has nothing to do with your account, but your grandmother has three outstanding library books."

"Oh. Have you mentioned it to her?"

Harper inclined her head. "I have and I sent her a text message. She's starting to run up quite a late fee."

"I'll take care of it." Gran had a bad habit of forgetting to turn her books back in. I'd have to go to by my parents' house and get them and return them myself.

"Thanks. That'll be one thing off my mind." She gave me a small smile. I couldn't help but notice that her words didn't exactly match her facial expression. The corner of her mouth kept turning down, and on close examination, her red-rimmed eyes betrayed she'd been crying. I highly doubted it had anything to do with my grandmother or that her phone call was with an employee—or at least I hoped not. If it had been, I'd highly misjudged Harper.

I couldn't help myself. My natural curiosity overrode my senses at times. Besides, politeness was part of my character. You see a friend in need, you act—it's the Southern way. I leaned closer to the desk and lowered my tone. "Are you sure that's all that's bothering you?"

"Yes. You're referring to my eyes." She smiled and emitted a little nervous giggle. "I have allergies. Ragweed is in full bloom this time of year. If I'd known Georgia's allergy season was practically year-round, I might not have moved here." She sniffed and fussed with her hair, smoothing it back.

Either she didn't believe I overheard her conversation or had decided to be in denial. Either way, I respected her privacy and decision not to share. "That's true. Sorry, you have a flare-up." I frowned in what I hoped read sympathy for her ailment and not that I suspected she hid something. She clearly didn't want to discuss it. "Are you staying for the club meeting?"

She gave her head a shake. "I wish I could, but I have a conflict." She placed the books on the cart next to her and paused, glancing up expectantly. "I'm surprised you don't too. I mean, with your mother's charity benefit going on tonight."

"Oh, Mother doesn't expect me to be there. She hosts so many events it would continually tie up my schedule." I smiled.

"That makes sense, I guess. Lyla"—she hesitated—"since we're chatting, could I impose on—" Harper stopped just as the doors opened and in stumbled an elderly woman. "Welcome. Is there anything I can help you with?"

"No, I know where I'm going. Thank you, sweetie." The white-haired lady moseyed on her way.

"Heavens. Listen to me prattling on while your hands are full. Here, let me take the other box." Harper made her way around the counter to help me.

"Thanks."

As I walked beside Harper to the conference room, I could clearly read she struggled with discussing what had her so upset. Her eyes kept skating back to me. I set the box on the back table next to the one Harper had placed and began opening up the boxes and setting out the refreshments. I noticed she hadn't yet left the room.

When her fourth glance lingered, I couldn't help myself. "Harper, hon, I wish you'd talk to me. I hope you know that I'm your friend and you can trust me."

She bit her bottom lip. "I really don't want to impose, and the meeting's about to start."

"We have time." I smiled and hoped for late arrivals. "Please. I'm all ears."

"Um"—she put her fingers to her lips and closed the distance of a few feet between us—"I was wondering if I could ask for a little free advice."

If by "free advice" she meant from my PI job, I was indeed all ears. I couldn't commit to any work without my Uncle Calvin's consent; being the boss and all, he had the final say on every case we took. "Sure. Have a seat and tell me how I can help." I took one of the vacant seats, and she perched on the edge of the one next to me.

Harper leaned closer, her voice edging on a whisper. "If I wanted to find someone, is there somewhere you'd recommend I look? Websites, forums, or whatnot?"

"Are we talking about someone close to you?"

She nodded her head a little too forcefully, and a few strands of hair escaped her bun. "Yes. My aunt. I *really* need to find her."

I studied her for a few moments, and she seemed a little jumpy. She always seemed like the nervous type, but this took it to a whole new level. The old adage Gran used to use, *"ants in her pants,"* came to mind. "How long have you been out of touch?"

"My God!" Laughter drifted into the room, and Mel breezed in with her arms loaded. "I'm so out of shape." She paused when she noticed us. "Lyla, you left your trunk open."

"Oh, I forgot about the coffee and tea." I rose and glanced apologetically toward Harper, who'd hopped up at the same time I had. I mouthed, "One sec."

"Don't worry. Amelia is grabbing it. She got here right after me." Melanie strode across the room. "I'm here bearing cookie confections and espresso fudge from that new little fudge shop on the square. I just can't get enough of that stuff." Melanie, my boisterous, chattering, never-at-a-loss-for-words best friend, brought immense energy to the room. We'd been inseparable since the first day of kindergarten. We'd been through everything together—first loves, first heartbreaks, major family issues, and her divorce. We always had each other's backs, no matter what. Figuratively and quite literally. Not only was her business right next door to Cousins, but my townhouse also backed right up to hers. She got me like no one else.

"Oh, hi, Melanie," Harper said, and took a step away from me. Her eyes kept skirting toward the door. "Rosa with you?" I wondered what that was about. Maybe she thought since Rosa worked for the police department, she could help too.

"No. Rosa has to work. How are you doing, Harper? You haven't been to the shop in a while. I've missed seeing you," Mel said while she began setting out the cookies she'd brought.

"I've been busy." Harper glanced around as if she were looking for an escape. It was so unlike her. Sure, she was usually quieter than the rest of us, but she'd become more vocal as of late. It was almost like she was climbing back into her shell.

"This coffee smells amazing." In strolled Amelia Klein, carrying the crate. She, Mel, and I were the core members of the group. We set every meeting and made sure our social media group remained active. Amelia and her lovely husband, Ethan, were transplants. Born and raised in Maryland, Amelia had been thrilled to find our little group a few years ago after her husband's job brought them to the metro area. She had a tight, curly mix of silver and black hair she'd decided to never color, big chocolate-brown eyes, and a flawless copper-colored complexion.

"Thank you. I got caught up chatting with Harper and forgot I left the coffee and tea in the trunk."

"No problem. I'll have this coffee brewed in a second."

I turned to the side, blocking the other's view. I kept my tone low. "Sorry for the interruption." Harper's wariness made me more concerned about her situation. "Would you like to continue this discussion in the other room?"

"No." Harper smoothed her hair back. "I better go finish up out front. Later, okay?

"Sure." I leaned in, "Are you sure you don't want to have a quick chat?"

"Yes. Quite." Harper glanced down at her watch. "I need to leave a few minutes early, so I can run home and change, and I have a couple of things to button up first." She pivoted around me and out the conference room door as if her hind end was on fire. *Okay, guess she's not ready to talk.*

"Hey, I wanted to run an idea by y'all." I informed my friends about a mini club meeting for Rosa and hoped it would draw attention away from Harper's odd exit. They both agreed, but I could tell it hadn't taken the spotlight off Harper. I busied myself, moving the refreshments around and tidying the table.

Mel furrowed her brow. "What was that about?"

I took a cookie from the box and nibbled it. A few crumbs fell, and I dusted them off my shirt and smoothed the front of my tan slacks. "I'm not quite sure. I wasn't able to get all the facts."

"She looked super stressed." Melanie tucked a blonde curl behind her ear, her eyes full of concern.

Amelia kept glancing around, a dead giveaway that she indeed knew something.

"Well, what did she ask you?" Melanie asked directly.

I studied Amelia as I answered Mel. "She just wanted some advice on how to locate someone. I got the impression she'd lost touch with a relative."

"Such a shame." Amelia shook her head. Her comment sounded casual, but her face told us she knew more than she was letting on.

"Amelia," Mel said. "What do you know?"

My curiosity had also been piqued. I glanced toward the door, hoping Harper wasn't in earshot and thinking we were gossiping about her. "Maybe now's not the time. Others should be arriving soon."

Amelia also seemed concerned; she tiptoed to the door, glanced out, and came back. I supposed the coast was clear.

"Lyla's right about the timing being wrong. And I honestly don't know anything for certain."

"But you know something." Mel narrowed her cool blue eyes. "I can read it all over your face. Harper's our friend. We need to know if something is up."

Amelia pursed her lips. "Fine. Last week Harper asked me about property values in her neighborhood."

Amelia had just recently gotten her real estate license for the state of Georgia. The previous license she'd operated under in Maryland had lapsed, not that she could use it here anyway. Six months ago, she'd decided to jump back in with both feet. She loved the work, and it suited her.

Melanie moved her head from side to side as if she were attempting to pull whatever Amelia was withholding from her mind. "And . . .?" She drew the word out.

Amelia relented. "And she asked me to contact her directly and not her husband, Leonard." She waved her hands. "Then she visited our church a couple of times"—Amelia leaned in—"alone."

I glanced curiously at Amelia. "You think there's trouble in paradise? Maybe that's why she wanted me to help her find the family she lost touch with. She's thinking of moving."

"I don't think her marriage can ever be described as paradise." Amelia rechecked the door. "Okay. This isn't gossip. I'm concerned." Mel and I nodded to show we knew. Then Amelia continued with a sigh, "She stayed over at my house two weeks ago after church. She said Leonard was out of town, and she'd locked herself out of the house."

"Okay."

We all edged a little closer.

Amelia shook her head. "But I don't think he was out of town."

Melanie folded her arms, looking bothered for Harper. "You think they had a huge fight or something, and she didn't want to go home?"

Amelia took a deep breath and nodded. "I didn't at the time, but Ethan said he ran into Leonard at the hardware store and casually mentioned Harper staying over. Leonard had no idea what he was talking about. Ethan said he looked irate."

"I wonder why she hasn't mentioned anything to me about it. She knows I've been through a messy divorce and would be there for her." Melanie looked even more bothered. "I thought we were closer than that."

"She never said anything to me about any marital problems either. I just read between the lines. And you guys know I'm not one to gossip, but I am an excellent listener, and people just seem to open up to me."

That was true.

"Well, that night, after Ethan went to bed, we had a cup of tea and watched Hallmark for a bit. That's when she asked about what she might get for the property." Amelia lowered her voice. "I told her I'd have to look up the comps in the area, and she'd need to have an appraisal."

"That's good of you, Amelia." Melanie patted her shoulder. "I'm glad you were there for her."

Amelia gave Mel a small smile. "While we watched the movie, I sort of got the impression that Leonard has some outlandish ideas."

"Outlandish in what way?" I took another peek toward the door.

We all got impossibly closer, huddling in a little circle.

"Well, she casually mentioned how Leonard would never approve of the outfits the actresses wore." We all shared a wide-eyed glance before Amelia continued. "I didn't pry but simply said a woman should be able to wear whatever she wants. I didn't want to upset her."

Melanie and I nodded our understanding. You had to be careful when broaching sensitive subjects with friends who were struggling.

"I sort of let it drop after that, and things seemed okay. But when I mentioned coming by the property and doing a walk-through, Harper nearly flipped her lid. She told me to forget she'd said anything, and begged me to not say a word to Leonard. Then it slipped out that Leonard likes to be the one to make those sorts of decisions, and she seemed really rattled and said she was tired and went to bed."

"Poor Harper." Melanie shook her head. I could tell she was disgusted with Leonard. "Now that you mention it, she did act oddly the other day when I asked if she wanted to go do some early Christmas shopping at the outlet mall in Woodstock with me. She said she mainly shopped online and Leonard liked to approve her clothing choices." Mel pointed at me. "Remember, Lyla? I told you about it."

"Yeah, I do, now that you mention it." That did sound troubling. "And her home life is rather unconventional." Harper told us during one of our meetings that Leonard's sister-in-law from a previous marriage lived with them as well as his daughter. It struck us all as odd that his ex-sister-in-law would want to live with him, especially after he'd remarried. She also alluded to other relatives staying with them off and on. But we couldn't get her to elaborate further.

"I don't like the idea of Harper suffering in silence. Nobody has the right to put restrictions on another human. Especially based on their gender. It's barbaric." Melanie sounded affronted.

I nodded emphatically. "You're not wrong," I said quietly. "But still, we don't know all the facts, and we wouldn't want to upset Harper further."

"Lyla's right." Amelia glanced toward the door before continuing. "And I'm not judging people's choices either. Anyone is entitled to believe and live as they see fit. All I'm saying is we should keep our ears open. And be there for her when and if she reaches out."

"Definitely," we all agreed, and I glanced toward the door, hating the thought of Harper being trapped in a bad marriage.

"Maybe I should go find her before she leaves. Make sure she knows she can call me day or night."

As if summoned, Harper peeked into the room. Mel, Amelia, I had shared a worried glance.

Harper's face was flushed, and we feared she'd overheard us. "I'm leaving now. Do you all have everything you need?"

I smiled, wanting to convey that we only discussed her situation because we cared. "Yes, thank you. If you want to chat a little later, you have my number, right?"

Amelia went over to the table, took one of the cups, and filled it with coffee from the large urn. Mel followed suit, allowing Harper the freedom to give me a single nod.

Harper was an attractive young woman. I'd place her a little younger than my thirty-two years. Why she married a man who was old enough to be her father and with the temperament of an old mule was beyond me. But, like Amelia mentioned, who were we to judge? Perhaps we were way off base, and she was feeling homesick. At times, and since our heads were filled with mysteries and true crime, and all of us indulged our imaginations, we could get carried away with our theories.

What wasn't a theory was that she'd requested my help, and I'd do my best for her. From previous experience with clients, I was aware of the precarious situation it placed the helper in. And if this was indeed a marital dispute, you had to tread lightly if the couple reconciled and suddenly they need someone to blame other than themselves.

"Thanks. I really appreciate it." She smiled, a little nervously, I noticed. "Sorry about earlier. It's been a day. I'll call you."

She waved to my fellow club members, who smiled and waved back. "Okay, well, I'm gone. I put the sign up on the desk to direct club members and visitors to this room."

"You want a cup of coffee and a muffin to go?" Amelia held out a cup and a large pumpkin streusel muffin.

"Yes, you should definitely take one." I was about to grab the muffin and cup of coffee from Amelia to pass to Harper when my bony little Gran, vigorously waving both hands, appeared in the doorway.

"Hey! It's my fellow Jane Does!" She scooted by Harper, giving her a little pat on the shoulder in passing.

"What are you doing here?" Gran didn't drive, and I glanced through the now empty doorway, searching for Mother or Daddy.

"Your daddy dropped me off on the way to pick up his dry cleaning." She embraced me, and I bent down to hug her back. "Apparently they got his suit mixed up with someone else's. I didn't want to miss the club meeting."

Gran technically was not a member of our book club, though she insisted she was since she'd attended a couple of times. Not that Gran ever read the club pick. She just enjoyed the wine, coffee, and snacks while pestering everyone with questions. Gran's a real card, and my club loved her colorful personality.

"Nice to see you again, Mrs. Moody." Amelia smiled and gave Gran a little hug. It warmed my heart that my group had adopted her as one of their own.

"Pfft. I told you gals to call me Daisy." She gave Amelia a pat on the cheek. And waved at Mel. "Ooh! Melanie, I like your outfit. Those jeans with holes in it look cool." Gran glanced down at her own outfit, knit gray pants and a peach sweater. "I'm going to take a pair of scissors to a couple pairs of jeans when I get home." I imagined my Gran in stylish jeans with her bony knees sticking out of the holes in her pants. Mother would kill me, but I'd take her to buy her a pair.

"Rock on, Daisy!" Melanie flashed a wide smile.

"Yeah, rock on!" Gran pumped her fist. "I'll go grab some snacks. You get us a good seat before everyone else arrives."

Chapter Two

This month was my turn to lead the discussion. Not everyone wanted to be placed on the roster, which was fine by the rest of us. *Crooked House* had been my suggestion for our classic month, and I was pleased to see not a single vacant seat. My opening went well, and the group embarked into lively discussion mode. I glanced around the room, full of smiling and engaged faces. Everyone took turns to eagerly share their opinions.

"What I want to know," Melanie said, leaning forward, "and maybe I was a little jaded since I'd been babysitting my cousin's twins while reading this novel—and for the record, the two are normally angels, but the experience taught me that children turn into demon spawn when they miss their naps."

Laughter spread through the group, and there were a couple of nods from a few of the mothers in the group who understood the importance of naptime.

Melanie continued, gesticulating wildly. "But am I the only who thought when digitalis-laced hot cocoa was used as a murder weapon that the little brat is the killer?"

"I did!" A visitor to the group waved. "But then second guessed myself."

"Who? What brat?" Gran glanced around the room as she devoured a giant chocolate chip muffin. Gran was a sweetaholic.

"I didn't. I went in a different direction with it. And Edith doing what she did was way out there," Amelia added. "She could have gotten the girl help or something. That would have been showing love, and I believed she did indeed love the child."

Murmurs of agreement from the left side of the room drew attention.

"Yes, but from what I gathered—and this is a completely subjective opinion—the prevailing idea during the time Agatha Christie wrote the novel was that insanity was an inherited trait, and therefore it's the dominating theme of *Crooked House*. I think the notes and journals provided evidence of the insanity, leading us to believe that perhaps Edith struggled with it herself. In her other works, Christie seems to use the theory that people are simply born, well, *wrong*." I crossed my legs. "Obviously, times have progressed, and now it isn't popular to subscribe to such notions."

Amelia scratched her head as she considered. "Yes, you're right. I can completely see that now. I was looking at it from a modern-day perspective."

"Wow. I agree with Aggie Christie here. Some people are born wrong. I'm going to have to read that book." Gran grinned and started clapping.

"It's Agatha, and yes, you definitely should read it."

"Well, I'm calling her Aggie. I'm sure all her friends did." Gran bobbed her head around gleefully. "And I feel confident that she and I would've been besties." She tapped her head. "Same mental thought processes."

I laughed and stood. "I guess that concludes this month's meeting. We'll have a poll up online for everyone on next month's club pick, so don't forget to check the web page." I clasped my hands together. "And thank y'all so much for coming."

Darkness had fallen after I cleaned up, and I drove Gran home. My grandmother lived with my parents. She had moved in with us when I was thirteen, after my grandfather suffered a heart attack. She'd been a coconspirator in all my endeavors and remained one of my best friends. Mother always said she deserved a medal for allowing Daddy's mom to move in with them. I always thought Gran was the prize. She certainly added a missing element with her presence.

I turned onto Mother and Daddy's street. They still lived in the same house I grew up in on a street of pre–Civil War, plantation-style houses. The structures were designed to handle Georgia's hot, humid weather, with large, deep front porches that boasted comfortable rocking chairs and whirling ceiling fans.

"You know," I said, glancing over at Gran, "the idea is to read each month's pick before the meeting."

"I like being surprised." Gran flipped on the overhead light to read from the back of the book. "Amelia loaned me her copy of *Crooked House*, since I misplaced mine. Oh, this does sound like a doozy of a mystery. Listen to this. The Leonideses are one big happy family living in a sprawling, ramshackle mansion. That is until the head of the household, Aristide—" Gran hooted. "What kind of name is Aristide?"

I laughed. "It probably wasn't so unusual when the novel was written."

She wiped her eyes, still chuckling. "Aristide is murdered with a fatal barbiturate injection." Gran sucked in a breath for effect before she continued reading. "Suspicion naturally falls on the old man's young widow, fifty years his junior. But the murderer has reckoned without the tenacity of Charles Hayward, fiancé of the late millionaire's granddaughter."

"I've read it, remember?" I shook my head, smiling.

"Yeah, yeah. Well, now that I know what I'm in for, I'm going to read it." She shoved the book into her handbag.

"Speaking of books, Harper said you were late with returning your library books again."

"I know, I know. I keep forgetting. I left them in your parents' new library. Maybe you can take them back for me. I won't be getting by there this week." She grinned over at me, knowing I would.

"I didn't know they finished with the construction of the library." My parents were doing a little renovation on the main floor of their home.

"Yep. It's a beaut too." Gran undid her seatbelt as I slowed down.

"Wait for me to park."

"I'm all right." She leaned forward, bracing her hand on the dashboard. "Looks like the event is still going on."

The street lined with cars forced me to park a couple houses down from my childhood home. "Wow. Mother must be raising a fortune tonight."

"She usually does." Gran and I shut the doors.

Gran tied the thin tie of her green sweater tighter around her waist. "I'd hoped this would be over by the time we got home. I'm not really in the mood to walk around and mingle with all those plastic smiles and stuffed shirts."

I looped my arm through hers when we met at the front of the car. "Oh, it won't be so bad."

Lights from a white van flew out of Mrs. Ross's driveway, nearly blinded us when they pulled on the street. Upon seeing us, the driver blew the horn. A squeak left Gran's lips as I wrapped my arms around her and hauled us out of the road, and we nearly tumbled onto the sidewalk.

"My God!" I stomped back onto the road. "You maniac!" I yelled at the van as it took the corner on two wheels. I could make out "Hewitt Electric" on the side as it passed by the streetlight.

Gran came huffing up beside me. "We should report that nut!"

"I will be." I put my hands on my hips.

Gran stretched, and I hoped I hadn't hurt her when I pulled her from the road. "Things like that really get the old blood pumping."

"Me too, but not in a good way. You okay?"

"Fine," she said but rubbed her lower back. When she saw me notice, she looped her arm back through mine. "I'd rather have an ache in the back then end up in the morgue."

She had a point there. "What was an electric van doing on the street tonight, anyway? I can't imagine an attendee showing up in a work van."

"I guess the Ross's are finally getting electricity run to their carriage house. I think they got jealous with everything your mom is doing to the house. She'll be hearing from me, and I'm sure she'll tear the company a new one." Our boots made clip-clop sounds as we walked up the lit bricked driveway, a necessity with the low-lit streetlights. "I love the Jane Does—they're so fun. They're more my crowd."

I couldn't help the smile that creased my lips as I squeezed her. "They love you almost as much as I do."

We mounted the brick steps Mother had lined with gorgeous burnt-red mums and crossed through the large white pillars on the brightly lit front porch. Gran let out a little groan of dread.

With my hand on the doorknob, I grinned. "There is a silver lining. Think of all that delicious catered food in the kitchen. You know how Mother always orders too much."

Gran's periwinkle-blue eyes brightened. "See." She pinched my cheek. "You get me."

The cacophony in the house hit us the second we crossed the threshold. My parents' first floor had high ceilings, an enormous foyer, and a sweeping open stairway. Sound traveled easily in this house.

The house was indeed packed. People mingled everywhere. The flow in the home was conducive to entertaining. We never used the grand dining room or the formal living room unless she hosted an event or holiday. The chef's dream of a kitchen, located at the back of the house, would be utilized by caterers. Adjacent to the kitchen was the place everyone gathered, the great room. The floor-to-ceiling windows brought in abundant light in the daytime. Off to the left of the great room, Daddy had converted the library into his home office, which he always kept locked. His office is what had inspired the addition of the new library. I'd been overjoyed when Mother had allowed my input in the design. The room had been the maid's quarters when the house was first constructed. With the expansion, it would open up onto a new patio with flagstone floors and a nice-size pavilion that included seating around the new outdoor fireplace. It would be a wonderful space when completed, and a perfect place to entertain. I was eager to get back there and have a look at the progress.

A woman came down the staircase from the second floor and waved to her date. I supposed she used one of the six en suite upstairs restrooms. The house, furnished in custom-designed furniture to mirror something out of *Southern Living* magazine, gleamed.

The mood lighting was perfect, and people everywhere were dressed for a black-tie event. The caterers were still weaving from room to room with trays of champagne and tapas. Clearly, to Gran's chagrin, the event showed no signs of slowing. I'd get her settled, exchange a few pleasantries with my parents, and whomever else they'd insist I greet, then make my excuses and leave.

Threading my way through the throngs of guests with Gran by my side, I waved and greeted as required. "Yes, I'm disappointed I had a schedule conflict. Am I proud of my mother and her efforts to raise money for the children's wing at Daddy's hospital? Exceedingly proud. No, I'm afraid I won't be able to stay for the silent auction. Yes, I still work for my uncle. No, I'm not married yet."

"Y'all take care. Lyla and I are expected in the kitchen." Gran saved me from a sweaty-handed gentleman who didn't understand societal personal space rules.

"Thanks."

"No prob, honey bun. I've got a major sweet-tooth craving. I hope Frances ordered those delicious double-chocolate truffles that were so popular at the literacy function."

As if conjured by Gran's words, Mother strolled slowly through the dining room, chatting with a woman. She looked gorgeous in her navy evening gown. My mother fits in this setting like a hand in a perfectly tailored Bespoke glove. Frances Moody enjoyed volunteer work like no one else on the planet. Not having a job outside the home since marrying my father, she'd dedicated her life to helping those less fortunate.

As I moved through the formal living room, I stopped in my tracks when I spied our chief of police, Quinn Daniels. It wasn't my old boyfriend who caught my attention; it was who he had hanging on his arm. Piper Sanchez, who graduated with Melanie and me, was the reason for his attendance, I suspected. I stepped to the corner, fighting the notion that I was behaving creepily and watched as she gazed up into Quinn's face, batting her long, dark eyelashes.

There was no doubt when it came to Piper's beauty. She was average height but way above average in figure, face, and hair. She had large brown eyes rimmed with those super long lashes, gorgeous olive skin, and a head of thick dark curls I'd kill for. The fact that men couldn't resist her charms is what had gotten her the position of lead reporter at *Sweet Mountain Gazette*. Although I'm sure she'd made her career advancements with her tenacious personality and sharp wit, her beauty did seem to help folks spill their guts at the crook of her little finger. Well, perhaps I exaggerated a bit, but that's how it seemed to me.

"Where'd you go? Oh." Gran leaned against my shoulder. "Looky who Quinn is snuggled up with."

"I wonder how long they've been seeing each other and what her angle is?" She'd never shown the least bit of interest in Quinn before.

"Don't know, but that gal changes men like the rest of us change our socks."

I let out a little chuckle that drew Quinn's gaze. With a little wave, which he returned, I followed Gran down the long hallway. On the way, I glanced up at Mother's latest artwork acquisitions from local artists. The piece was tastefully lit from above with a satin picture light. Exquisite.

"I've got to run to the bathroom. Be back in a sec. If they're getting low on those truffles, grab me some." Gran scooted away at my nod.

To my left, among the low chatter, I thought I heard sniffling. Pausing, I turned to see Harper wiping her eyes with a tissue. She stood there with the man I'd seen outside of Smart Cookie earlier this evening. He was tall, on the lean, wiry side, with dark brown hair and black square frames perched high on his nose. He ducked his head and spoke to Harper just as Mother came back into the room.

Who is this guy?

My pulse sped up. The way the man was regarding my mother had me on edge. His jaw was set, his head leaning forward in an aggressive posture. Her head jerked back slightly at something he'd said. Harper had stood there, watching the exchange with an odd expression on her face.

I did not like this one bit. No one spoke to my mother in that manner. After two advancing steps forward where I'd intended to give that man a piece of my mind, Mother whipped something back at the man. Wow. He nodded, his face relaxing, and then moved on.

Harper nearly crumbled when he left the room. Mother pulled her off to the side with a grip on her arm. I moved inconspicuously to the left, to keep an eye on them, and caught an exchange between them that I couldn't make out. I could tell by Harper's reaction that she took comfort in whatever my mother had said. She wiped her nose and tucked the tissue into her palm before giving Mother a single nod and lifting her chin almost resolutely.

And I had no idea what to make of what I'd just witnessed.

Harper noticed me after Mother, who hadn't seen me, left the room. "Hey." She glanced down at the bodice of her long black satin dress, where there was a damp spot. "I thought you weren't coming tonight." She began furiously wiping at it. Satin wasn't a forgiving fabric.

"I'm just dropping my grandmother home." I focused on her trembling fingers. "Are you okay?"

"Yes—no. Yes." Harper glanced up and gave me a shaky smile. "Leonard and I had a tiff. He's been avoiding me all evening." She glanced around in search of her husband. Amelia's concern seemed warranted now.

"Who was—" I started to inquire about the gentlemen she and Mother had confronted, when Harper interjected. "I'm sorry, Lyla, but I really must find Leonard."

"Oh, okay. I can hang around if you want to continue our earlier discussion. I'd love to help you if I can."

"Thank you." She nodded and rushed past me.

I felt unsure of what to do next. On the one hand, I wanted to let Harper come to me in her own time. On the other, if her marriage was a dangerous one, I felt I should do more. I just didn't quite know what. At the very least, I would be conducting a background check on Leonard Richardson.

"Lyla, come on." Gran pulled me from my thoughts as she swooped next to me and took me by the hand. "We're going to miss all the truffles." She dragged me through the dining room, where I craned my neck around, hoping to see where that man went. I also wanted to know who he was and what his business was here. And why in the world he'd been waving at me earlier.

Gran shoved us through the kitchen door. "Jackpot." She began moving around the workers and filling her plate with cream puffs, chocolate-dipped fruit, and her beloved chocolate truffles.

I propped myself up at the end on the island, still thinking about Harper, the mystery man, and mother. I wondered if a domestic issue had occurred here, and as the hostess, Mother had gotten involved. Though, that didn't quite jive—especially with local law enforcement present. It must not have been a severe altercation if one had occurred. Perhaps, like me, Mother saw Harper in tears and stepped in then. I'd hang around for a bit and do a little digging.

I tried to stay out of the way as the caterers did their jobs, pouring myself a glass of red wine and nibbling on the truffle Gran insisted I try.

Staff began weaving around us after Gran had eaten her third truffle.

"Sorry," I said to the man, trying not to glare at Gran behind him. "We'll get out of your hair. Come on, Gran. I want to check out the new library anyway."

"Yeah, and grab those library books," Gran reminded me.

We moved down the small hallway off the kitchen and past the back staircase toward the open door of the new addition. "Someone left the door open. No one should be going in there since it leads to the back patio. It could be dangerous since it's still being remodeled." My parents had torn down their old screened-in porch, and the area could be hazardous.

"We'll close it back off after you have a gander inside," Gran said while wiping her mouth with a cocktail napkin. "Brr. Do you feel a chill? I bet one of the crew left the back doors open. I'll fix that."

The sound of breaking glass caused me to pause and take a couple steps backward. Then rough scolding came next. I glanced into the kitchen to see crystal shards all over the floor and the head chef chewing out one of the employees, who had started crying. Bless her heart.

I shook my head and went back to Gran, who stood frozen at the doorway of the library. When I saw how pale her face was and that the desserts she'd been eating now lay in a heap at her feet, I almost panicked.

"Oh God." I rushed beside her and gripped her shoulders to peer down into her face, fearing the beginnings of a stroke. "Gran, speak to me!"

Her lips were moving slowly, and I started to yell for help when she managed to utter in a gasp, "So . . . someone's in th-there."

"What?"

Slowly she lifted a finger, pointing to the floor in the low-lit space. A candle burned on the small table beside the large floor-to-ceiling mahogany bookshelf. I squinted and took a step to move in front of her, stumbling over something in the doorway. A man's sizeable brown loafer lay on the at my feet. With my knuckles, I slowly pushed the second French door further open. A little shriek left my lips. A body lay awkwardly in front of the

Chesterfield and next to the fireplace. I spied bloody footprints leading out the open doors to the patio. "Oh no!"

Gasps came from behind me.

I glanced back to where Gran stood and saw the catering staff huddled together in shock. They'd seen more than a glimpse. "Everyone remain calm. You," I said, pointing to the dark-blonde woman in a black chef's coat, "dial nine-one-one." I barely recognized my own voice. Her head jerked forward a couple of times as she pulled a cell phone from her pocket. "You," I said to the man beside her, "don't allow anyone else in here. And Gran"—she stared, blinking—"get Quinn and Daddy. Now!"

Gran managed to regain her faculties and moved with a purpose. Having received my CPR certificate six months ago, I felt compelled to check on the man. Stepping over the long red blood smear, I moved closer to the body. Wind whipped into the room from the open back door, slamming one of the other doors. I jumped. He must have hurt himself and become disoriented going in the opposite direction of the door.

Puddles of vomit lay where he'd collapsed. I did my best to step around them. The pungent odor of sickness and blood forced me to put an arm over my nose and mouth. My head spun. *Get it together, Lyla. Bend down and check for a pulse.*

There was a long scratch where his watch should have been on his left arm that lay over half of his face. I also noticed his suit jacket appeared torn, and one of my mother's brass candlesticks lay beside the man, the base covered in blood. Spots flew across my vision as I stooped down next to the body. Shaking my head, I focused on my task and checked for a pulse. *Nothing.*

I took a shuddering breath and lifted my gaze. Something caught my eye in the man's hand. It might have belonged to his attacker. A tie or rope? When my eyes moved to the man's face, I gasped. The man's eyes were frozen wide open, his mouth agape.

Oh God! I stumbled backward until my back hit the brick fireplace. My ears were buzzing, and my stomach lurched. *Oh no—no no no!* Leonard Richardson was dead.

Chapter Three

Police and medical personnel swarmed the house. The guests were corralled into the family room, formal living room, and front porch. Mother, Gran, and I were standing in the hallway off the kitchen. Mother stood stoically, her gaze distant. Soft murmurs echoed down the hallway from the formal living room. The indelible image of Leonard Richardson, I feared, would be permanently imprinted on my brain. I'd seen crime scene photos before, but I'd never in my life experienced what I had in my parents' library. I was no expert in forensics, but from my assessment, the man had been robbed and beaten to death. Perhaps his head injury had caused him to be sick. I wondered how in the world no one heard the struggle that obviously took place so close to the kitchen. It made no sense. My stomach twisted into knots as Gran and I held hands.

The audible intake of breath from the other room sounded ominous. We turned to see a gurney with the deceased zipped up in a black bag. I took Mother's hand with my free one as we heard a wail that sounded a lot like Harper from the other room. My heart ached.

"That poor girl. Poor, poor, girl," Mother whispered. "I just can't believe this is actually happening. We have the entire hospital board here tonight as well as some of the most prestigious families in the South." It sounded like a bit of a stretch to me, but I understood her meaning, and I did indeed feel horrible something like this had happened. Mostly for Harper, but also for my mother. She detested any kind of scandal or drama. *"Here in the South, behind closed doors, every family had their secrets, and decent people aren't interested in airing their dirty laundry to the world or catching wind of other folks who do."* I'd heard that all my life. Well, the macabre scene out back would be gossiped about for ages.

"I'm still in shock." I tried to keep my tone even. After I said it, I wished I'd hadn't. This wasn't about my discovery. The Richardson family had experienced a tragic ordeal and a great loss. I echoed Mother's sentiments on Harper. That poor girl. Her husband had died. No, had not just *died*—but been *murdered*. I swallowed.

Mother turned and stared me straight in the face, her expression an odd one. "You had a club meeting tonight?"

"Yes, ma'am. But Daddy dropped Gran off at the meeting, and I drove her home."

"Oh . . ." Mother swallowed. "And you said you're the one who found Leonard Richardson?"

This conversation seemed strange because she knew I'd found Leonard. She must also be experiencing shock. "Yes, ma'am. I went back to see the library and to retrieve some library books for Gran."

She blinked a few times and gazed off. Gran raised her brows as she glanced from me to my mother. My shoulders rose, then slumped. There was so much here I couldn't explain. Who could have had the gall to attack the elderly man with all these people present? I knew most of the people here. Well, almost everyone. My mind went back to the man I'd seen earlier.

I cleared my throat and asked Mother about him.

She put her hand on her forehead. "I spoke to a lot of people tonight."

"The tall, thin one with dark brown hair. He was in the dining room with you and Harper."

"Oh, right. Now I remember." Her brow furrowed. "I think he's a writer of some kind. He's researching a story. Some of our guests were complaining about his incessant questions. I kindly explained this wasn't the appropriate time to have such discussions."

"Research? What story?"

Mother shook her head. "Lyla Jane, I don't know if I'm coming or going right now." Her bottom lip quivered.

"It's okay, Frances, dear." Gran patted her arm reassuringly.

"Oh, Moth—" I hated to see my mother cry.

"I need to powder my nose," she interrupted, and abruptly left the room.

"Bless her heart. She doesn't have a strong constitution like you and me." Gran moved closer to me and wrapped her arm around my waist, hugging me tightly. "It's a good thing she didn't find the body. We'll have to help Frances through this."

I nodded. "I agree and we will." I kissed the top of my grandmother's head. Gran knew as well as I that my mother and Uncle Calvin had a tragic past. Something relating to their childhood. She didn't speak about it often, and though I've asked over the years for her to confide in me, Mother insisted that neither my uncle nor she desired to relive those days, especially not through my eyes. I'd respected their wishes, as had Gran. I tried not to let it bother me that she didn't feel comfortable confiding in me.

"I can't b-believe this is ac-actually happening." Harper's sobs brought me out of my reverie. I glanced up as she came around the corner and rushed straight for me. Gran moved aside, and I froze as Harper threw her arms around me.

"I'm sorry. So very sorry." I hugged her tightly. I didn't try to tell her everything would be okay. Nothing would be okay for a long time.

She wiped her face and moved between Gran and me. "Did he look . . . did he look as if he suffered?"

My gaze skidded around the room as I tried to formulate an appropriate answer. I needed to choose my words wisely, not wanting to say anything wounding. "I, uh, I don't think so."

Harper nodded and seemed to take some solace in my words. Though how, I hadn't a clue. "They said he was robbed. Robbed! Someone took his watch, wallet, and wedding ring."

"Who said that?" Gran asked.

"The police." Harper glanced between Gran and me. "They asked me about his watch and wedding band and if he had his wallet on him."

"My God!" Gran shook her head.

Harper took in a shuddering breath. "It's horrifying, and they wouldn't let me see him before t-t-taking him away."

"It's good that you didn't. Leonard wouldn't want you to see him that way." I gave her arm a squeeze.

She dabbed her face and nodded. "I guess you're right. It's just that I said some awful th-things to my Leonard tonight. We had a fight, and it got nasty. And now I'll never be able to apologize. He died with anger and pain in his heart because of me." She gave me a slight frown as she said, "I did love him."

We stood there, the three of us, for some time, all around us the sound of people barking orders and officials rushing here and there. Sniffles and sobs from the grieving widow. Gran murmuring condolences while I stood silently; my thoughts were in a tumult.

A large man in plainclothes, with smooth amber-brown skin and a shiny bald head filled the front doorway. He turned and spoke to an officer before moving through the room as if he owned the place. His commanding presence seemed obvious to everyone as they shrank back and parted to allow him to pass. *Detective*, I instantly thought. All the other police officers were in their navy-blue uniforms except for Quinn, who'd been dressed in a suit. He advanced toward us, and I noticed the gold shield clipped to his belt—definitely a detective.

"Chief Daniels," his gravelly baritone voice called down the hallway. So low and deep that I wouldn't be surprised if the booming tone rattled the floors beneath my feet. My head swung around to see Quinn moving toward the man with a serious expression. He didn't seem to recognize him.

"Detective Battle?"

A clipped nod. "Crime scene?" the man asked tersely.

"One minute." Quinn disappeared, and I wondered where he'd gone. The detective gazed around at the people, who took notice of his scrutiny. Heads were swiveling back and forth, and whispers were audible.

"Okay, you can come through." Quinn's voice brought me out of my contemplation.

The detective's eyes met mine as he strolled past. Sharp, intelligent eyes regarded me. Was he wondering where I fit in all of this? Everyone he came in contact with would be a suspect in the homicide. And rightfully so.

"This is a . . . a nightmare. Things just got so messed up." Harper's words pulled my attention away from where the detective had gone to view the scene. She dug through the clutch attached to her wrist, looking for a tissue. I fixated on the simple little black wristlet. Something about it eased my concerns, and I couldn't pick out what or why. I let out a slow, controlled breath.

"I'm sure he knew you loved him," I heard Gran say to reassure Harper.

"Of course. Everyone argues." I tried to focus on consoling her, but my mind raced with scenarios. One thing was certain. Whatever had happened, this situation would alter her life forever.

Harper shook her head; her face looked red and blotchy. "You don't understand. I told him I was leaving him, that I couldn't take the life anymore. I don't know how I can go on now."

"It's going to be all right, honey." Gran patted her shoulder. "Lyla's right. Couples argue, and some marriages don't work out. You can't own everything. Let's deal with one thing at a time. Sweetie, this is a lot."

"Right. One thing at a time." I stared at my Gran and smiled in awe of her clarity. Those were wise words. "You'll get through this. We'll help you. And whoever did this will be brought to justice."

Harper stood back and stared at us through watery eyes. "That means so much to me." She took us both by the hand and squeezed. "I've felt so alone for so long."

Gran patted her hand before Harper released ours. "Well, you're not alone now, sugar."

Harper wiped the tear tracks from her face, and we stood in silence for what felt like an eternity. I kept glancing back toward the restroom, hoping Mother was coping okay.

"This the widow?" the detective's voice boomed, and both Harper and I jumped. Quinn and the detective appeared in the doorway. I bet everyone around him lived and worked on pins and needles.

"Yes. Harper Richardson." Quinn stood to the left of the detective.

The detective nodded toward me. "And you're the one who discovered the body?"

I opened my mouth, but Quinn answered for me. "Yes. Her name is Lyla Moody. This is her parents' house."

"Well, technically, Quinn." Gran lifted her hand and waved it. "I thought I saw someone in there first. I didn't know who it was, though. My eyesight isn't the greatest. Then Lyla here went in to see if she could help the poor man. God rest his soul."

"You two stay put," Detective Battle said to Gran and Harper before pointing to me. "And you come with me."

"Okay." I followed the large man back into the kitchen. He dug a pair of blue booties out of a box on the island and handed me a pair. "I'm going to need you to put these on and walk me through it. Step by step. You understand?"

"Yes, I do," I said numbly. Everyone in this room wore the blue shoe coverings and thin disposable Tyvek suits to prevent contamination of the scene. I dutifully slipped the booties over my shoes and followed him into the little hallway to the library, now cordoned off with crime scene tape. Seeing the outline where Leonard Richardson's body had been had my head spinning a little, and I braced my hand on the wall.

"You need a sip of water or something first?"

"No." This couldn't be over fast enough. I stood up and slowly walked into the room. I described, in as much detail as I could recall, what I saw and how Gran had behaved, pointing to the melted truffles on the floor. I left nothing out. "After I instructed a caterer to dial nine-one-one, I sent Gran to go alert Quinn."

"Chief Daniels and your father?"

I nodded. "That's when I walked in here to see if"—I swallowed—"Leonard was still alive. I stumbled back when I s-saw he was, um, deceased, and slid down that fireplace there." I pointed.

"Did you touch the body?"

"Yes." I met his gaze directly. "I checked for a pulse."

"Nothing else?"

I shook my head.

"Can you describe the body?"

I stared at him for another moment and took another deep breath.

The detective put a hand on my shoulder and bent to peer into my face. Not many men I came in contact with towered that much over me. "I understand this is difficult," he began softly, "but it's imperative for me to know exactly how you found the body."

The body. Slowly I forced my head to bob. "Okay." I swallowed again and turned back toward where Leonard Richardson had been, clearing my throat. "He was on his back, with his arm slung over the left side of his face. His arm was scratched here."

I pointed to my own arm, to show where his watch was missing. "I noticed because a stream of blood trailed down onto his face." I took in a shaky breath. "His jacket was torn, and he had something in his hand." I felt my brows draw together as I struggled with how to describe it. "A rope or maybe a hoodie strap. I'm not sure. But I am positive he had it gripped in his hand. And the candlestick was there." I pointed to a spot on the floor. "The base was covered in blood."

His eyes sharpened. "Candlestick?"

I nodded slowly. "Yes. It matched this one." I pointed to the one on the mahogany mantle above the fireplace.

"You're positive you saw a candlestick?"

Was I? Yes. "I'm absolutely positive. My boot hit against the heavy brass as I kneeled next to the body.

"Thank you, Miss Moody. I'll need you to hang around a bit longer. We'll need to speak again."

"Oh. okay."

Chapter Four

I left the room in a hurry, with the detective right behind me. I could almost feel his energy. Strong. Eager. Alert. I forced myself not to glance back at him. Harper and Gran stared in my direction when they noticed me returning. He had quick quiet words with Quinn, and neither of the men looked happy. An ominous feeling took up residence in my midsection.

"Mrs. Richardson," Detective Battle said softly when he and Quinn concluded their dialog, and I felt better about him showing kindness to her. At least he was treating her with respect, as the grieving widow. "If you wouldn't mind coming with me, please."

Harper glanced from me to Gran. We both nodded in encouragement for her to go. She'd have to do this on her own. There was no way they'd let us accompany her, not being related to her in any way. In fact, I'm not sure they'd let us even if we were part of her family.

As Harper followed the detective out of the room, the weight of the situation overtook me. Fully aware of the heinous crime committed here and how I hoped they'd find the culprit swiftly. Gran moved closer to me and whispered, "How'd it go?"

"Fine. The detective just wanted me to recount what I saw." I didn't feel like going into it all.

"I wonder why they don't haul us all down to the police station to question us, like in the movies? Any one of us could have killed that man." Gran wasn't a fool. Although she hadn't seen the condition of the body, nor had I described it to her in detail, what she had witnessed had been enough.

"Technically, that isn't accurate. Neither you nor I were here when Mr. Richardson was attacked."

"Everyone else was. Even James will be suspected." Gran looked worried about that.

"Daddy will be questioned, but I doubt the police will seriously suspect him. I do find it surprising that the catering staff didn't see anything before we arrived."

"Yeah, that is odd. I bet one of them did it."

"Shh." I shook my head. "Let's not start throwing blame around." I didn't want us to be overheard and rumors to begin to spread.

"Well, I can't help wonderin'. And I bet they'll drag to the police station whoever they narrow down as suspects." Gran moved aside to allow a woman and her husband to pass by us. She was really obsessed with the idea of people being forced down to the police station.

I pursed my lips. "Maybe. For now, I just think it's probably easier to speak to us all here to start with. Even with the blatant foul play, it's standard procedure to speak to the witnesses right away. The first forty-eight hours are crucial to any investigation.

People have a tendency to forget valuable pieces of information as time passes."

Gran nodded, gazing around. "Wow. You've learned a lot working for Calvin."

She was right: I had. I'd gleaned a wealth of information regarding police procedures and the law. I'd also learned that what made Uncle Calvin and me different was that at Cousins Investigative Services, we weren't constrained by some of the legalities imposed on law enforcement."

"So, let's see. One of these people is probably the killer." Gran narrowed her eyes and scoped out the people in view.

I rubbed my forehead. "The probability is high that the culprit was in attendance at some point during the evening. Probably fled the scene shortly after the attack. With blood spatter like I saw, it would be impossible to keep your clothes clean. And the scene certainly didn't appear to be premeditated. Or the killer is here and managed to sneak out and change clothes, then returned to the event so as to not be suspected. That's what I'd do."

"Hmm. Yeah, that'd be smart. I'd do that too. See that woman there?" Gran pointed down the hallway, to a short, stocky woman with wispy snow-white hair coiled at the top of her head, who was whispering to a much younger brunette. They both looked to be in a bit of shock. Pale and unsure of where to look.

I covered her finger with my hand and pushed it back onto her lap. "Don't point at Leonard's family."

"Yeah, we don't want to tip them off that they're suspects." Gran turned to the side. "Isn't it weird that Edna, the sister-in-law of Leonard's first wife, still lives with him?"

"Yeah, I know it isn't the norm. I've seen Edna around town on occasion, but I've never seen Leonard's daughter up close." I felt awful for the grieving Richardson family.

"No, it ain't normal. The woman never married. Never even dated, I heard. She could've killed him. Maybe she's just been biding her time."

Edna looked older than Gran and didn't look strong enough to kill a fly. "Please don't go around saying things like that."

"Hush. I'm being quiet. Or"—Gran glanced around as if in search of someone—"well, I don't see him here, but his son should be a suspect."

I sighed. "Why should Leonard's son be considered a suspect?"

"Well, I hate to be a gossip"—Gran loved to gossip—"but what happened to Leonard made me think about it, something I heard the other day. Sally Anne said that Leonard's only son has a thing for Harper. And the way she heard it, they sneak off for a pickle-tickle from time to time."

"Eww, Gran."

She shrugged. "Just what I heard."

"This is not the time."

"Okay, okay. I just thought since we needed to talk about everything while it's fresh, it might be a good idea to explore options." Gran pulled a napkin from her purse and began eating a truffle. She hadn't been so shaken up that she didn't sneak back and grab another handful of her favorite treats and hide them in her bag.

She held it out to me. There was no way I could eat anything at the moment. "No, thanks." My head swam with thoughts. I couldn't get what Harper had said to the person over the phone out of my head. *"Don't you dare. You'll be sorry."* I wondered if she'd been speaking to her husband then, and that's one of the things she'd referenced regretting. I couldn't imagine her pain.

"Too bad your honey isn't here." Gran ate her truffle. "He'd sure be a help to us."

"He's working on a big case at the moment. I won't see him until date night at the Klein's with Mel and her new fella." Brad, "my honey" as Gran referred to him, was deep into a case. Both our jobs kept us busy, and the fact that we both understood how important the other's work was gave our relationship stability. Neither of us was in any hurry to speed things along, and Brad respected my choices and career. That my parents and Gran seemed to genuinely like Brad made the relationship all the better. Honestly, it was difficult not to like Brad when he set his mind to winning you over. Gran was right, though; Brad would find it difficult to stand idly. I was eager to discuss this with him.

"Oh, who's little Mel seeing these days?" Gran sounded keenly interested. She loved hearing about who "her girls," as she referred to Mel and me, were having fun with.

"Mel is going out with Wyatt Hanson."

Gran waggled her penciled-in eyebrows. "Oh . . . he's a looker. Just like his father was before he lost his hair and gained all that weight."

"Gran!" I shook my head at my grandmother in a chastising fashion.

Quinn waved in my direction, and I started to walk toward him. "No. I need Mrs. Moody." I gave Gran's hand a squeeze as Quinn nodded toward the detective who had joined us.

"Mrs. Moody, this is Detective Battle—if you wouldn't mind going with him." Quinn made the introductions.

Detective Battle extended a hand toward Gran and gently shook hers as he smiled. "I just have a few questions for you."

"Sure." Gran nodded her head but swallowed. She looked nervous, and I felt helpless.

"I'll accompany her." I took her hand when he released his grip.

"No." Detective Battle said.

I met his gaze, indignation filling my body. "Why?"

Before he could utter another word, in stalked my daddy with his longtime attorney, William Greene. "Chief Daniels, my mother and the rest of the Moody family will be glad to sit down with you and the detective here with our family attorney present."

"Chief." Mr. Greene nodded to Quinn. "Detective," he said by way of greeting to Detective Battle. "Which would you care to begin with? Perhaps, in the interest of time, we could all sit down together. I could even bring in the lady of the house, and we could get this whole thing wrapped up in a nice bow for you."

Detective Battle stared at Mr. Greene and then focused on Daddy. "Is there a reason you believe your family needs representation?"

"Yes," Daddy answered firmly. "When it comes to dealing with law enforcement, it always benefits everyone involved to have someone in the field of law mediate." My daddy was a firm believer in utilizing his right to have an attorney present no matter the circumstances.

"You have a lot of people here, Detective. That's an awful lot of interviews to conduct. I'm only here to streamline things and be helpful." Mr. Greene met the detective's stare with unwavering self-assurance. How I envied that ability.

"I'm aware of how to conduct an investigation. I'll begin with Mrs. Moody." Apparently, Detective Battle didn't care to be told how to do his job. He'd all but glowered at Mr. Greene. But we were drawing attention, and the detective relented, "Mr. Moody may accompany her."

"Very well. I believe Mr. Moody has agreed to make his office available for interviews."

After I watched my father lead the way to his office, I stood there, staring up into Quinn's frustrated face. "Daddy is only trying to protect his family."

Quinn kept his tone low. "I understand that, and I'm trying to find out what happened to Leonard Richardson."

"You sound irritated. This detective seemed upset when I described the scene."

"What do you mean?" His cool blue eyes narrowed. "He said nothing to me."

I shrugged. Obviously I was mistaken. "Nothing. I guess I'm just not accustomed to dealing with someone like him."

"He's good at his job, and he knows it." His lip curled ever so slightly, and I wondered why he'd called the guy in if he had misgivings about him. So, the man's prowess wasn't exactly in question. Quinn had problems with the size of his ego.

I glanced around, feeling much better knowing I'd been mistaken about my concerns with the candlestick. I cleared my throat as I spied Piper Sanchez with her phone to her ear, and that tall, thin man next to her doing the same. "Um, Quinn?"

He ran his hand over the back of his neck. "Yeah?"

He tensed slightly when I took his arm and leaned in closer. From his open expression, I assumed it was more out of surprise than apprehension to my closeness. "I don't want to start anything, and if you're seeing Piper, I think that's great. But have the two of you discussed how you'll handle the conflict of your jobs?"

"What?" Quinn's eyes narrowed again.

I briefly pointed in Piper's direction. "She might be on the phone with her editor as we speak. The story will be everywhere in the morning."

His head whipped around just in time to see Piper slip out the front door.

"Oh hell, and that writer is with her." He started to bolt, but I kept my hand on his arm; he glanced down at me. His eyes were hot with anger, not directed toward me, I could tell.

Mother had been right. "What kind of writer?"

"Mystery, I think. He blew into town last week. He's been pestering people all over about town secrets for a book he's writing." He scowled. "I told Piper not to bring him. He came into the police station twice, chatting up Sergeant Landry." Quinn's lips thinned into a white line. "I've got to go."

"What book?" I dropped my hand as he rushed after Piper. I wondered why Rosa hadn't mentioned him before the book club meeting. I bet that guy was glad he decided to show up here. He had some new material now. Small-town murder. He could spin this so many ways.

Mother sidled up to me, and I jumped. "Where's Quinn going?" She sounded weary.

I put my hand over my thumping heart. "To make a faulty attempt at stopping Piper from running a story." I turned to her. "Are you okay?"

She nodded. Her emerald-green eyes were bloodshot as she tucked a caramel-brown curl behind her ear. "Have you seen your father?"

"He went with Gran and Mr. Greene. She's being interviewed."

"They're letting your father stay with her?"

"Yeah." I nodded. "Mr. Greene is a powerful force."

"That's good. I need to speak with you alone." She leaned in. "Come with me."

"Where?"

She took my hand, guiding me to the upstairs hallway and away from the prying eyes of others.

"Lyla, honey, listen to me. We don't have much time. I'm so sorry you found that man."

I search my mother's big, round eyes. "I'm okay. Don't worry about me."

"I can't help it. Something like this . . ." She hugged me close and rubbed my back in a soothing fashion. I froze. My mother wasn't the most affectionate person. She'd never showered me with lots of hugs in my childhood. In fact, she detested effusive behavior and said so. She loved me—I knew that—but she wanted me strong, and for some reason she felt too much coddling resulted in the opposite effect.

She whispered, "I'm going to ask you to do something for me, and it's going to sound insane."

My stomach lurched, but I said, "Of course."

"Don't mention anything you overhead Harper say at the public library."

"What?" My blood ran cold.

"She told me she approached you about locating a family member and that perhaps you overhead her having a rather heated discussion on the phone."

Okay. Harper had suspected I might have caught bits of a sensitive conversation. *"You'll be sorry."*

"Lyla."

I pulled back, shaking my head. "I hear you but don't understand what you're asking."

"You need to understand that her marriage with Leonard Richardson was a situation the police would never be able to understand."

"What do you mean?" A shiver traveled up my spine. "Mother, lots of people get stuck in bad marriages."

My mother emphatically shook her head. "No. Not like this."

"I can't withhold information. It'll come out anyway. And I'm sure if Harper just tells the detective how unhappy she was, and is honest, he'll clear her as a suspect." Even as the words left my lips, I knew she believed me to be naive. Still, I always thought the truth would prevail. I had to believe it would.

"Honey, you know that isn't true. You of all people know that sometimes things don't work out."

Me of all people? What in God's name was going on here? Harper's declaration of a troubled marriage, her rage at the library, some writer poking around, a murder, and now Mother's request had my head spinning. *Why would she be behaving this way if she doesn't know something?* I had to ask. I whispered so low I could barely hear the words: "Did Harper kill him?"

"Frances, Lyla, are you both up here?" Daddy called from the stairs, unable to see Mother and me tucked away in the shadow.

Mother's tone, barely above a whisper, matched mine as she replied, "Do you honestly believe that young woman could hurt anyone, let alone kill them?"

"No."

Mother grabbed my forearms and her gaze bore holes through mine. Her tone dripped with contempt when she spoke next. "That man doesn't deserve our sympathy." My bones chilled. I'd never seen this side of my mother before.

"But—"

Mother leaned her forehead against mine. "Do I have your word?"

Terror gripped me. "Yes . . ." I cleared my throat. "Yes, Mother."

She dropped her arms and squared her shoulders. "We're in here, James."

Who are you? I stared at her back.

Chapter Five

Close to eleven, the rest of the guests gave their contact information to the officers and were sent home. I, being the one who had discovered the body, had been asked to stay. Now, I sat across from the detective in the dining room. William Green sat next to me. I'd already given my statement more than once on the record, answering the questions regarding where I'd been before reaching my parents' house, whom I'd seen at the library, and everywhere I'd gone afterward. I'd told him how Harper had seemed before she left for the day. I didn't lie. Couldn't. I told them she'd been upset about a staff member not showing up for work. And how she seemed stressed with having to perform two jobs. However, I did omit the overheard conversation. I walked him back again through my discovery and felt positive both Gran's and the caterer's versions would corroborate mine. I repressed my need to ask questions regarding their statements.

"What made you venture into that part of the house, Miss Moody?" Detective Battle asked again.

"Miss Moody has already answered that question, Detective Battle." Mr. Greene leaned back in the high back chair. "And it's getting late."

"I realize the late hour, and I'm affording the Moodys a courtesy by giving their statements here. I could easily move this to the police department."

How disappointed Gran must be with his decision to keep us all here. "It's fine." I shivered despite the warmth in the house—the aftereffects of shock, which I'd become accustomed to quickly. "I don't mind answering again. Like I said, before our club meeting, Harper mentioned that Gran had incurred some late fees for overdue library books. Gran mentioned to me that she'd left the books in the new addition. Plus, I'd been eager to see the finished product. The event was still underway, but we didn't dress for the occasion, and it became clear we were in the way of the caterer's, so I decided to check it out."

"That's when you saw him?"

I nodded and swallowed as the image raced back to my mind's eye. "Yes. Gran didn't look well standing right outside the door of the library, and when I discovered that she indeed hadn't had a stroke, I turned to investigate what had freaked her out." I took a breath. "And because I was concerned that he might only be injured and needing help; I went inside to see if there was anything I could do. I'm CPR trained." My shoulders slumped forward as the weight of fatigue settled into my weary bones.

"You went inside the room before or after you instructed the caterer to dial nine-one-one?" Detective Battle asked.

"After."

"Were any of the catering staff missing at that time? Did anyone seem unusually nervous or behave strangely beforehand?"

I furrowed my brow at the new questions he'd just thrown my way. "How would I know if anyone would be missing? Ask the head chef. And the only disruptive behavior I witnessed was when the head chef chewed out one of the servers for breaking a crystal glass."

He scribbled down something onto his little pad.

"After you went inside the room, did you immediately recognize the victim as your friend's husband?"

I shook my head slowly. "No. I hadn't spent that much time around Mr. Richardson. And it was only when I"—I paused, swallowing a sip of water—"got closer that I managed an identification. His, um, profile had been altered."

He maintained eye contact while I exhaled.

"You say you haven't spent much time with Mr. Richardson. What about his wife, Harper?"

I let out a weary sigh. "Yes. She's a friend of our group. Harper recently joined the Jane Does." When his eyebrows rose to his nonexistent hairline, I explained, "The Jane Does is a book club. We read true crime, mystery, and thrillers. Harper joined a few months ago, but her attendance is sporadic at best. Before that, I saw her whenever our group would meet at the library."

"Has she ever mentioned trouble with her husband to you or anyone in your club?"

Warning bells. I cocked my head to the side as if I really needed to ponder the question.

"In my experience, ladies tend to talk a lot when they're in large groups," he pressed.

"Excuse me, Detective Battle," Mr. Greene rose. "I need to use the facilities. We'll pause the interview."

Detective Battle tapped the recording app on his phone.

I studied him the same way he was studying me. "Surely you don't think Harper is guilty?"

"I don't know what to think. You mentioned earlier that you saw a"—he glanced down at his pad—"brass candlestick. It's funny, because no one else seems to recall the item being in the room."

I sat up straighter. "What?"

He opened his mouth and then paused, moving his hands together in a praying fashion before tapping his index fingers to his lips. "We should wait for your attorney before discussing this any further."

I put my hand on the table. "Hold on. You mean Quinn and the other uniformed officers didn't see it? Or just the other eyewitnesses?"

"You want to continue without your attorney?"

"I want to discuss this now. You can turn your little recorder on after he gets back." I patted the table with my fingertips.

"Very well." He glanced back down at his pad. "It seems either you imagined the candlestick—"

My eyes went wide. "I didn't."

"Well, we don't have it in evidence, and I don't have another single statement that mentions it being in the room or missing from it."

Suddenly, my bravado vanished and was replaced with confusion and fear. Had someone snuck into the room and removed it from the crime scene? Perhaps the guilty party? Mother's words came back to me: *That man doesn't deserve our sympathy.*

I didn't believe for a single minute that my mother could be involved. But would she interfere for the sake of what she perceived as justice?

"Do you have a theory?" he said, baiting me.

I couldn't sit here silently for very long or he'd ask more questions. Questions that I feared might lead to my conversation with my mother. It wasn't completely outlandish to believe we might've been overheard. I didn't think we had been. Still, it wasn't worth the risk. I sat up a little straighter and glanced around. "Not a theory. I have my observations."

He folded his big hands together and placed them on the table. "Such as?"

"I have no explanations regarding the candlestick. And I could almost swear that I saw it. Now you've given me pause." I chewed on my bottom lip and wished to God I hadn't opened my mouth without Mr. Greene. I was such an idiot. I persevered. "I understand your need to press me now. The amount of blood around the body would rule out a lot of potential suspects, and a desire for a speedy apprehension forces such behavior on your part."

"Rule out suspects like your friend, Harper?"

"Yes. Her dress was spotless." I raised my hand. "And before you say she might have changed clothes, it would have drawn attention if she'd shown up in one gown only to leave in another. Women notice other women's dresses." I didn't want to continue to think about my mother. Still her plea kept circling in my mind. Then a thought occurred to me. "Don't you find it odd that before I arrived, no one else noticed anything?"

"I do." He nodded, and I leaned forward.

"He was sick—he vomited. Perhaps he went through the library to pop outside to get some air and—"

"And?" the detective prompted.

I shrugged. "And maybe there's more to this than meets the eye."

Mr. Greene cleared his throat from the doorway, and my face flushed.

"Why would you say that?"

I glanced back at my father's lawyer, who sighed. He did not look happy with me. "You may continue, Detective. Nothing she said while I was out of the room is admissible."

The detective turned the recording app back on and asked me the question again.

"I don't know." I sat back against the chair. "His shoe was off. It was the shoe that gave me the sense of foreboding first. It's weird. That's all."

"Interesting observations. That's why you sent your grand-mother after Chief Daniels?" This time his tone was gentler. And I felt as if he were laying a trap.

"Yes."

"Your mother said Harper spent a lot of the evening with her."

I shook my head and said with all honesty, "I wouldn't know about that. It makes sense. Harper's what you would categorize as an introverted personality. Mother would have wanted her to feel welcome and comfortable here."

"Meaning she keeps to herself?"

"Yes, mostly. I mean, she participated a little more each time during our book club meetings, but nothing personal ever." I coughed and took another sip of water. "Excuse me."

I placed the glass back on the table. "She isn't the type to discuss her troubles. At least not with me." I held my breath, hoping he wouldn't delve deeper into that particular line of questioning. I did not want to lie to this man. *Did not.* Nothing good ever came from lying to law enforcement. But I also wanted to keep my promise to my mother—now more than ever—though I wished I'd pressed her for more answers. Her request spoke volumes regarding her connection to this case, or maybe she just pitied Harper. Still, I didn't want her to compromise herself or an investigation out of some misguided loyalty. And I had no idea how I was going to deal with any of this. Yet.

"What's your line of work?" The detective leaned forward, and I got the distinct impression he leaned in for the kill.

I crossed my legs as my stomach did a flip-flop. "I work for Cousins Investigative Services."

The detective scrutinized me with his intense dark gaze. "That's the private investigation firm owned by Calvin Cousins?"

Did he think I would cover up a crime? Or perhaps was guilty? "Yes."

"You're working with GBI Jones on the Interstate Eighty-five cold cases?" He'd done his homework on me—and fast for this time of night.

I folded my hands on the table, mimicking his posture. "Our office does work with the Georgia Bureau of Investigation on cases here and there. When we can."

"That would mean that you're familiar with police procedures." He sat back against the chair, looking so relaxed.

Uh-oh. I met his gaze, lifting my chin and then leaned back. "Some. Surely you aren't implying that—"

Mr. Greene covered my hands with his and squeezed. "Okay, detective. I believe that's enough for tonight. If you need to speak to my clients again, you know where to reach me."

The detective rose. "You do know not to leave the state, correct?"

He's just trying to rattle me. To see if I'm hiding anything. Lord, help me. I am hiding something. I pushed up from the table, standing. "I have no intention of going anywhere. Goodnight, Detective."

Chapter Six

When I crawled into bed in the wee hours of the morning, my mind whirled with thoughts. I reached over and unplugged my cell from the charger and called Brad. It went straight to voicemail. "Hey, it's just me. Um, something happened tonight." I told his voicemail the condensed version of what had transpired. I figured I'd get more detailed when we spoke next. We had out date night scheduled at Amelia's, and I could fill him in beforehand. When I disconnected the call, I felt better. I lay there, staring at my ceiling and beginning to second-guess myself. Had I really seen the candlestick? When I'd asked Mother before leaving the house, she said she didn't recall it ever being in the room. And Gran said she never notices such things. How could I be the only one to have seen it? I tossed and turned and tried some deep breathing exercises. I needed to get a few hours of sleep. I closed my eyes and waited.

* * *

Late Saturday, I woke to my phone ringing. Melanie was calling to announce she was outside my front door, because I'd neglected to hear her pounding. She stomped over from her identical fifteen-hundred-square-foot, two-story, cookie-cutter, white-washed brick townhouse that had the same open floor plan: a living room, a kitchen, and a dining room on the main floor, and a bedroom and bath on the second floor. It wasn't my dream home or anything, but it was comfortable and close to work.

"Why are you beating my door down?" I asked as I swung the door open. "I thought you had my spare key."

"Not since you had your locks changed." She waltzed past me. "I spoke to Harper this morning. She told me she asked you to come by."

I yawned as my current predicament came whirling back to my mind—the events of yesterday and then Harper calling me at seven this morning, asking me to come over.

I scrubbed my face with my hands. My eyes felt like there was sandpaper under my lids. "Sorry. Yes, Harper called and asked me to come by and have a chat."

Melanie slung her purse onto one of my bar stools. "She said the police mentioned something about cause of death to her."

I felt my brow furrow. "Poor thing. Harper didn't mention that to me. I guess she must have received the call between the time she spoke with me and when she called you." I tied my robe together. "And it was probably the preliminary report. Nothing official yet. But from the condition of the body, I guess it was cut and dry for the coroner. Did she say if they had any suspects?"

"No." Mel shook her head. "I can't even imagine the night-mare she's living through." We both sighed and gave a commis-erating head shake. "Anyway, before Harper told me about your meeting, I suggested bringing by some food so she wouldn't have to worry about cooking. She seemed to like the idea and said she wouldn't mind if we all just came together. I already called Amelia, and she'll meet us here after her last showing today."

Since Harper didn't have any family close by, I could see her wanting friends near, but it did surprise me that she didn't wish for some privacy during our conversation, because she came off as such a private person. And I'd gotten the impression she had something serious to discuss with me. Maybe she'd decided that the desire to be surrounded by friends outweighed her privacy needs. I could see that.

"Wow, you do look wiped. Your eyes look awful." Mel's meticulously groomed brow wrinkled with concern.

"Thanks, Mel." I patted my puffy eyes.

"Sorry, I didn't mean it the way it came out. I shouldn't have woken you the way I did. I should have considered how tired you were. After I did my shopping, I assumed you were up and ready to go."

I swatted the air. "It's fine. I should have been up." I yawned yet again. "I need a strong cup of coffee before I can go into this again or go anywhere. Is Wyatt coming with you to Amelia's tonight?"

Mel smiled a little. "Yes. I don't want to talk too much about it just yet. You know how superstitious I am, and it might jinx the relationship."

I laughed. "Okay. You let me know when the planets align just right, and we can chat about it." I made the universal sign for crazy just to mess with her. Mel was one of a kind.

"Stop!" she scolded, but she laughed along with me. "You said that the detective wanted to go over your statement again. Why?"

I put a pod into my Keurig and hit the button for a strong brew. "I found the body. That's the way these types of investigations work. And Mel, if you'd seen Leonard." I shivered. "All I can say is that anyone with eyes could see his death was no accident. And the more I think about it, the more the robbery angle bothers me." Last night, the indelible image of Mr. Richardson had haunted my dreams. In one frightful nightmare, the man had even sat up and started talking to me. I shivered at the memory while I waited for the coffee to finish brewing.

"So now you think somebody didn't rob him?"

"No, someone robbed him. But if there was some petty thief in attendance, why wouldn't he rob other people besides Leonard? Robbing just one guy—I don't believe it would be worth the risk."

"Unless it was some drug addict. They lash out like that."

I cocked my head to the side. "I think someone in such a desperate state, one that would bring the person to attack a man, whether he was an addict or not, would have stood out in that crowd. I mean, I could be wrong, but I'd think the desperation would show in some form. There has to be more to it. Like maybe the robbery simply covered up the real motive."

Melanie kept shaking her head at the bar. "Crazy. When you first told me, I could tell this rattled you. I mean, it would have rattled me." She lifted both hands. "And I'm not discounting the fact that the murder took place in your childhood home, but later, I thought it probably affected you even more because of Harper." Mel tilted her head, considering. "Now, I see this has really got a grip on you for all those reasons plus the mystery of the case."

I sipped from my mug. Mel knew me well. And even I hadn't considered all that. "You hit the nail on the head. It does have to do with Harper and that it happened in my childhood home, not to mention the ripple effect it will have in our community."

Mel shivered. "Well, it goes without saying, I'm here for you. Harper didn't sound like she's gotten much sleep either. I don't think she's even slept more than a couple hours in total."

"I'm not sure I'd be able to sleep in her position either." I turned with my mug in hand. I'd been surprised when I'd received her call earlier today. She'd insisted that I come by, and her tone told me how desperate she felt. In her place, I probably wouldn't know what to do. What worried me was that she mentioned speaking with my mother before she called me. Originally, after Mother's insistence that I should keep silent, a move entirely out of character for her, I feared the worst. Now what I feared more was that she might be getting sucked into a situation she didn't understand. Not that I'd mention any of this to Mel. Yet.

Mel studied me, rubbing her temples. "Hmm. Okay. Now I'm processing this. Just saying, if this was just a robbery, crazier things have happened, but no one else saw anything?"

"Not to my knowledge. And since I'm the one who found the body, it appears not. But I agree; somebody would have had to. The struggle would have drawn attention. The man was just lying there dead when Gran and I showed up. Everyone kept going on about their business. I won't describe the scene since it's someone we both knew. No one should have images like that in their head."

"I appreciate your discretion. But since you believe it's more than a robbery, you're worried about Harper."

I nodded.

Mel's gaze sharpened. "Okay. Well, I'm going to lay this out here. Harper told me she and her husband argued beforehand. Not at your mom's, but before they left the house. And he avoided her at the event."

I nodded again. "Harper mentioned that to me and Gran too." I raised my brows and added, "Right after."

Mel scrunched up her face. "The police aren't going to like that. She'd have to know that, right?"

"Of course, but it would be nearly impossible for her to be involved in the crime directly. The . . . um, the scene made that fact evident. Not that the police won't run down other options concerning where she theoretically could be. It's good that she does seem to be avoiding being seen in public right now. She mentioned taking a leave from work. Though I wonder if she shouldn't be requesting a consultation with an attorney just to be on the safe side."

"Mm-hmm." Mel went to my refrigerator and got a bottle of water. "We should mention that to her. She isn't popular with *his* family. You know, the Richardson family."

"I got that impression too. The aunt and daughter were at the event, and they weren't rushing to console her." We both shook our heads. "Poor Harper. I bet she feels so alone. Did she mention asking me to locate her family? She did to my mother."

"No. But I figured if Harper invited us to all come over together, she would. Or"—she paused and took another sip—"maybe she's discombobulated by everything." Melanie shrugged. "She did ask me if the detective spoke to me or anyone else in the club."

My skin broke out in goose bumps. If Melanie or one of the other club members had mentioned to the police what I'd told them about Harper requesting help locating her family, I'd have some explaining to do. I could say I didn't think the two situations were related. They wouldn't buy that, but I could. Or I could say that she was approaching me as a client, and our records were confidential. But no money had changed hands, nor had any documents been signed, so that would not stand up in court. I'd have to come clean, sounding as casual as I could manage. Then there was Amelia; she had her own story about how Harper wasn't so happy in her marriage. I'd have to speak to my mother. There was no way I could keep my word about withholding information. My reputation was on the line.

I took a deep breath to slow my spinning mind. I needed to take this one step at a time. I'd begun to see this like one of the Jane Doe cases up I-85 and had become obsessed with finding the answers. I'd always been obsessed with true crime cases. So much so that my parents made me see a therapist for a while. Stupid, if you ask me. They make docuseries about criminals for a reason—people are interested. But I won't deny the fact that my interest had been the reason Quinn and I had ended. I believed that had a lot to do with my mother's influence since Quinn was in law enforcement, but whatever. I'd moved past that now.

I couldn't care less about those who found fault with my desire to work in the field. Finding the truth was something I *needed* to do. And the Jane Doe cases needed someone to care— to restore their stolen identities. But right now, no one had asked for my help. And this was not one of those Jane Doe cases. Still,

I had difficulty halting my speculations, perhaps because Harper had requested a visit.

"Yoo-hoo! Earth to Lyla!" Melanie waved her hand in front of my face.

I blinked. "Sorry. I got lost in my thoughts."

"It's okay. I get it. I'd be the same if I stumbled on our friend's husband's body at my folk's house and the entire Sweet Mountain social elite was there." She rolled her eyes and added, "Not that anyone would've crossed the threshold of the pathetic excuse my parents had for a place when they had one."

I put my hand on her shoulder. Some people should not procreate. My sweet best friend had lived the childhood from hell. Both her parents were drunks and self-centered jerks who'd spent every dime they managed to make or steal on themselves. Scum is what they were. Mel had spent most of her time at my house, and Mother had made sure she had what she needed when Children's Services placed her in her grandmother's custody. Mel adjusted as well and even began calling her grandmother mom. God only knew where her parents were now. Mel hadn't heard from them in nearly fifteen years. And I for one believed that was a positive thing.

Mel gave me a small smile and shook her head, her signal that she wanted to let the topic about her parents drop.

I would respect her wishes. Always. "I think one of Mother's concerns is that this could potentially make national headlines. I mean, think about it: with the writer snooping around and all, the twisted tale he weaves could be a *New York Times* bestseller."

"Hold. The. Phone." Mel's eyes widened. "What writer?"

I paused with my mug halfway to my lips and explained what I'd learned about the man. "And it's not as exciting as it sounds. And I haven't exactly spoken with him directly, so nothing more to report on that front." I shoved the idea off for now for fear of how the writer might portray the town—the fallout unimaginable. "What I can tell you is that the detective who is in charge of the case is sharp. And from my interaction with the man, he'll have no compunctions asking the difficult questions and ruffling a few feathers, including those of our Sweet Mountain's elite. The nosy writer is the least of their worries."

There was a knock at the door.

"Get that, will ya? I'll run upstairs and throw myself together. Won't be fifteen minutes."

* * *

We took my car, Amelia and I in the front seat and Mel in the back. We'd already picked up a fried chicken family meal with all the fixings plus dessert at a local Southern food restaurant. While we waited in the drive-through, Amelia had been fascinated with the presence of a writer in town and could hardly contain her giddiness.

Melanie suggested that if indeed he turned out to be more of a friend than a foe—foe in the sense of disparaging our town instead of balancing the gruesome events from the other night with Sweet Mountain's better qualities—we ask him to come and speak with our book club.

We'd never had a budding author discuss a work in progress with us before. And I had to agree it would be exciting. I didn't share that something about the man gave me the willies or that he'd been outside Mel's cookie shop just hours before the ordeal. I didn't want to add fuel to any rumor fires until I knew what he was up to for sure.

The chatter in the car continued. It consisted of concern, speculations, and gasps as Amelia and Mel shared theories. I avoided describing the scene and explained tactfully, the best I could, that we needed more information before leaping to judgments. Amelia reached out and squeezed my arm as the GPS instructed me to take a left turn in four hundred feet. "How haunting. I probably would've fainted on the spot."

"A little, yeah." I nodded. "I operated on pure adrenaline, thinking Leonard possibly could be alive and might need aid. When I realized he was no longer with us, I went down like a ton of bricks." I turned on my left turn signal as I took a deep breath, remembering. "I didn't lose consciousness, but I sure felt woozy. The scene was like something out of one of our true crime case logs." I shifted in my seat. "I won't be able to enjoy the new addition without thinking of it. Even after a thorough cleaning."

"No, I wouldn't imagine you could." Amelia looked sympathetic. "I bet your parents won't be able to either."

"Your poor parents." Melanie shook her head. "Your mom spent a fortune on the tranquil space." Melanie had a soft spot for my family.

"Yes. And knowing Mother, she'll probably spend another fortune to renovate the renovations to erase the horrific memory. If they stay in the house." No one had mentioned a move to me; they'd lived in the same house since I was born, but I wouldn't be shocked if the idea of moving came up in the foreseeable future.

"Well, the good news is, in the state of Georgia they wouldn't be required to disclose the death to potential buyers, like they have to in other states." Amelia shifted to face me. I caught the move in my peripheral vision as she continued, "I will be glad to help if they do."

"Interesting," Mel said from the back seat.

"I'll be sure to mention you if they decide to go that route." I shrugged. "You never know. This is uncharted territory in the Moody family. My mother didn't even like me watching horror movies growing up."

Mel snickered. "It's true, Amelia. Lyla and I hauled her TV into the closet to watch the old Halloween movies one year. Her gran nearly scared us to death when she swung open the door."

"I bet Daisy didn't rat you guys out." Amelia smiled back at Mel.

"Nope. She joined us and brought popcorn."

I smiled at the memory. Gran was something else.

Rosa's ID came up on my navigation screen. I hit the "Answer" button on my steering column, still smiling. "Hey, Rosa."

"Hey. You busy?" Her voice sounded strained. "I hear car noise."

"I'm driving, but I can talk." I cast a glance to Amelia, who lifted her brows. "We're all here," I informed Rosa. "Mel and Amelia are in the car with me. We're on our way to see Harper."

"Oh. Hey, y'all." Rosa cleared her throat. "Harper is the reason I'm calling."

All of us shared a wide-eyed glance while we waited for the traffic light to change.

"Okay," I said slowly.

"I only have a few minutes. I'm sitting in my car on my break. Something's up with her husband's case. Something, um, *big*."

"Define 'big.' Has there been a break in the case?" I swallowed and instantly thought about the missing candlestick. Amelia had said when she'd spoken to Rosa last night, she'd been shocked at the calm way Rosa discussed the murder. When questioned, Rosa explained her time in the army had desensitized her to a lot of things. I'd admired Rosa for her strength and fortitude. That was the reason her nervous tone alarmed me so much.

"Or does this have to do with the cause of death?" Melanie leaned forward. "Harper mentioned something about it over the phone to me."

Amelia asked, "Do you all have a suspect in custody?"

"Cause of death hasn't been determined. There is no suspect in custody. But yes, to answer Lyla's question, there has been a break in the case. I can't go into much detail, but I wanted to give y'all a heads up. It's been a madhouse around here. An all-hands-on-deck situation. Chief Daniels is walking around like he was castrated by the detective taking over the office. And he's the one who put him in charge of the case. I have no idea why he's behaving that way. Unless it's the detective's methods he doesn't care for."

"What do you mean?" I turned up the volume.

"Detective Battle is hell-bent on closing this case, and fast. From what I gathered, he has a close relationship with the DA, and their success rate is off the charts. And—oh. Hold on a sec. Hey." We heard Rosa's window roll down and a few muffled sounds. She hadn't put us on "Mute," and we all sat deadly silent at the intersection, trying to discern the tiniest clue from the sounds. "Okay, I'm back. Sorry about that. I have to be careful. Leonard Richardson's sister-in-law, brother, and I think the brother's son came in this morning. And whatever they handed over to be submitted into evidence created a flurry of activity unlike I've ever seen in this department."

"What?" My mouth gaped.

"Oh my God!" Melanie let out a huge gasp. "What kind of evidence?"

"I don't know. But I heard the words 'search warrant' being uttered in the same sentence as Harper's name." I let out a little breath. Not the candlestick. Why would they search Harper's house if they found Mother's property, potentially covered in the victim's blood?

I blinked and noticed Amelia staring at me oddly.

I gripped the wheel. "I'm sorry, what was that, Rosa? I missed that last part."

"I said Detective Battle is all geeked up about the evidence." She got silent for a breath before she said, "Guys, are we sure Harper had nothing to do with Leonard's murder?"

Rosa's question left the car speakers and encompassed us. Street noise and the sound of the tires on the pavement seemed to get louder. Amelia fiddled with her nails, making a little ticking sound. I kept my eyes on the road and slowly hit my brakes at the next traffic light.

It was Mel who broke the silence, which felt like it had lasted a century but was probably more like less than a minute. "Yes!" Melanie threw her hands in the air, and one of them hit the back of my seat. "We've all spent time with the woman. She doesn't have a mean bone in her body. Not a single one. I can't believe you'd even ask such a thing, Rosa!"

"Calm down, Mel." I cast a quick glance in the rearview mirror. "Rosa is giving us information, and we are so grateful for the heads-up."

Amelia shifted in her seat. "I do find it difficult to believe Harper would be capable of such involvement. She's the one who found homes for all those stray kittens someone dropped on my door last spring. She's adamant about volunteering her time at the animal shelter with me. And we've all seen her shy away from confrontation at the library."

While I waited at the stop sign for my turn to go, I listened to Rosa and Mel go back and forth, Rosa hemming and hawing, and I began to wonder what else she might be privy to. She wouldn't divulge anything that would compromise her job, and I respected the limits of friendship in relation to her position on the police force.

"Okay, take a chill pill, Mel. I was simply asking a question. People aren't always as they seem, so I'd be careful being cavalier in your assumptions." Rosa's tone came out as authoritative.

Amelia shook her head slowly as if she couldn't wrap her head around such a notion. And I could understand the struggle. Mel crossed her arms across her chest. Her face said she wasn't too happy with being spoken to that way. Emotions were running high.

I cast another quick glance in my rearview mirror to see Mel's brow wrinkle and then smooth. "I didn't mean to lash out like that, Rosa. I'm sorry. It's just, y'all didn't hear Harper on the phone. She sounded devastated." I didn't remind Mel that I'd seen Harper when it occurred. And I had to agree in that respect. The poor woman had seemed devastated.

"This is it; I believe." Amelia pointed to the next street on the right just as the robotic voice of the GPS said, "Turn right and you have reached your destination."

With a sigh, Rosa said, "All right. I gotta go anyway. Just please be careful. Something is mighty strange about that family."

"We will. Thanks, Rosa." I disconnected the call.

"I love Rosa to bits, but I wonder if her perspective is a little skewed because of the detective's influence." Mel tightened her high ponytail.

"What's he like, anyway?" Amelia asked.

"He's a man you wouldn't want to come after you. I got the impression he trusts his instincts for good reason. And I think Rosa's just looking out for us. We'd be remiss not to consider her perspective."

Chapter Seven

B arnard Drive was a long, winding dead-end street with only three or four houses on large wooded lots. The lawns were sparse in the grass department, with large exposed areas of Georgia red clay caused by tree limbs' overgrowth blocking the morning sun.

"That must be it there. It says three-two-zero-eight on the brick mailbox." Amelia leaned over and pointed to the last house on the left. We pulled into the driveway of an old, three-story, clapboard, Queen Anne–style home that had a brass sign on the facade reading "Circa 1900."

"I'm going to look up the comps on this street," Amelia said. "These properties could bring in a pretty penny. No wonder Harper was curious about listing the property."

"Wow." Melanie leaned up between the seats. "I had no idea she lived in a house this large. Harper's always talking about conserving everything. I pictured a more minimalistic type of place. And it looks like she has company too. Huh."

"Yeah. Probably people are dropping off food and offering condolences, like us. Maybe her coworkers at the library."

I parked behind a green Jeep Cherokee. There were three other vehicles in front of it, and a large white work van nestled beside the garage.

I wrinkled my nose when I shut off the ignition and got a whiff of something rotten. "Do y'all smell something?" I glanced around the car. Something in here smelled beyond foul. The air freshener I'd bought had done its job while the car had been running. I'd fork out the extra cash for another when the time came.

"Yeah, I do smell something. Did Mrs. Kreger not pick up after her dog again?" Mel started checking her shoes.

That'd explain it. That woman was the worst about not taking bags out with her when she walked her little Yorkie. "We're going to have complain, Mel. It's getting crazy. Now I'm going to have to have my car detailed again."

As we took in the large home and exited the vehicle, Mel commented, "It must've cost a fortune to renovate. The Richardsons must be loaded."

Rosa had sparked new concerns, and if the family was indeed well-to-do, that did not bode well for public opinion regarding Harper, the young widow. Especially since she was the second wife of Leonard Richardson and barely married for two years. Add that to the deceased man's elderly sister-in-law and brother casting suspicion her way and *yikes*! Then an odd thought occurred to me. *How eerily similar to our club read.*

"Well then, they should've done a better job with their front lawn," Amelia said absentmindedly, bringing me back to the present. None of us wanted to think about the ramifications of what might happen if the detective obtained a search warrant. In Harper's already fragile state, it would crush her.

"Curb appeal is essential," Amelia continued as if we were simply here for a visit. "It can bring in an additional ten K with some properties. And Harper will want to get top dollar. She'll probably be eager to sell now . . ." Amelia's voice trailed off, and worried glances were exchanged. Now, with her husband gone, she should have no trouble putting the property on the market. We all hated to think that way.

As we unloaded the trunk, each of us grabbing a bag, the pungent order I'd caught a moment ago assaulted us. I checked my shoes, and they were clean. Amelia handed me the little bag she'd been carrying so she could inspect hers, and I nearly gagged. "My God! This is the smell." I held the bag at arm's length.

Melanie leaned over, sniffed, her face nearly turning green. "Yep. That's it. What the hell is that?"

I tossed the bag back to Amelia, and she rolled her eyes. "It's Valerian root tea. It's a natural way to help Harper get some sleep. It's called nature's valium. It has a real earthy fragrance."

"Earthy? Mel thought we'd stepped in dog mess. There is no way I'd drink that. Um, wow." I took a step back just as a black Lexus, blasting some sort of rock music, pulled up beside us. A man about our age, wearing sunglasses, got out. He flashed a movie star smile. "Can I help you ladies with something?"

"We're here to see Harper." I smiled back.

"About what?"

"Um, we're her friends. We're here to support her." Melanie's eyes narrowed, and she sounded annoyed by the question.

The man, whoever he was, seemed to be rather protective of our friend. I stepped up and shuffled some bags around before extending my hand, my smile still in place. "Hi, I'm Lyla Moody, and these are my friends Melanie and Amelia. We know Harper from the library."

He shook my hand lightly before removing his sunglasses and running a hand through his wheat-blond hair. "Oh, hey. I think I recall Harper mentioning you guys." He nodded at our little group. "I didn't mean to be rude. Harper's had such a rough time with my Dad's death. And a couple of reporters have been by."

His dad?

"We understand," Amelia said, but looked a little taken aback by the "dad" comment too.

"Oh. I'm LJ . . . er, Leonard Richardson Junior," he said, shrugging, "but everyone just calls me LJ."

"Nice to meet you." I gave him a sympathetic smile. "We are so sorry for your loss."

"Yeah, thanks." He frowned appropriately, but the sadness didn't quite reach his eyes. Odd.

"We won't stay long. It appears you already have company." I nodded toward the cars.

"Nah, those belong to the family. Welcome to our home." He put his glasses on top of his head. "You all can follow me." He turned and started for the large white front porch, *whistling*.

"Our home?" Amelia raised her brows.

I shrugged.

"He doesn't seem all that torn up about his dad, does he?" Melanie said under her breath.

He certainly didn't.

LJ took the steps two at a time and shoved his key into the front door, which had a stained-glass oval window in the middle.

Maybe the news hadn't sunk in yet. Some people needed more time than others to process trauma.

The three of us slowly walked inside after him. A green marble fireplace with an old-fashioned painting of an unsmiling Harper and Leonard hanging above it greeted us as we entered. Leonard must've been close to sixty or so when they'd had this painted, making him thirty years her senior or more. I tried not to pass judgment.

To the right of the fireplace was a small window and a set of stairs where LJ went. He put his hand on the white railing and yelled loudly, "Harper, you have company!"

We all jumped and glanced around with full hands, shifting uncomfortably. The floors looked to be all original, as did the fireplace. A snorting sound came from our left, and I glanced through the open French doors into what appeared to be a formal living or sitting room. A peek inside revealed an expensive rug, antique lighting, and velour furnishings in earth tones. Edna was asleep in a settee with rounded arms.

While LJ still called up the stairs to Harper, I mouthed to the others that Leonard's sister-in-law was asleep in the next room.

After another yell, he turned to us. "No need to wait here. Make yourselves at home. Go on through there." He pointed to the little hallway in between the entryway where we were and the sitting room. "Put the food in the kitchen. I'll go up and get her. She's probably in the shower or something."

We all exchanged another glance after he disappeared up the stairs. We moved down the long, narrow hallway, passing the formal dining room off the room Leonard's sister-in-law, Edna, snoozed in. It had high ceilings like the rest of the house and was painted emerald green with white trim. It, too, had a fireplace.

"I wonder why Harper didn't mention that his son lived with them." Melanie looked concerned.

I shrugged. "She told us about Edith, and we had a lot of questions as to why. Maybe she thought it would lead to more questions, or perhaps it's a recent development."

Mel's eyes went wide, and I knew what she was thinking when I goofed. The name of the sister-in-law of *Crooked House* was Edith, and there were so many similarities here.

I didn't want to get caught up in the similarities of the novel and rushed to correct myself. "No, not Edith, Edna."

Mel nodded and softly mimicked the *Twilight Zone* theme song.

Amelia sidled up behind us and we nearly gagged. That tea was an affront. "Since Rosa said his brother and sister-in-law turned in evidence, I wonder if the brother lives here too."

Mel slowly raised her shoulders.

"I have no idea." I turned my head, not able to take that odor one more second. "Move that bag, Amelia."

"Gosh, you're like a child. It's not that bad."

My eyes were watering. It was indeed that bad. The sound of water running caught my attention, and we slowed. We kept glancing around when we heard the creaking of a door opening. But there wasn't a door on the right-hand side of the hallway.

I saw the young woman I'd seen with Edna the last night come out a paneled wall door to our right. The room would be impossible to notice when the door was closed. I wondered if a lot of old homes had hidden places like that.

The girl was tall, thin, and pale, with chestnut-colored hair. I fought to control my eyes from going wide at her attire—a vintage, green, fringed flapper dress. The light bathed the black and white tile flooring, exposing a small powder room. Up close, she appeared much younger. I'd guess she was anywhere from sixteen to nineteen, with almond-shaped eyes, which she'd lined with jet-black eyeliner, and sparkly gold shadow glittered on her eyelids. She cast an odd look our way. We all smiled instinctively.

I cleared my throat. "Hello. We're friends of Harper's. You must be—"

She sniffed, cutting me off as she lifted her nose and continued down the hallway. Apparently, to her, our presence was of no consequence.

Amelia frowned. "Who was that?"

I leaned closer and whispered, "It's Leonard's daughter."

Melanie let out a little giggle, something she does when she's nervous. "This family just keeps getting weirder. I have no idea how Harper stands it."

"I'm not so sure she had a choice." Amelia made a face of disapproval as we continued down the hallway.

"Who are you?" a wheezy voice asked us. And we halted beside a galley way that appeared to be a butler's pantry. An elderly man sat slumped in a wheelchair; a burgundy crochet afghan lay across his lap, and his finger pointed at us.

"Um, hello, sir. We've brought food for the family." I hoped we'd brought enough for the additional mouths we hadn't known we needed to feed. I'd remembered about the sister and daughter but hadn't known that the son or this elderly man would also be here.

"Harper." He sliced his hand through the air. "That little gold digger. She ain't gettin' one red cent if I have anything to say about it." *Oh my.* He must be one of the ones who went to the police station with so-called evidence. "I told Leonard to watch out for her. She'd been aimin' to take this family's fortune all along. Well, I'll contest the will if I have to. She ain't gettin' nothin'! That money belongs to the family, not her. Not her, you hear! She ain't ever been one of us. The little hussy."

Melanie let out a little another giggle, and I shot her a stern glare over my shoulder. My friend tended to laugh when she got scared, nervous, or at the most inappropriate times—mostly when Mel wasn't sure how she ought to react. It wasn't her fault, but under the circumstances, I'd hoped she get a better handle on her little affliction.

She seemed to take the hint and glanced down at her feet while pinching her lips together. I did feel bad for her.

"We didn't mean to upset you, sir. You are?" I asked with a smile.

"Me?" He squinted his eyes at me. "Who wants to know?"

Melanie snickered again, but I could tell she'd wrestled with the one that got away.

"I'm Lyla Moody." After his rant about Harper, I withheld the information regarding our friendship.

"Moody, huh?" He glanced up at the ceiling as if trying to place the name. Suddenly, he shrugged as if he'd given up. "You got a cigarette on ya, Moody?"

More snickers from behind me.

"Um, no, sir. I don't smoke."

He sliced another hand through the air. "Nobody smokes anymore. Leonard smoked. Beatrice smokes, but she only smokes those fancy French cigarettes." He crinkled up his nose.

"I apologize about the cigarettes, but we do have some food, Mr. . . . ?"

"No 'Mr.' here. I'm just Felix. Leonard was my only brother." His face crumpled, and his head slumped forward. He used a handkerchief in his left hand to wipe his eyes. "Sure gonna miss that son of a bitch."

"We're so very sorry for your loss." I felt helpless. "We're going to take this food to the kitchen and give you some privacy."

He sniffed loudly, and despite his cantankerousness, my heart ached for the old guy.

Amelia stepped up beside me. "If you'd like, we could make you a plate."

He nodded his head. "That'd be good. Thank ya."

"Um, would you like us to help you into the kitchen?" I offered.

He shook his head. "Nah. Those two fools are in there. I'd rather be in here."

We all moved slowly down the rest of the hallway. All of us seemed to be processing our encounter with the young women and the little old man. I paused several feet from the kitchen when I heard a hushed conversation and the rustling of paper. "There's nothing in here about how he died."

"And you were expecting there to be?" The person asking sounded like a woman with a low husky voice—then more rustling.

"Yes, woman. That's why I said it." I'd been right. It was a woman. I glanced back at my friends. Everyone had the same "should we stay, or should we go?" expression. "Idiotic newspaper. There aren't any pictures of the body or anything. That detective fella said someone brained Leonard. What kind of fool reporting is going on in this town?" They must be the fools Felix Richardson had referenced.

"They were hoping to find crime scene pictures in the local paper," Amelia mouthed.

"This is nuts!" Melanie whisper-shouted, and I nodded in agreement.

"You all find it?" LJ called. His boots echoed in the hallway.

"Yes." I continued into the large country-style kitchen with a large square table in the center. A couple, the one we'd overheard, sat sipping coffee and reading the local paper.

"Hey." LJ moved around us, then glanced back at us and grinned. "These are Harper's buddies. They brought food." He moved to the refrigerator and pulled out a beer, cracking it open and taking a deep sip. "Harper will be down in a minute."

The couple at the table eyed us with palpable scrutiny.

"Oh, sorry." LJ swallowed quickly. "This is my cousin Kenneth and his wife, Janice. They're staying with us for a while."

"Hello. Hi." We all stumbled in unison with the greetings. Too weird. All these people behaved as if they owned the place.

"Just put those bags down here." LJ took the bags from us and placed them on the table, shoving the newspapers and mail out of the way.

"We so terribly sorry for your loss," Amelia said to the couple while placing the apple pie and the bag she carried down.

"Don't waste your sympathy. Anger is what you should feel." Janice ran her hand through her frizzy bleached-blonde hair. "That little gold digger is to blame. Don't believe me—just ask Charlie. He knows all about it."

"Janice!" LJ scowled.

She raised her hands. "I'm not saying she killed him. But she was supposed to be looking after him. He wasn't himself these last few weeks. What was she thinking? Taking him to a party in his condition was absurd." I wondered if she, too, had been involved when the others went to the police. This family certainly didn't think highly of Harper, and the thought troubled me greatly.

"Yep. My dear uncle and I were working on a project together. I do hope I have enough notes to finish it. He would have wanted that." Kenneth attempted a dutiful expression though he didn't quite make it. "Smells good." He began picking through the bag closest to him and paused. He waved his hand over his nose. "Shew! Did dad mess his pants again?"

"I ain't done it!" Felix bellowed from the other room.

Janice laughed as Kenneth found the bag. "Shew! Here it is! What's in this bag? I ain't eaten it!"

"It's an herbal tea." Amelia's face flushed. We'd warned her.

The old man got up and tossed it into the trash and tied it up. "This needs to go out now, LJ, you hear?"

"I'll get right on it." LJ blinked rapidly above the can. I guess the odor was still emitting through the black garbage bag.

"Well, I hope y'all enjoy the food. We"—I waved to include my friends—"didn't want the family to have to worry about cooking or anything during your time of grief." We certainly hadn't brought enough food for all these people for more than a single meal.

"Excuse me." All eyes turned to Amelia. "The elderly gentlemen in the other room asked for a plate. Would you mind if I made him one?"

"Uncle Felix has got to eat too." LJ finished off his beer and went to take the trash out. It didn't escape our attention that he kept the bag at arm's length.

Kenneth shrugged. "Sure. He's right. My old man has to eat too. And while you're at it, take a plate to Aunt Edna. She'll wake up when she smells the food. Plates are over there." He waved to the cabinet beside the white ceramic sink and took a drumstick right out of the box. Amelia went to retrieve a plate and some flatware to dish out the food.

"I'll help you, Amelia." Mel began taking the food from the bags.

"What did you say your name was?" Janice twirled a finger through her hair.

I hadn't, but I didn't see the harm in introducing myself. "Lyla Moody."

"That your natural color? It's a unique copper color." She squinted at me as if investigating my roots.

"Yes, ma'am."

"Quiet, woman." Kenneth pointed at me. "Moody." He scrounged around for the newspaper and pointed. "You're the little gal who found Uncle Leonard."

"You be quiet!" Janice cast him a murderous glower.

Uncomfortable, I folded my hands in front of me, and my heart began beating like a drum. I didn't know how Harper coped with living here. The vibe in this house caused my skin to crawl. "Yes, sir." I fought to control my irritation with the Neanderthal.

"What'd he look like?" Kenneth popped a couple of pieces of fried okra into his mouth. Janice glanced up then as if she, too, were interested in my answer.

And when I cast a glance over to LJ, who'd just come back in, with hopes of him saving me from being rude, he raised his brows and said, "Well?"

Why in the world would his son want to know something like that?

"Um," I glanced back at my friends as they left the room, off to deliver the food to the senior residents of the house.

"It wasn't . . . well . . ." I stumbled over the words. How did one describe such a sight to the supposedly grieving family members? I honestly didn't desire to go into it at all. *What type of family behaves this way?*

"Hey." Harper entered the kitchen, saving me from continuing. Our fellow club member had swollen red eyes and wore a long, belted, denim dress. Seeing her settled all my doubts that had been raised by Rosa's call.

"Harper. You poor thing." I hugged her. "How are you holding up?"

She shrugged and laid her head on my shoulder.

"We brought some food. Are you hungry?"

"I don't think I could eat just now." Harper released me. "Why don't we all go sit outside for a bit."

"Okay." Anything to get out of this house.

Chapter Eight

The four of us sat on her oversized screened-in back porch with cups of tea. Harper didn't have any coffee in the house, and I felt terrible for not having asked if they needed anything from the store. I could tell Amelia did too. The three of us sat stiff as statues, clearly uncomfortable to the casual observer. Harper gazed out over the backyard, covered with fallen leaves. A large rope swing, tied to a limb on the large oak tree in the center of the yard, moved with each gust of wind. Standing by the tree stood Leonard's daughter, smoking a cigarette in one of those old-fashioned cigarette holders.

Harper noticed us staring as she sipped from her antique rose teacup. "That's Bea. She's Leonard's youngest child. She's a sweet girl. But she bucked her father's rules at every turn. She just broke Leonard's heart with her wild, rebellious ways."

Bea must've noticed us staring, too, because she walked into the small carriage house at the back of the property.

"The police were here again today." Harper turned in her seat toward me. "They kept asking if I knew whether Leonard had had any enemies, or could I think of anyone who would rob him."

"Oh" was all I could think to say.

"Who could have done this at your mother's charity event? It was by invitation only."

The three of us shook our heads, and I said, "I don't know, hon."

"It's just unimaginable. And Lyla, this happened right under the chief of police's nose. If anyone should have noticed something suspicious, it was him. How dare he!" Harper put her hand to her mouth. "Sorry. I didn't mean to raise my voice. It's just the police are beginning to sound more and more accusatory."

"Have any idea why?" Amelia asked and cast a worried glance my way before focusing on Harper. We were all recalling Rosa's warnings.

Harper shook her head, looking helpless.

"None of this makes sense. And nothing I can say will make it any better. But you'll have some closure when the police get whoever did this. The police are just following protocols. Try not to take it personally," I said, attempting to reassure her.

Harper nodded; her shaky fingers gripped the cup.

I hated this. *Hated* it. If I dwelled on the crime long enough, I understood Harper's anger. It could have been my father lying out in the library, or any other attendee. But then, I thought back to Rosa. The evidence the family had turned over gave me pause in that line of thinking.

"It's surreal. I keep thinking Leonard's going to walk through that door at any second. I wanted out of my marriage. That much is true. But I didn't want him dead." Harper wiped a tear from her cheek.

"Oh, hon." I moved around Amelia to sit to the left of Harper and took her hand. I had to do something. "Have the police said anything about the evidence they recovered at the scene or about any suspects?"

Mel and Amelia looked on with keen interest as Harper shook her head. She dropped her face into her hands, and I wrapped my arm around her shoulders and held her while she sobbed. All three of us shed tears along with her. Her pain palpable, Melanie wiped at her eyes, and Amelia handed tissues around.

"We're going to get you through this. You aren't alone." I squeezed her tighter.

A minute or so later, rustling in the blinds caught our attention, and Harper lifted her head and began mopping her face with her tissues. Kenneth peeked out while he took a bite of what looked like pie.

Harper frowned. "They'd kick me right out if they could. They never approved of our marriage."

"Who? Leonard's family?" I glanced toward the window.

She nodded, and Kenneth stuck his tongue out at us before letting the blinds drop.

"My God. He gives me the creeps." Melanie shivered. "Do they all treat you that way?"

"Well, LJ is different, and Bea seems to like me. But the rest of the vipers are a nightmare. They're always here with their hands out. None of them pitch in for anything. Dead beats." Harper wrapped her arms around herself. "LJ is the only one I can depend on." I wondered about the rumors of an affair. Especially by the way her face softened when she'd said LJ's name.

Harper," I said softly, "are you sure you want to stay here? You could come and stay with one of us for a while." This family certainly seemed to have it in for her.

"No. It's fine." Harper sniffed. "This is my home, and I won't give it up to those vultures."

"I can respect that." Melanie leaned forward. "But isn't it too much to cope with? I mean, it's got to be awful staying here with the likes of Kenneth."

Harper shivered and surprised us by whispering, "It is. You all can't imagine what it's like living the way I have for the last year. I'm getting rid of them as soon as I can. That'll serve them right."

"Good for you!" Mel nodded.

I put my cup next to where Amelia had placed hers. "Bless your heart. I can't even imagine the strength it must take to endure all this. And the offer stands. If you ever need a break, you'll always have a place with one of us."

"Thanks. Your mom said the same." Harper glanced up and gave me a watery smile. "You have such a nice family."

I smiled. "I am lucky." I wanted to ask about my mother but didn't feel like the timing was appropriate.

She nodded and rubbed her finger around the brim of the cup; her eyes remained downcast. "It's like I'm a stranger in my own house now. When Leonard was here, it was different." Mel passed the box of tissues over to Amelia, who handed it to Harper.

"You told us about Edna and Bea living with you, but not the rest of them. Has Leonard's family always treated your home as if y'all had a revolving door?" Melanie scooted to the edge of her seat after a quick glance toward the blinds behind her told us we were no longer being watched.

Harper shook her head. "When we first got married, it was just the two of us, Edna, and Beatrice. Edna took some getting used to." Her shoulders rose and then fell. "I managed to adjust. We had a nice little house in Chapel Hill, North Carolina. I had my job as a receptionist at the rehab facility, and we were close to my aunt. One day, it simply changed. Leonard started going to late-night meetings and started asking me to dress differently. I wanted to make him happy, so I complied." She sighed. "He floored me when he up and told me he'd bought a house in Sweet Mountain, Georgia, and put our old house on the market; He'd never even discussed it with me. That's when I found out about the severity of his impulsiveness. He said he was *led* here."

"Led here by . . .?" I asked.

"He said he felt this is where we needed to be. That he'd been guided by a higher power." Harper twisted the tissues in her hand.

I glanced briefly over at Amelia, who raised her brows.

"Leonard sometimes said things like that. He felt we should do this or that. He claimed to have some psychic discernment." Harper shrugged. "I just thought it was a quirk. Leonard was very good with money and retired early. He spent a lot of time reading up on different ways of life and enjoyed it. I supported it. But he got caught up in some weird minimalistic movement from years ago. I can't remember the name now, but I think the police raided their compound like forty years ago or something. I'm talking kooky stuff."

I shivered at the notion of Harper being controlled by a man with strange ideas.

"So when did the family move in?" Amelia asked gently, tucking a single stray silver curl behind her ear.

Harper let out a shuddering sigh. "They were already here when we got here. Leonard said people in that movement study he took part in lived this way. I thought it was weird, you know?"

We all nodded.

"But then after Leonard explained that having family close by meant we'd always have a strong support system and would always be close, I thought that idea was sort of nice. I'm an only child, you see, and my aunt raised me after my parents died in a car wreck when I was four."

"Oh, Harper." Amelia squeezed her hand.

"It's okay. I don't even remember them. But having so little family, I thought it would be kind of nice to be close to my new family." Harper dabbed her eyes. "And it was at first. Then things got weird." She gulped from her cup as if she needed a second to scrounge up her courage. "A couple of months after we moved here, I was getting homesick. Plus, it was feeling a little overcrowded in the house." We all nodded in sympathy. "That's when I started talking to Leonard about taking a trip home and spending a few weeks with my aunt. Just she and I, like we used to. I thought it would do me some good. He hit the roof, yelling and saying that part of my life was over now, and we had a higher calling. We had no room in our lives for those who didn't believe the way we did." Her voice hitched.

Amelia sucked in a sharp breath.

"What he meant was the way *he* believed." She put her fists to her chest. "Because I didn't have any idea what he believed other than wanting to keep me all to himself. I knew then that I needed to leave."

"So, did you?" Mel leaned forward.

"I called my aunt and told her everything. She told me she'd come and get me. I needed about a week to get my things in order. I packed a small bag, things Leonard wouldn't notice missing. But she never showed up. I called her cell more times than I can count. I called her friends, and they hadn't seen her. I even called the police. She simply vanished."

"When was this?" I felt my brow furrow. "Is this who you wanted me to help you find?"

"Yes. My aunt went missing last year. Her neighbors started noticing her newspapers piling up on her front stoop. Everyone thought perhaps she'd had an accident or heart attack or something. They called the police, and they broke the door down. She'd just gone. Her bank accounts were cleaned out, and her clothes were all gone."

"She just left without a word?" Amelia looked shocked.

"They said she must have left. They had a hit on her credit cards. Still, Phyllis never wanted to leave the house she shared with my late uncle. She was sixty-eight for heaven's sake. Settled and happy. But the police wouldn't do anything. As much of a fuss as I made, they just put out a missing person's report." She let out a loud sigh. "After that, I felt stuck. And Leonard knew it. I wasn't supposed to express my opinion outside our marriage quarters, and never in front of the family. Then he started telling me who I could and couldn't be friends with." She glanced over at Mel, who wiped her eyes.

"Why didn't you tell us?" I said gently.

"I felt so ashamed. I had a weak moment a few weeks back at the market. Your mom was there, and when she showed me kindness, I spilled my gut. She offered to help me, and we began making a plan for me to open a new bank account, and she said she'd help me find a place. I made her swear not to tell you. I'm sorry."

"It's okay, and God, I'm so sorry you've been living through such hell." I gave her a sad smile as my heart broke. No wonder Mother had taken such a stance to help her. It all made sense now. To think that she'd been living such an oppressed existence for years was horrifying.

"It wasn't all bad. Leonard could be charming sometimes." She gazed out over the back lawn. "The strange thing was, all this time I thought Leonard just wanted us to lead a simple life. You know, embody some of the minimalistic qualities— getting rid of superfluous things or sharing housing—but really, I think he was losing his mind. I was changing my lifestyle and dress because of the ravings of a madman." Harper rubbed her forehead.

"How'd you find out?" Amelia asked as she wrapped up tighter in her thick gray sweater.

"I found a journal he'd been writing in. He scribbled a lot of crazy stuff in there. It was turned over to the police this morning. Perhaps it was early onset dementia or something. I don't know."

"You sure you won't reconsider and come to stay with me? I hate to think of you staying here after all the crap you've been through." Melanie looked as though her heart was breaking. My tender-hearted bestie would move heaven and earth for a friend in need.

"You such a good friend, Mel. And I promise you this: if it becomes too unbearable, I will."

Melanie nodded. "Okay. I won't smother you with constant calls and visits. But I'm available day or night."

"That goes for all of us." I smiled, and Amelia patted her arm.

"The reason you invited me over in the first place was to see if I could find your aunt. That's what you were going to ask me about at the library?" I hated to tell her that if her aunt hadn't been seen in over a year, the likelihood that she was no longer with us was great, although the credit card hit did shed a glimmer of hope. Especially if there was more than the one hit, and recently.

Harper nodded. "Maybe Leonard threatened her, and she left out of fear. Maybe she's been on the run all this time."

"Do you think Leonard could've done something like that?"

"I just don't know." She met my gaze directly; her hazel, almost green eyes were red and watery. "But I have to find out. And when they arrest the person responsible for Leonard's death, and this all blows over, I can go home, and so can she."

In my opinion, and if Leonard's family had anything to say about it, nothing about this case was going to blow over.

"Will you help me?" Harper pleaded.

"Yes, I'll do my best to help you find her."

Chapter Nine

"It was awful. I felt so helpless." Amelia tapped the shoulder of her husband, Ethan, and pointed to the wine bottle decanting on the sideboard behind him. "Our suspicions about Leonard seem accurate by Harper's account. And that family—wow."

Melanie and I nodded in agreement with our friend.

"Ethan, you should have seen her. She was such a mess. She just sobbed and sobbed." Amelia cleared her throat. I could tell she fought for control over her emotions.

"You have such a tender heart. Don't go blaming yourself for not getting involved. Even I could tell from the little time I spent with Harper how private she was. She isn't the type to confide easily, and you're not a mind reader." Ethan handed her the bottle of merlot and kissed her on the cheek. He always regarded her with such love, even after ten years of marriage. Melanie and I kidded Amelia that her tall, dark, handsome man, with dark chocolate-colored eyes and steel-colored hair, was the last of his kind.

I'd genuinely felt that way until I'd started dating Brad. I smiled over at my date, glad to be ending this day on a better note. He'd arrived at my house right when I'd finished washing the day off me and putting the finishing touches on my makeup. He'd looked so good in his dark blazer and navy slacks that I wished we didn't have to leave my house. But plans were plans, and Amelia would have been miffed with me. Now, my heart warmed at being surrounded by some of my nearest and dearest.

I gazed down the mahogany table lit by candlelight, taking in the moment of normalcy. The Klein's dining room was tastefully decorated in muted tones of tan, cream, and browns. Sconces and framed designer prints adorned the walls. Amelia invited us to dinner at least once a month. Usually Rosa came, sometimes stag and sometimes with a date. Since she had to work this evening, it was just Brad and me, Mel and Wyatt, and of course Amelia and Ethan.

We always had Italian—lasagna Bolognese, to be specific— the dish Amelia had perfected from the cooking class she'd begged me to take with her last spring and abandoned after the scalding water burn incident. Not that I minded—I hated to cook. Mel and I always enjoyed coming over to their home. The love she and her lovely husband shared was an inspiration.

We continued discussing Harper and her situation, and Melanie, in typical Melanie fashion, let her opinions about the family living with Harper be known. "I've never in my life met anyone like the Richardson family, and that's saying something. The mixed bag of nuts I call my relatives don't even hold a candle to that family." Mel hit the nail on the head. That family had a creep factor off the charts. "The whole family was just peculiar." Melanie shivered. "And that house had a vibe like—"

Amelia, Mel, and I all said in unison with wide eyes, "Three Gables."

"It's from a book we were reading," Melanie explained to her date with a little smile.

Brad, who was sitting next to me, let out a loud belly laugh as he set his beer glass on the table. He had the best laugh in the world. A deep rumbling sound that was infectious, and his smile knocked ten years off his face.

"It's true." I tried to keep a straight face. Because now, after I'd said it out loud, I could see how absurd and hilarious it sounded. "All kidding aside," I said, smirking at Brad, "they have eight adults living in that house. Well, seven now that Leonard has passed. And none of them were torn up about his death."

This got his attention. "What do you mean?"

"Exactly what I said. The family seriously didn't seem to care a bit."

"Except for Harper and his older brother, Felix." Melanie rushed to add. "That old guy was something else."

"Right," I agreed. "Leonard's brother and, of course, Harper were upset. But we overheard cousins, or whatever they were, talking about seeing crime scene photos and how disappointed they were that the paper hadn't managed to print any."

Brad furrowed his brows.

"Exactly." I shook my head.

"Though none of them are fans of Harper except LJ, the son." Amelia's brows rose. "But Felix disparaged Harper with no compunctions." Amelia dipped a breadstick in the leftover sauce on her plate.

"True," I agreed. "Felix called Harper a gold digger."

"Hold on. You mean the family, other than the brother and wife, weren't in mourning, and someone murdered the man?" Brad cocked his head toward me.

I nodded. "That's what I'm saying. Oh, everyone in the house is interested in who's going to inherit his fortune but no one seemed to be missing him."

"Not even his children?" Ethan put his fork down. "You said he had a son and daughter, right?"

"His son wasn't upset." Amelia wiped her mouth. "And I couldn't tell about the daughter. She was as unique as the rest of them, dressed in a flapper dress and using one of those French cigarette holders."

"Are you sure you gals weren't projecting your book onto the family?" Brad looked amused. His eyes were crinkled around the corners as he took another drink of his beer.

"It's God's honest truth." Melanie leaned around me to give Brad a dead-level stare, but her lips twitched. "This old sister and brother live there along with his weirdo ass son, daughter, and two cousins. They were the strangest group of people ever. We weren't projecting anything; they were like the family in the book."

"Wow, that does sound far-fetched, Mel. You gotta admit that," Wyatt said. His curly blond mop of hair bounced around as he shook his head. Wyatt and Mel lived next door to each other after she moved in with her grandmother. They'd dated for a while in their teens. Back then, I thought he'd be the one, but it fizzled out as teen romances seem to do, and they went their separate ways. When they saw each other across the dance floor last month at a Western bar on the outskirts of town, Mel said it was an instant connection. Sparks flew, as Mel put it. They looked well together—both blonds with bright blue eyes.

"It does sound crazy." Mel giggled. "It was just a wild experience that I don't think you can appreciate unless you were there."

Wyatt smiled and shook his head.

"This is the type of family you'd see featured on one of those TLC shows. Everyone would watch." Melanie wiped her mouth. "It was an eerie experience."

Amelia nodded in agreement.

"Mel's right. 'Odd' and 'eerie' are adjectives I'd use to describe that family." I sipped from my glass. "They'd certainty attract viewers if they had a program. The most difficult part for me was leaving Harper there. I'm concerned for her." I went on to explain our suspicions regarding the family and the journal the family submitted into evidence.

"Rosa said the family turned over this evidence, correct?" Brad's face altered from amused to his GBI scrutinizing expression. Not much fazed Brad except a good case that got his blood pumping.

I nodded.

"Are you sure this journal Harper mentioned was what she was referring to?"

"I have no idea."

"Hmm." Brad put his glass down. "I would think you'd need more than something like that to acquire a search warrant. Do you have the specifics on her aunt's disappearance?"

"I do. Harper forwarded me the contact info of the police department in charge of the case." I put my fork on the plate. "I'll do my best for her. Harper seems to hold out hope for a reunion still." Brad and I shared a knowing glance. We both knew the chances of that were slim if there wasn't any recent activity on her credit cards or bank records. In this day and age, people just didn't disappear—especially people with little to no means.

"It was so nice of Lyla too." Melanie finished her lasagna and smiled. "And I know Harper appreciates your help."

I smiled down the table at my oldest friend. Fierce and loyal, that's our Mel.

Chapter Ten

Monday morning, I got a call from my uncle. We were having issues with the wiring at the office, and Calvin was trying to get us an appointment with an electrician ASAP. Problems in the old building were something we'd grown accustomed to. Luckily the new virtual private network I convinced him we needed to purchase was up and running and allowed us to access our system. It would be getting a test run today. He seemed happy when we spoke that we could now work from our computers securely, wherever we were. Calvin worked old school style, and I'd done my best to bring us up to modern processes.

While I waited for my coffee to brew, I called the police department and inquired about Harper's aunt. The officer I spoke to told me that the case had been reclassified three weeks after her niece reported her missing. She'd used her credit card to book a hotel room and at a gas station on the outskirts of town. The clerk remembered her and a gentlemen friend she had with her. I'd be checking to see if there were any recent hits to said cards later.

"Coffee ready?" Brad came into the kitchen, and I slid a cup across the counter and began unzipping my dress. He raised his brows over his mug.

"Don't get any ideas. I'm working from home today, so I might as well be comfortable."

He glanced down at my tablet, where I'd taken notes from the call.

"As far as the Chapel Hill Police Department is concerned, Phyllis Johnson isn't a missing person. She simply doesn't want to be found." I sipped from my mug. "That begs the question—"

"Why?"

"Exactly." The toaster popped, and I put the hot bagel onto the plate and opened the fridge to retrieve the raspberry cream cheese Brad liked, and passed it to him. "Somebody certainly scared her away. It doesn't make sense that she would turn her back on her only living relative. I plan to do some digging."

"You're thinking Harper's deceased husband threatened her to keep her from interfering in his plans?"

I shrugged. "Makes sense. Harper certainly painted a picture of a controlling man. He didn't want her to go home to see her aunt after they moved here." My cell rang while Brad took a bite of the bagel I'd made him and perched on a barstool.

I slid my finger across the answer icon. "Cousins Investigative Services." I kicked off my right black pump.

"Is this Lyla Moody?" asked a deep gravelly baritone voice I recognized.

"It is. How may I help you?"

"Miss Moody, this is Detective Battle."

"Hello, Detective. What can I do for you?"

"I was hoping I could stop by your home this morning. I have a few more questions for you. It won't take long." I wondered how he knew I'd be home. "I went by your office a few minutes ago, and your uncle said the office was closed today for some wiring issues." Wow, could he read minds too? "Sergeant Landry will be accompanying me."

"Sure, Detective. I'll be here." I shoved my foot back into my pump and zipped my dress back up.

"Good. I'll be there in an hour. We have one other stop first."

"See you then." I disconnected the call.

After I relayed the conversation to Brad, he tried to talk me into moving the appointment. I could see how much he wanted to be here for the meeting. Sheer curiosity had been eating away at him since I'd discussed everything with him last night. It'd been nice to talk it out with an objective person who not only appreciated my invested interest but encouraged it.

But now, as we went around and around about how it could be advantageous to everyone involved if he were here, I was beginning to become annoyed.

"At the very least, you should call your family attorney. Him dropping by like this makes me wonder what he's up to or looking for." Brad scratched his jawline.

I considered his words. The detective had bypassed Mr. Greene by calling me directly, and I did wonder why. I could call Mr. Greene at any time or could shut down the detective's questions by evoking my right to counsel. Not that I believed I'd need it.

"Nope. Like you, I'm curious about what he's up to as well. I can handle it. Besides, I might get some idea of what the family turned over. Whether it's simply the journal or something different all together. It could help Harper if I do this." I wiped down the counter and put the cloth on the sink divider.

"Lyla," Brad said in a chiding manner I didn't care for.

"I'm not getting into this with you again." I rinsed out my mug and put it in the dishwasher.

Brad put his coffee mug down on the bar with a thud and rubbed the scar that ran down from his left eye. He'd once told me that all these years later after his car accident, it still ached sometimes. "What would it hurt for you to wait for me?"

"Look," I said, propping against the counter and folding my arms, "I love working cases together. I do. But this one doesn't concern you."

"If it concerns you, it concerns me. I'm a little upset that you didn't call me while you were on the scene."

I studied him. "You didn't say anything before."

"I'm saying it now."

I considered his comment for a couple of beats. No, I hadn't called Brad, but then I hadn't called anyone. "I called you when I got home."

"That's not the scene. And I have a history with Detective Battle. You had to figure that out when he mentioned me."

Here we go. Now we were getting somewhere. "Oh, it makes perfect sense now. You didn't move your schedule around to be here as a supportive boyfriend, though you did take advantage of that title for the last two nights," I teased, yet still felt a tad irritated. "You're still here because the case and the lead detective interest you. And for the record, how was I to know you have a history with the detective when he simply mentioned your name?"

"Because it makes sense. And come on." He shook his head, not buying my outrage. "We had a lovely dinner and hike yesterday. And if I recall correctly, you jumped me last night."

Okay, that part was accurate. I smirked. "Whatever. I won't hold it against you that you find me irresistible, but why are you so insistent on this case? Perhaps there's something there on the detective you have a history with, or maybe you have a vendetta against him or something?"

He stared at me, flatly. "No. He's tough. We worked on a case together about five years ago. He won't relent in his pursuit of the killer."

"Good."

Brad cocked his head to one side. "Well, that depends. I've seen Battle tear families apart to get to the truth. And sometimes just to find a direction. He isn't going to be kind here. And we're talking about your prim and proper family who would rather swallow their tongues than disparage their reputations."

"That's not fair." God, he was right about that.

"If you think the detective is going to play fair, think again. How does it look that a murder and robbery took place right under everyone's noses? The scene of the crime was at your parents' place. And no one saw a thing." He gave me a stern look. "Not the police, an entire house full of guests, or the catering staff. Then you walk in and stumble on the scene and mention a potential murder weapon that just up and disappears." I'd only just confided in Brad about that little tidbit.

I placed my hands on the island. "I know it doesn't ring true, Brad. Even now, I still can't believe that not one single person witnessed anything suspicious. If I were to step back and examine this objectively, I would suspect a massive cover-up. And I won't lie and say it hasn't crossed my mind more than once." I pushed off the counter and rubbed my forehead. "I just can't make sense of it yet. But I will."

"So why not wait for me?" He softened his tone. "We make a fabulous team. You said so yourself." He wagged his dark brows at me, and I couldn't help but smile. We did—that was true. Brad and I had worked out the kinks in our professional relationship over the last year. The cold cases we worked on were time intensive. Our job entailed reconstructing the cases to discover the identity of and then hopefully arrest whoever was responsible for robbing these victims of their lives.

Brad took his job seriously. He had worked homicide for seven years before moving to a different department. That's probably where his path had crossed with Detective Battle's.

"I love working cases together. But I'm not working on this case. I'm a witness. Nothing more."

He gave me a "yeah, right" look.

"I'm not."

"You won't be able to resist. Do I have to repeat where the crime took place and that the victim is your friend's husband, whose family suspects her of killing him?"

"No, and enough about this. I'll speak with the detective and keep you posted. Have you received the preliminary report back from the Jane Doe discovered off the industrial road last week?"

He shook his head. "Not yet. I'm expecting to get them back today. You gonna have time to work it?"

"I should, yes." There were about twenty-seven Jane Doe cases to date that had gone cold. They call the area that runs along Interstate 85, mostly near the state's northern tip, the dumping grounds. Brad and I had closed three cases, a real feat. I had no intention of slowing until every Jane or John had their identity restored and their families had some closure.

He came around the counter and placed his plate and mug in the sink. "You can push Battle off by a day. Come on." His brown gaze warmed, and I began to melt as he wrapped his arms around my waist, nuzzled my neck, his stubble grazing my cheek. Brad always seemed to have stubble. He wore the cologne I'd bought him. Playing dirty, he was. "I might be able to see something you'll miss," he murmured in my ear.

Spell broken. I put my hand on his chest, pushing Brad away. "Listen, buster. This won't work. I'm not waiting for you. Sorry."

"Seriously?"

"Yes, Brad, seriously. How can I ever prove myself as a competent investigator if either you or Calvin is constantly shadowing me?"

Brad put his hands on his hips and nodded. "I see what you're saying."

"Plus, if I wait for you, your background with the detective could prove a distraction and detract from the focus of the case. I've been having this weird feeling about the family since Harper began divulging the secrets of her life."

"You really think there's something odd at the Richardson house? That maybe someone there is involved?"

I folded my arms and considered. "The family dislikes Harper in the worst possible way. Well, except for LJ, but that's another story in itself. She has off-the-chart trust issues. It's so hard to say. The robbery throws me, and to get a clearer picture, I think I need to know what sort of *evidence* the family turned over."

He gave me a devilish smile. "You sure you don't want my help?"

"Just because we're"—I swished my hand between us— "doing *this* doesn't mean I'll rearrange a potential case just because you ask. Though I appreciate your offer"—I closed the space between us and took the lapels of his sport coat—"and I will keep you in mind if your services are required." I brushed my lips against his.

When I pulled away, he winked. "Wow. I see how it is then. Detective Battle won't know what hit him. I better get on the road. I have to be in Nashville before five; the Jane Doe had a punch card for a deli up there. I'll probably just grab a hotel for the night."

"That makes sense. Otherwise, you'll be spending over ten hours in the car. Besides, we're having an impromptu club meeting for Rosa since she had to work when we had our regular meeting."

His phone chirped on the counter. Brad kissed me again before stepping aside to check his message. He clipped his phone to the holder on his belt and slid his arms into his coat. "I've got to go."

"Okay." I turned and unlocked, then opened the door.

Before he got into the driver's seat, he called, "Be careful and remember, you promised to keep me posted."

"Right back at you." I waved as he pulled out of the lot. The wind blew, and I detected a faint scent of rain in the air. Rumbling thunder and the darkening sky informed me I'd assumed that correctly.

Mrs. Kreuger came out of the building across the street and walked her little dog around the corner. It didn't look like she had a small cleanup bag with her either. I glanced over at Mel's empty space. She'd have a fit if she witnessed the woman violating our community laws.

Sighing, I started to cross the parking lot to have a word with her and froze. A black sedan idling beside a maple tree near the pool area caught my attention. The window rolled down, and someone flicked ashes from a cigarette onto the ground. The headlights flashed as if trying to get my attention. I wondered for a second if LJ had driven Harper over, but then recalled he drove a black Lexus, and this car was the wrong make and looked a lot older.

Big fat raindrops began to fall. The lights flashed again and kept flashing like a strobe light. I shivered, but it had nothing to do with the temperature or the rain.

I backed slowly toward my front door. Mrs. Krueger's violation didn't seem all that important now. I had every intention of taking a picture of the creep in the car and reporting him as I scrambled, grabbing my phone and rushing back onto my stoop, but whoever it was had gone. That fast. Which made me even more suspicious of his intentions.

Blowing out a breath, I closed my front door and glanced around, needing to do something. Anything. Clean—I'd clean. I didn't want the detective to think I lived in a pigsty. By the time I'd tidied up a bit, I began to wonder if I'd overreacted in my concerns about the car. It could've been a kid playing a prank; clearly, worrying about Harper and thinking about her husband's murder had my imagination in overdrive.

I picked up the books on the floor next to the sofa. I found a tube of lipstick and my plaid scarf on the rug. Things had gotten a little passionate last night. I couldn't help but smile. Brad had undoubtedly spiced up this gal's life. He'd showed up at a time when the same ole homeboys weren't cutting it for me anymore. I even enjoyed our little spats. They were lively and never got nasty. Fun. Life was fun with Brad.

Chapter Eleven

My stomach growled, and I got up from the dining room table and stretched. I did a double take when I glanced down at the time on my phone. It was almost three, and the detective had yet to show. I'd finished up the data entry for my uncle's backlog cases and began my file on Phyllis Johnson, Harper's aunt. A public records search showed a single filing for divorce when she was in her early twenties; she had no criminal or civil charges filed against her over the years. So far, I'd found no state or federal tax liens, judgments, bankruptcies, or notices of default or hidden assets. I'd placed several calls to neighbors who still resided on the street; they, like Harper, seemed to think the idea that Phyllis Johnson took off to start over some- where sounded absurd. This was not a promising start and one I'd hoped to avoid. Harper had enough to deal with without having to face that she might not ever see her aunt again.

I sighed and put my laptop aside. After a quick mental debate on whether to call the detective directly, I decided to try Rosa first, since she was planning to accompany him anyway. The call went straight to voicemail. Anxiety made my stomach churn. Perhaps

Detective Battle and Rosa had just been held up by something. Highly possibly—still, this wasn't an appointment where they'd scheduled a window between noon and four. A quick check at my phone logs didn't show Harper had called, and I felt confident she would call if something significant had taken place.

I'd see Rosa later anyway, and I would ask her what happened then. I showered and changed clothes, then decided to drive into town to pick up some food for tonight's meeting. I needed to have an ordinary and fun evening: food, good wine, and book chat with my best girlfriends. The phones had been quiet, so I didn't foresee any problems with skipping out a little early. Our operation wasn't a nine-to-five sort of business anyway.

As the rain subsided, the temperature dropped, making me glad I'd worn my oversized gray hoodie. My favorite specialty food shop was bustling with shoppers. The lighting and presentation made this shop a pleasure to frequent—everything decorated in white and muted earth tones, making for a perfect backdrop for appealing food displays. The lighting made the colors of the food pop, and the sampling cheese counter made selection easier for those domestically challenged. I'd selected a double cream brie and a few wedges of hard cheese recommended by the lovely young man working the counter.

By the time I was on my way to the wine section, my mood had considerably lifted. As I turned onto the wine aisle, I noticed Piper Sanchez chatting with one of mother's neighbors. Craning my neck around, I could see they were deep in conversation. *Hmm.* When my cart hit something, I sucked in a shocked breath.

My eyes met the tall, thin man's behind his square black frames. And *he* was on the *floor.* "Oh, I'm so sorry!" My cheeks warmed as I bent down next to him. Humiliation overwhelmed me—I'd knocked the man down. "I wasn't paying attention. Are you okay?"

He placed his hands on the floor, smiling and shaking his head as he stood, bringing me up with him. "Yes, I'm fine."

I put my hands to my cheeks. "I'm so embarrassed. I hope I didn't hurt you."

He laughed and dusted off his slacks. "No harm done. I shouldn't have stooped down so low to read the labels." He extended his hand. "Charles Hammond."

I took his hand and gave it a light squeeze. "Hello, I'm Lyla Moody."

"It's nice to meet you, Lyla. I wanted to make your acquaintance the other night, but"—he shrugged a shoulder—"it didn't seem appropriate." He glanced in my cart filled with cheese, premade antipasto platters, shrimp cocktail, a couple of packages of spiced nuts, crackers, and a loaf of French breach. He reached over and chose a nice Chianti and a Cabernet Franc. "The acidity will work extremely well with salty foods."

The writer didn't seem like a pest or rude at all. Perhaps my first impression had been wrong. I took the bottles and placed them in my cart. "You know your wines."

"It's a new passion of mine." He stepped back and put his hands in his pockets. "My protagonist enjoys the finer things in life." He glanced around. "This shop is simply delightful, and a gem one would not expect to find this far away from the city. I might use the store in my current work in progress."

"Oh." I wondered what else he'd be using.

"Charles! There you are." Piper, wearing an accusatory expression, stood at the end of the aisle. She literally tapped her foot theatrically, which I found amusing.

"Here I am." He smiled and turned to pick out a couple of bottles of wine.

"We're going to be late for our dinner engagement." She huffed as she checked her watch before focusing on me. "How are you doing, Lyla? You're good friends with Harper Richardson, right?"

I met her gaze straight on. "We're friends. That's true."

"And you found the body. Interesting. I've meant to come by and offer my condolences to you and your mother. That couldn't have been easy on either of you."

"That's incredibly kind of you." My tone dripped with sarcasm. "But it's Harper who is truly grieving. And I'm afraid our calendars are pretty full. I'll get back to you."

"Ouch." Charles smirked and stepped aside to allow me to pass. "Nice meeting you."

"Nice meeting you too." I tossed a smile over my shoulder and went to check out. Piper and I had once been close friends. Right now, that felt like a million years ago. I began to wonder what had happened to our friendship. Things like that happened, I supposed.

I walked down the sidewalk of the square, carrying my bags and moving toward my car. As I waited for the stoplight to change, a silver Cadillac parked around the side of Sweeties Market and Deli caught my eye. The car looked like Mother's.

A glance into the window of the market confirmed my suspicions. Mother sat at the table directly to the left of the dining room. To say I was surprised by her outing would be an understatement. Quizzically, I peered through the window. The ladies she dined with were her usual crowd. Part of me felt glad she'd managed to get out and about. The other part worried sick she might be struggling to deal with what had happened and could react badly. Some things trigger Mother's past trauma, and she'd lose herself for a few days. At least that's how Daddy described it. Thankfully, my mother always found her way back.

Mother beamed at the table, and I, too, began to smile. My smile faltered when Charles passed by the window. He waltzed right up to their table and took a seat in the middle. Hadn't Piper said they had a dinner engagement? I scanned the room and did not see her. Huh. Perhaps she'd said "our dinner engagements"—plural.

The table greeted Charles as if they had been awaiting his arrival. I still saw no sign of Piper, and that was a relief. The women began to laugh at something Charles said. Boy, would he have some material to work with now. You'd think he would have mentioned this to me. He seemed nice enough, but I still, I didn't care for the idea of his unguarded access to the old families of Sweet Mountain who loved to gab.

Someone bumped into me, and I stumbled forward. "I apologize." A woman flushed with embarrassment and took her child by the hand. "Say you're sorry, son." The little boy, who wore a blue ball cap and had giant doe eyes, said, "Sorry," before ducking his head behind his mother's leg.

"It's fine. No harm done," I assured them. The light changed, and I cast one last glance back toward the deli. Charles stared right at me, and our eyes locked. They were penetrating and eerily unwavering. Part of me wanted to storm in there and find out what was going on, but that would only make another scene, giving him more material. I smiled as if everything was perfectly fine, hoping that were true, and waved before turning my back on him. I'd have to deal with this situation later. I crossed the street as the wind blew, and an ominous feeling overtook me that the gray sky could perhaps be an omen. I hoped not.

* * *

The core group of the Jane Does—Mel, Amelia, and I—were all seated on my tufted group sofa. We were still waiting on Rosa. I'd just finished telling them about my encounter with the writer and how later I'd seen him with Mother and her ladies' group.

"Oh my God," Melanie cackled. "You ran him over!"

Amelia smirked and picked up one of the bottles of wine he'd selected—not that I'd shared that part of the encounter. "Be honest. You sure you didn't want to run him over?"

I threw a napkin at Amelia. "No! But after seeing him charming the senior ladies of our town for information, I might have reason to again."

"Oh well, that would be a little nutty, Lyla. And when have we ever had this opportunity before? Maybe we should have him come to our club meeting." Melanie lifted her hands in the air. "Or better yet, maybe he'll let us beta-read his novel! We could influence the story. Give him a genuine perspective of our hometown life. I mean, if he's going to write it, he might as well involve us."

I glanced from Mel to Amelia, who raised her brows. "She has a point. And honestly, the story will probably only be loosely based on Sweet Mountain."

"Well, I hate to burst any bubbles here, but I googled him and didn't find a single title he's published." I took a sip from my glass.

"That doesn't mean he won't—or maybe he publishes under a pseudonym. Lots of people do that, as you well know." Melanie wasn't having her bubble burst.

"You're right. And it's something to consider, I guess. Charles did seem nice." I glanced back at the clock. "Where is Rosa? This is her second no-show today."

Mel crossed her legs, and her concern replaced her amused smile with a frown. "I'm starting to get worried. It isn't like her not to call, and her phone is still going straight to voicemail."

"She's just a half hour late. Let's not freak out yet." Amelia attempted to be the voice of reason, but her seemingly calm demeanor had a crack in it. She kept tapping her index finger on the sofa.

"More like forty-five minutes." Mel didn't even try to remain calm as she violently tapped on the screen of her phone. She placed her phone back on the end table with a giant sigh. "Voicemail."

We'd all grown closer over the last year after the death of a club member. The tragedy bound us, and we were more than merely club members now. We were like sisters—sisters who could read each other well.

The knock on the door made all three of us jump. I leaped to my feet and answered it. Rosa stood on the other side, still in her blue uniform. "Oh my God! We were so worried," I said.

"I'm sorry." She hugged me, and I let her pass. "My phone died, and I didn't have my charger on me."

Mel and Amelia hugged her next, then Rosa took a seat next to Mel. "It's been a day from hell."

Melanie poured a glass of wine and handed it to her.

"What happened to you and Detective Battle this morning? He called and said y'all would be here, and then nothing." I kicked off my Mary Janes and sat on the chaise lounge, tucking my feet underneath me.

"He didn't call you?" Rosa stared at me for a moment, confusion written all over her face. When I shook my head, she said, "Huh," and took a deep sip from the glass.

"He said he was going to. I guess it slipped his mind. It was *that* kind of day." Rosa put the glass on the coffee table. "Two of our officers and Chief Quinn called out sick with the nasty stomach bug that's been going around. Detective Battle took me off desk duty, and we had to hire a temp to cover the front desk. It was madness."

"Oh no." Amelia's eyes went wide. "A couple of ladies from my church had that bug running through their families last weekend. They said it was awful. Had their entire family down for the count for three days."

"Yikes." Melanie scooted away from Rosa.

"I don't have it." Rosa gave Melanie a look that said she didn't appreciate being treated like a leper. "And I'm starving." Rosa got up and made herself a plate from the food I'd laid out on the bar. "I missed lunch and came straight here from my last call."

"Nothing too horrible, I hope," I said.

Rosa shook her head. "Some domestic over on the outskirts of town." She grabbed a napkin and perched on a barstool. "Did you find anything on Harper's aunt?"

I gave her the lowdown on what I'd discovered and how even I found it difficult to believe that a person could simply vanish in this day and age without a trace, and that those closest to her agreed with Harper's and my assessment. "Though I'm not ready to rule anything out yet," I continued. "All it takes is one critical piece of evidence to alter an investigation completely." I truly wished to be able to locate the woman for Harper.

Rosa nodded. "That's the truth." She tossed a couple of olives stuffed with blue cheese into her mouth.

"Well, did it feel amazing to be in the field?" Melanie asked Rosa. Mel seemed to have gotten over her worry of contracting the illness going around.

Rosa shared with us that after her stint in Afghanistan working as military police, she needed a break from any field duty. She never went into details about what she'd been through, and we never pried. We admired her and gave her the freedom to share whatever she felt like and whenever she was ready to.

"Yeah, it did. I liked being on desk duty. I needed the reprieve for a bit, but now, I think it might be time for a change." She turned toward me. "Lyla, you have any water?"

"Yes, in the refrigerator." I smiled at her growth. "Sweet Mountain will be lucky to have you keeping us safe."

My friends echoed my encouragement, and Rosa grinned over her shoulder. "Y'all are the best."

While she went to retrieve the bottle, I wrestled with what would be appropriate to ask about the Richardson case. I cast a glance toward Mel and Amelia, who also seemed to be having the same trouble.

Rosa turned around, the bottle to her lips, and stared at us for a few blinks. "Y'all, I can't say anything more, so please don't ask me to. I probably shouldn't have called the other day. Can we please just chat about the book? Or if this is too difficult, I'll understand and go."

Mel, Amelia, and I exchanged a glance. None of us wanted her to leave. And as her friends, we needed to respect her position.

"Please, stay." I smiled. My friends chimed in with similar comments.

"So, what did you think about the story?" Melanie said, directing the conversation to its stated purpose.

Rosa beamed, and we all let out a little sigh of relief. "It was so good. I don't have the book with me, but I finished it. I had my suspicions but did not see that ending coming."

The fears of the day became distant as we delved back into discussions of *Crooked House*. Having my townhouse filled with friends enjoying food, and listening to my book club chattering, made everything seem more normal somehow. The energy in the room was the medicine we all needed. And later, Melanie took great pleasure in telling the story of how I ran over the writer at the market.

We were all still laughing, the warmth of the wine spreading throughout my body, when my phone rang from inside my purse. I let it go to voicemail, not wanting anything to spoil the evening. But as soon as the ringing ended, it began again.

"Take it. It might be important." Rosa said, still chuckling as she got up to use the restroom.

"Sorry, y'all." I reached down and dug into my bag to retrieve it. A Facetime call came through from a number I didn't recognize, and I almost declined it, when something changed my mind. This call could have to do with the disappearance of Harper's aunt. I'd given my number out to several people. I swiped the phone icon right, to answer. LJ's face came on the screen.

"Lyla, this is LJ. I'm calling at Harper's request. The cops are here with a search warrant!"

"What?" I was on my feet.

"They're tearing the house apart!" The screen view flipped, and Harper's pale face filled the screen, her voice high and shrill.

"They showed us a warrant. Something about new evidence they've uncovered." The camera turned, and we could see Detective Battle and another officer as they came down the hallway toward the camera.

"Harper Richardson, you are under arrest for the murder of Leonard Richardson." I couldn't believe my eyes or ears. My heart began to race as my friends and I crowded around my phone to watch helplessly as the officer continued reading Harper her rights while another officer cuffed her in the living room of the Richardson home.

Harper glanced up at the phone with flooding eyes. "What's going on? You have to help me, Lyla! I can't believe this is happening. I'm mean, I worried someone might try and frame me, but—" Before she could finish her thought, the police interrupted. Her face crumpled, her bottom lip trembling uncontrollably.

"It's okay, Harper. Listen to me. I'll do everything I can to help." She tried to focus on the phone. Just then, her legs gave way, and the two officers held her upright by her arms.

Sharp intakes of breath echoed from my friends as my hand holding the phone shook. Horrible thoughts raced through my mind as we watched Harper being taken out the front door and placed in the back of the police cruiser. Never will I forget the look on her face when the officer said she was under arrest. The entire Richardson family stood idly by. They'd even wheeled out the elderly gentlemen onto the front porch to watch the officers put her into the back seat, the officer's hand on the top of her head as he pushed her in. The only one who seemed to care was LJ. He'd rushed the police, shouting profanities, phone in hand, until he too was threatened with an arrest himself.

"LJ!" I shouted to get his attention. "She needs a lawyer!"

He shoved his hand into his hair, a panicked expression on his face. "What?"

"Harper needs a lawyer." I gripped the phone too tightly; my fingers were white. "Do you need me to help you with that?"

"No. I've taken care of that." He appeared frantic. His head kept shaking, and the phone screen trembled. "I've got to go. Harper begged me to call you and let you know you'll be hearing from her lawyer. We need your help." The sound of loud breathing came over the phone as we watched him run toward his car. "I can't believe this. I effing can't believe it!"

"Okay, try and stay calm. Let me know—" I managed to get in before LJ disconnected the call.

I stared at my friends, all of us at a loss for words. Amelia sat down on the sofa, hard. The whites of her eyes were showing more than usual, and she panted a little. Melanie blinked rapidly and looked like she, too, might faint.

A million things went through my mind. With Harper charged with murder, would LJ have access to the family account? Did he have his own money? Would he contribute to her defense? She was going to need all the help she could get, emotionally and financially. By the way he'd reacted to her arrest, I believed he would. I wondered who her lawyer was and when she'd retained him. She hadn't mentioned anything about seeking my help, other than for her aunt's case. I guess with the new development that had changed.

I needed answers. While at the Richardsons', I'd resisted asking about the rumor of an affair. I'd hoped we'd have another chance when she'd settled down a bit. It would surely come out now. Everything would come out now. Not that I judged her for it. I had no idea how I would survive in her position.

Rosa slowly made her way back into the living room. All three of our heads whipped around accusingly. "I told you Detective Battle had evidence for a potential search warrant. I told you not to be cavalier in your assumptions. The case is solid. And that's all I can tell y'all." She walked over and grabbed her purse off the sofa. "I better go."

None of us said anything as she walked out the front door. We all just sat there, processing what had transpired.

After Mel and Amelia left, I called Brad and left a voicemail. I got into my coziest PJs and washed my face and brushed my teeth. I couldn't do anything for Harper until her lawyer called, so I decided to check in on my mother, who seemed to be in a rush to get me off the phone after I told her I saw her at Sweet Market Deli. "Well, you should have come in and said hello. Everyone would have loved to see you."

"I had groceries and didn't want to disturb your meeting with the *writer*." I let that hang out there, hoping she'd elaborate on the discussion.

"Lyla Jane, please don't be patronizing. Have you heard from Harper? Is she doing all right?"

"Patronizing? I simply inquired as to why you lunched with a writer. You, Mrs. Ross, and Mrs. Waters were all sitting at a table with him. And while he seems like a nice man, I'd be careful. Some things can't be retracted."

"What? James, turn that up." I tried to remain patient.

"Oh my stars. The police arrested Harper this afternoon." She sounded shocked and a tad out of breath.

Guess it made the nightly news. "I know."

"You knew! You knew and didn't tell me." Mother sounded distraught.

"I was about to. What's between you and Harper? You discouraged me from drawing any attention to her. Had me withhold information from the police. I don't understand, and now—well, they're going to leave no stone unturned. You do realize how, from the detective's perspective, this case looks like a massive cover-up. If you know something more, you'd better tell me right now." My pulse raced as I waited for her response. I couldn't imagine what she'd say, but the foreboding I felt spoke volumes. I loved my mother. But I didn't exactly *get* her.

"There is much you don't understand. And that young man, the writer you were asking about, he seems to understand everything."

"What are you saying? Everything about what? Harper? I can't—"

"Lyla Jane, I have to go." She hung up. For the first time in my life, my mother hung up on me. I stared at the phone. What was going on? I worried now more than ever. She hadn't denied a cover-up. Was it possible? No. I gave myself a mental shake. My mind went round and round with thoughts I couldn't ascertain. I closed my eyes, willing clarity to come.

When the phone rang again, I nearly leaped out of my skin. I assumed it was Mother calling back. I didn't even check when I doubled-tapped my earbud. "I can't believe you hung up on me."

"What?" a male voice said. My mouth felt dry, and I checked the time and who was calling. It was almost eleven. I must have fallen asleep.

"Sorry, Uncle Calvin." I yawned. "I thought you were someone else. We're working from home again tomorrow?"

"I'm afraid so. I'm sure you saw the news about Harper Richardson."

"Actually, LJ called when she was being arrested and gave me a heads-up that she needed my help."

"He called me too, and so did Harper's attorney." Well, that made me feel better. "The attorney—Jenkins is his name—he's just a step above a public defender, and he sounded overwhelmed to me. They retained him before her arrest. I suppose they saw a charge coming." I'd wondered about that. "And Jenkins officially requested our help turning up leads to build a defense."

I sat up straight in the bed. "Oh!"

"But honey, they don't have the money for it."

I gripped the blanket. "I can do a lot of the legwork pro bono."

"I knew you were going to say that, and I wouldn't be able to stop you from running with this on your own." My uncle knew me so well. "But Jenkins claims there may be some funding coming down the pipe in a couple of days. Not a ton, but if he manages it, we'll make it stretch."

"I'd hug you right now if you were here. You're turning into an old softie."

He snorted. "Jenkins would like us to meet him at the police station in the morning for a consultation. No promises."

"Okay. I get it." I grinned so hard my face ached. After the exasperating conversation with my mother that had worried me to death, this was finally something I could affect. "I'll be there."

Chapter Twelve

T he police station was silent when I walked through the double doors of the little brick building Sweet Mountain Police used for their station house. They didn't need a large building, so when the small Baptist church moved locations when their congregation outgrew the building fifteen years ago, the city renovated the building, and the police department moved in. I stood in front of the large, vacant mahogany desk in the poorly lit front room and waited for Rosa to return to her post. I glanced up at the wooden plaque that hung above the glass separating the desk from the waiting area. It read:

"The Sweet Mountain Police Department's focus is:

"To protect and serve our citizens with a high level of integrity
"To utilize a community policing philosophy
"To strive for excellence in all that we do
"To become less incident driven and more proactive in preventing crime"

"Hey, Lyla." Rosa's smile didn't make it up to her eyes as she retook her seat and smoothed her thick, dark, wavy hair away from her face.

"Good morning, Sergeant Landry. I come bearing gifts." I presented Rosa with a cup of her favorite brew. She always complained about the coffee they served in the police station. "I'm sorry about the way I reacted last night. We all are. We felt a little blindsided, and you had nothing to do with that. You did try and warn us."

"This coffee is your peace offering?" On my nod, she smiled again. "Thank you for saying that. You can't imagine how conflicted I've been feeling." Rosa took the paper cup of mocha java and sipped. She closed her eyes, savoring. "You are my favorite person right now." She sighed. "Are we okay?"

"Glad to hear it, and yes, we are one hundred percent okay. I get it. You and I are both dedicated to our lines of work. I want you to know I respect you and understand completely."

"But do Mel and Amelia?" Her shoulders sagged.

"If they don't, they will. This tragedy has been tough on all of us. You included."

She took another sip from the cup. "It has been challenging. Harper has always been standoffish around me. I guess that's why I felt concerned before any of y'all did. Not that I don't wish things were different. I do. But we can't focus on the things we can't control, right?"

"Right." I rested my hip against the desk.

"Thanks for coming by and bringing coffee. You didn't need to make a trip over, but I'm glad you did." She went back to typing but in a moment looked up again. "Is there something else you want to talk about?"

"I'm sorry." I hesitated, surprised by the question. "I didn't mean to interrupt your workday. You want me to have a seat?" An odd vibe rolled off her.

Rosa's hands froze over the keyboard. "Wait a minute. You aren't here just to speak with me, are you?"

I cocked my head to one side. "No one informed you that Cousins was requested to confer with the defense?"

"No." Her brow furrowed.

"Well, they have."

"If that's true, why didn't they call you?"

"Mr. Jenkins called my uncle and asked us to come down. Calvin should be here soon." My voice trailed off after 'soon.' Something felt off. "What am I missing?"

Rosa pursed her lips and held up a finger. She rolled her chair back to check whether anyone nearby could overhear us. A sense of dread crept up my spine as she moved the chair back to her desk and leaned forward. "There was an incident with an *inmate*. County lockup called for an ambulance, and the *inmate* went to Piedmont last night." Rosa appeared to struggle with how much to share. She kept glancing back toward the door behind her.

My fingers went to my parted lips as I whispered, "How bad is she?" Had Harper been so terrified that she had a heart attack or something? I had no idea of her medical history. Or had another inmate harmed her? I'd never or such a thing and couldn't fathom it.

"I honestly don't know."

"What happened?" I asked, then shook my head immediately. "Forget it. I don't want to get you in trouble."

Another officer came through the door. Rosa straightened. "I'm not at liberty to give out that information. Good day, Miss

Moody." She wheeled her chair back to retrieve a paper from the printer.

"Good day, Sergeant Landry."

As I left the building, I fumbled through my purse for my phone and had to fight with my shaking hands.

"Miss Moody! Lyla!"

I glanced up, shocked to see Charles waving to me from the parking lot. Off to the left of him, her back turned to me, stood Piper with her phone to her ear. I lifted my hand in a wave and strolled toward my car.

The way Charles looked at me put me on edge as he trotted over. He smiled, exposing a row of perfectly straight teeth, as he reached me. "What a surprise to see you here."

"Yeah. I'm surprised to see you too. I just dropped off some coffee for my friend." I gave him a small smile and kept my tone casual. I didn't want to convey that I knew anything about Harper. The last thing she needed was more attention from the press.

"How nice of you. You must get your kindness from your mother."

My smile faltered.

"She is eager to help me with my new novel." His smile broadened. "I think it will be a big hit too."

I hiked my purse higher on my shoulder and folded my arms across my chest. "You should be careful about where you get your information. A lot of the seniors around here love to tell stories with lots of embellishments."

He grinned. "True. While I enjoyed speaking with the group"—he leaned over—"I'd much rather spend time getting to know you and hearing your perspective on things."

I'm sure he would. "You know," I said, "I'm familiar with all the big names in publishing. Your name doesn't ring a bell. Unless you publish under a pseudonym."

"You googled me." He stepped closer; his face took on a more serious expression as he cast a glance back toward Piper, who hadn't noticed us yet. "Listen, all kidding aside, I'd like to sit down with you as soon as possible. I think we have a lot to talk about it." Something odd swam in his gaze—something pleading.

"Um, I'm kind of busy at the moment but—"

Piper shouted some obscenities into her phone, then noticed us and called out, "Hey, Lyla," before rushing over to me. "Could I get a quote for the Sweet Mountain Gazette?"

"Quote on . . .?" I turned my back on Charles and sped up my pace, glancing around the lot for my car.

She pursed her lips and followed me, holding the phone near my face. "Come on. Leonard Richardson was murdered in your parents' house. They just charged his second wife, a friend of yours, with the crime. Her stepson says you're helping her case. I heard a little rumor that something was missing from the murder scene." I flinched, and she smiled. "Surely you have a comment." Charles had caught up with us, and he kept his gaze intently on me.

"I'm afraid I don't." I hit the key fob and started to open the door. I was irritated by the manipulation while my friend fought for her life. Piper threw her hip against the door, slamming it shut. Frazzled, I fought to control my temper.

"Lyla, we've known each other forever. And I know you're on your way to Piedmont Hospital like we are." She tossed her hair as if to say, *we're way ahead of you.* "And as we are both aware, when something is going on in Sweet Mountain, *everyone* has a comment. You are working in the PI field now. You found the body. Surely you understand this playing dumb isn't going to cut it."

I hiked my purse higher on my shoulder. "Not everyone likes to feed the rumor mill, Piper. Harper deserves privacy and a right to due process uncompromised by a skewed public opinion."

"Uh-huh." Piper held her phone in my face. "What does your mother have to do with the Richardsons, and why is she protecting Harper?" My gaze flew to Charles, who in turn gave his head a small shake. Was he saying Piper hadn't gotten anything from him? Whatever. I wondered what Mother had told him. Piper caught the little visual exchange and turned toward Charles; he pushed his square black frames up on his nose, revealing nothing.

Enough of this. I squared off against the buxom brunette accustomed to getting her way. "Nothing, and she isn't."

"Are you so sure about that? I heard from a little bird that she's very involved. She's even offered to help with bail. That is, if Harper's attorney manages to convince a judge she isn't a flight risk." Triumph radiated across her face, and I fought the urge to slap it right off her.

"Wow," I said dryly. "No wonder you can't manage any career advancements. You believe everything any imbecile spouts off." I glared from her to Charles. "Now, if you'll kindly remove your sizeable rump from my door, I'd like to be on my way."

Piper huffed, her face flushed, but to her credit, she pulled herself together in record time. She smiled, slow and coolly. "You don't want to make an enemy of me, I assure you of that."

"Why?" I tossed my hair over my shoulder and cast her a dead-level glare. "You gonna sit on me?" I'd gone for the shock factor and achieved it. Not that I was proud of reverting to adolescent behavior.

Charles let out a snort of laughter and shoved his glasses back up on his nose as he stepped around Piper, who'd moved away from my car. "Here." He thrust a card at me with a wink as he jerked open the door. Piper had rattled me with the comment about Mother, and I needed to shut her up to give myself time to find out what the hell was going on. I didn't buy the enemy-for-life bull. She played tough because she had to. And if it turned out I was wrong, oh well. I'd deal with the repercussions then.

Chapter Thirteen

Forty-five minutes later, I pulled into the parking garage of Piedmont Hospital. Nerves clenched within my stomach as I worried for Harper. My phone rang through the speakers in the car. I hit the "Answer" button on the steering column. "Hey." It was my uncle Calvin.

"Where are you?" He always sounded uptight when something went awry with a case. This one technically hadn't even begun yet, and we were already dealing with a nightmare.

"I'm at the hospital. When I arrived at the precinct, I found out they transported Harper here from jail. I don't know anything more yet. I was going to call you, but I ran into Piper Sanchez, and she said the oddest thing that had me mentally whirling. I'm sure there isn't any truth to it. She claimed Mother had offered to help with Harper's legal fees."

"That's the first I've heard of it." He didn't sound happy. "I did receive a call about Harper from Mr. Jenkins. He's still trying to get to the bottom of what happened. Be careful. He warned me of a large press presence around the hospital."

I glanced around and could see a couple of media vans. "Okay. I'll keep my head down as I go inside."

"Good girl. I'm not sure they'll give you any information on her condition. Mr. Jenkins is on his way there now. He raised hell with the county, and he probably is still doing so in transit. I'd advise you to wait for him. I can meet you both after eleven—Jenkins is aware of that. He has drop-in office space in one of the buildings few a few streets over." When a car slowly rolled past me, I thought it looked similar to the car I'd seen at my townhouse—or at least I thought it was. My heart sped up.

"Okay." Turning in my seat, I scoped out the scene behind me. Nothing odd stood out. Shaking my head, I inwardly chastised myself. Nerves. *Get a grip, Lyla!* "Got it. Did Mr. Jenkins say where he'd meet me?"

"No, but I figured perhaps the cafeteria. You'll blend in there."

That made sense.

"Did you get anything on what the police have on Harper? It took a lot of effort not to question Rosa." I shifted in my seat.

"I bet it did. Yes, I did get an overview from Jenkins, and you're not going to like it."

Chills spread across my skin, and I adjusted the heat.

"From the tox screen they ran on the victim, he discovered someone poisoned Leonard."

"What?" I couldn't believe my ears. I'd imagined he was going to mention that the candlestick had been found in the house, with Harper's prints on it.

"Yes. And the toxicologists never would have been able to search for the particular drug if the victim's brother hadn't turned over a bloody crocheted purse—" Blood thrummed loudly in my ears, so loud it drowned out my uncle's voice. I'd seen Harper with her crocheted purse at the library. The image of what I'd thought was a rope in Leonard's hand flashed in my mind. The remnant had been the perfect size for a purse strap.

As my breath came in small gasps, I muted the phone. *Oh my God!* That was why I'd found comfort in noticing Harper's wristlet at the charity event. Subconsciously, I'd recognized the purse strap.

"Lyla!"

I cleared my throat. "I . . . I'm here. Sorry."

"I told you that you wouldn't like it. Do you recall seeing a torn strap near the body? Or did Harper say anything about drugs Leonard might have been taking?"

"Yes to the strap. No to the drugs." I focused on his words.

"That's not good. Not good for you or Harper."

I shook my head. "I didn't withhold anything." I cringed and thought back to my conversation with Mother. "Not about the strap, anyway. I honestly believed it to be a rope or jacket tie. And another thing that doesn't make sense is that when I saw Harper, she was carrying a clutch, not her crocheted bag."

Uncle Calvin grumbled in irritation. "Tell me you included that in your original statement."

"They didn't ask me about her purse. And yes, I mentioned seeing something in Leonard's hand. I told the detective every-thing." *Oh, Harper.* "And Calvin, before you pull out of the case, Harper thinks Leonard's family is trying to frame her. Anyone who's spent time in that house and around that family would have no trouble finding the notion plausible. How did Leonard's brother come to possess the purse?"

"I believe the brother, Felix, is on record as reporting finding the evidence somewhere in the house."

I rolled my eyes. "See! If you killed someone, would you hide something of such importance where others could find it? No! You'd get rid of it. Another thing, Leonard's brother, Felix, is a feeble older man in a wheelchair. He doesn't have the capacity to search a house that size. It doesn't make sense."

"Okay. That's something to dig into, right? Reasonable doubt is all we need to present *if* we take the case. And that's a big if. Perhaps the family is on the side of justice, and Harper has fooled you."

"Oh puhlease . . ." I put effort into debunking that ridiculous notion. "But to show you I'm on the side of justice, I'll question her thoroughly. I met those people; you did not. I'm telling you, something is up with that family. And I'll prove it."

"Okay, okay. I hear how set you are on helping the girl, and if the family is 'our reasonable doubt' at present, we need to spend more time in that house."

"That shouldn't be a problem for me. LJ is cooperative."

He grumbled again. "There's truth about the rumors, then?"

"I don't know, but I am suspicious they are true. I'll find out from Harper for sure. It's something we'll need to get ahead of. I'm sure her attorney has thought of that. If he's aware of it, that is."

"We'll find out. I'm not committing to anything. Yet. You need to be prepared for the DA to want to speak with you as well, and if something more damning comes to light—"

"I hear you. I'll jump ship if I determine Harper's guilty." And I'd already thought of my deposition with the DA. "I'll be prepared for the DA. But is Mother?" I said this only to show him I was thinking ahead.

"What are you getting at?" Calvin sounded wary.

"I'm just saying. Mother's acting oddly."

He cleared his throat. "I'm sure I don't have to remind you of the importance of having your father's lawyer, William Greene, present."

"No, Uncle Calvin, you don't. Mr. Greene was present during my original interview. The police are aware if they need to speak to me again to go through him. I've got this. Relax." I decided to keep to myself the meeting that I'd agreed to yesterday with Detective Battle, because it had never taken place. No harm done. However, I shuddered at the thought of what my reaction would have been if he'd posed the question about the purse. If Detective Battle had dropped that bomb, I'm not sure I could have held it together.

"Good. Your father will take care of making sure his household is represented." That was true. "And you know the word 'relax' isn't in my vocabulary. Call me when you're on your way to his drop-in office."

"Of course." I disconnected the call.

* * *

As I walked through the dark, dingy parking garage, my heels echoed loudly, giving me a nervous alone feeling, and I sped up my pace. I'd never been a fan of parking garages and took a deep breath as the clear, bright blue sky greeted me. My thoughts drifted back to the case. If Felix had turned over the purse, what did the police need the search warrant for?

I spied reporters and a couple of uniformed officers standing around the front entrance, and my stomach lurched. The uniformed officers were doing their best to move the group back from the double doors. Slowly, the group begrudgingly retreated several yards back from their original position.

Come on, Lyla. I shoved my anxiety aside. Zipping my phone into my purse, I pulled my scarf up, put on my sunglasses, and made my way toward the crowd, being careful to keep my chin tucked down. As the entrance neared, no one stopped me, and my guard began to slip. Then a dark-headed woman shoved her phone in front of my face. "Miss Moody! Why did Mrs. Richardson murder her husband?"

Keep it together. I steeled myself, pivoted, and went to the left.

"Did Mrs. Richardson try to kill herself?" *Oh sweet Jesus.* Another pivot.

They swarmed, and I felt like a character in *The Walking Dead*, trying to make it to the safety of the building. "Is your family concealing evidence to protect a killer?"

"No. And I was under the impression that in this country a person is innocent until proven guilty."

"Is the Richardson family involved in communal living?" someone shouted.

I got bumped but managed to remain upright. "No. What sort of question is that?" People were losing their minds.

"What does your mother have to do with this case?" Phones and microphones moved closer to my face. Lights flashed in my eyes.

With my hand up to block the flashes, I fought through the sea of extended arms. "Other than hosting a benefit, nothing."

"Is it your statement that your mother has no prior involvement with Mr. Richardson? Were they lovers?"

The world had gone mad! *Enough.* I halted my advance and faced off with the reporters. There was no way I was going to allow these vermin to muddy my upstanding mother's reputation. "No. Absolutely not. Lady, you need to get your facts straight."

I spied Charles Hammond off to the side, watching. *Wow, they must've flown here.* He popped a stick of gum into his mouth. I didn't see Piper, but she must be close by and waiting for her opportunity to pounce. I bet all these reporters beating her to the punch chapped her hide. I waded closer to the entrance, where a man stood in a red ball cap, glancing around suspiciously, his hands in his pockets. I thought he looked like LJ, but I couldn't manage a better glimpse.

News cameras swung in my direction. "Lyla! Lyla! Are you helping the defense?"

"No comment. Come on, people. I need to get through." I weaved my way between a shorter gentleman and a taller woman about my height, ignoring their questions.

My steps sped up as I navigated around reporters. The officers were seriously understaffed here—*utter chaos.*

Finally, the double doors were a few yards in front of me. The reporters were mostly held back, and I could breathe a little better. That was, until Charles faced me. I could see the whites of his eyes. His mouth opened wide. I stumbled and tried to discern what was going on with him.

He leaned forward, his arms pumping as he went to the balls of his feet. What was he doing? He started yelling. His hand flung forward as he pointed.

A loud shout went up to my left, and everything seemed to happen in slow motion. I turned to see Quinn running toward me as well. Odd, because I'd thought he was ill. *What in the world?*

Screams echoed around me as I turned to see who Charles had been pointing at, and before I could figure out what was going on, a man in a black ski mask barreled into me, holding me upright. Stale breath hit against my face. "Strike at the shepherd!" Something stuck into my side. Every muscle in my body seized up like a full-body charley horse. My teeth rattled in my head a microsecond before everything went dark.

Chapter Fourteen

"You seem okay." The ER doctor said, and clicked his little light off. "No signs of a concussion that I can tell. But a scan will tell us more. Sit tight."

"Thank you, Doctor." I held the ice pack to the side of my head, where a rather large egg-sized knot formed, while he pulled the curtain closed behind him. The paper-lined table made a crinkling and crackling sound as I gently lay back down. My head was seriously thumping, and I waited for the painkiller they gave me to kick in. I closed my eyes for a second and saw the man in the ski mask. I shuddered.

"Lyla."

I jumped.

"Y-yes?" I gripped the ice pack.

"It's me, Quinn."

"Oh." I let out the breath I'd been holding. "Hey." I struggled to sit up as he pulled the curtain back and peeked inside. The room spun a little, and for a minute I thought I might be sick.

His deep blue eyes were filled with concern. "You want me to get someone? A doctor or nurse. You don't look so hot."

I put the melted ice pack to my face, willing my stomach to settle. "The doctor just left." I let the pack drop to my lap. "I'm okay. You don't look so hot yourself."

"I'm fine. You're sure you're okay?"

"I think so. And"—I held up my hand, attempting to forestall him—"I don't want to be rude, but if you're sick, keep back. The last thing I need to deal with is a stomach bug."

"I kicked it. But I'll stay back." He cleared his throat and ran a hand through his slightly graying black hair. "No real injuries?"

Quinn and I had a complicated relationship. We'd gone out a decade ago, from my late teens into my early twenties. He'd made noises about us giving it another try, but I wasn't keen on the idea. I'd been straight with him, which he seemed to be okay with. We were trying to find a balance in our working relationship.

"I don't think so. Other than a bump on the head, a scraped arm, and my hip being sore." I examined the abrasion on the side of my right forearm. "I'll probably have an ugly bruise." I glanced down at my picked-up skirt—nothing to be done about that now. At least my high boots had protected my legs. "They're going to run a CAT scan to be sure."

He nodded.

I swallowed and met his gaze. "The guy used a taser on me?"

"Yes."

I closed my eyes. "I had no idea how awful that could be. Did they get him?" My shoulders slumped forward.

Quinn nodded. "Yes. That Hammond fellow reached him before I did. He gave the guy a solid slug to the jaw. Slowed him down a bit and gave the Atlanta PD time to snatch him as he rounded the corner, attempting to flee."

I thought back to Charles running toward me. Charles kept turning up everywhere I went, but this time I felt gratitude. "Why'd the perp say he attacked me?"

"He isn't saying anything. He pulled a knife on an officer, shouting nonsense and threats that broke out into a brawl. They had to use force to restrain him." Quinn shrugged a shoulder. "He's unconscious now and in the hospital."

"This hospital? Never mind—he would be." I rubbed the space between my brows. I felt discombobulated.

Quinn cleared his throat. "It got crazy after you dropped. I went straight for you, or I would have grabbed the perp myself. Reporters scattered and visitors were screaming. It was bedlam."

I winced. "Oh my God. Reporters."

"Don't get upset."

My phone rang, and I scanned the room, relieved to see my purse over on the chair in the corner. "I bet my assault is all over the internet now." I'd seen, on a video Uncle Calvin had me watch, how someone losing muscle control looked after being hit by a taser. "I'm so embarrassed."

Quinn gave his head a shake, and he stepped between me and my bag. "Don't be. And leave the phone for now. Let's make sure you didn't do some serious damage when your head hit the pavement, before dealing with incessant reporters."

Sound advice. I settled back on the table.

"You still need to give a statement. The officer is outside. You ready?"

"Yeah, okay. Let's do it." No point putting it off. The sooner they had my statement, the better. That nutjob needed to be off the streets and away from people for good.

The curtain pulled back, and I realized that Quinn had meant 'outside' in the literal sense. I felt odd that the Atlanta officer probably overheard our entire conversation. Well, it couldn't be helped now. And in the grand scheme of things, it didn't really matter.

The officer smiled, her big brown eyes softening. "How are you, Miss Moody?"

"I'm alive."

The officer smiled and began her questions, which I answered in a monotonic, almost absent voice. "One minute, I was fighting reporters to get to the entrance, and the next, the man had a vice-like grip on my arm and tased me."

"What did he say before he hit you with the taser?" The female officer had high, sharp cheekbones and seemed young. From the way she questioned me, I got the sense she did many of these types of interviews and felt extremely comfortable doing so. For as young as she appeared, that told the tale of the crime rate in the city.

I shook my head and, when the room spun, instantly regretted it. "I'll never forget it." I put the ice pack to my head and wished for a new, colder one. "'Strike at the shepherd.'" A shiver ran up my spine.

"That goes along with what he yelled at the police." She showed me an image on her phone. "Have you ever seen this man before?"

The mugshot of a twenty-something Hispanic male with a large spiderweb neck tattoo stared back at me. His hair stood up all over his head, and his eyes looked bloodshot and vacant. I said with all sincerity, "Never seen him before. Who is he?"

She clipped her phone back to her belt. "The perp's name is Geraldo Morales. He's got a rap sheet half a mile long for breaking and entering, assault, and possession of narcotics with intent to distribute."

I glanced up at Quinn, who'd moved to the corner of the room, with arms crossed over his chest. He didn't look happy.

I glanced back at the mugshot and then at the officer. My scalp crawled, and I wrapped my arms around myself. "That's an odd rap sheet for a random attack like this one."

"It is and it isn't. His street name is Spider," the officer said. "He has an odd background we need to look into more thoroughly.

"With a street name like Spider, I guess the tattoo makes sense—though getting it was not too bright if he didn't want to be identified. I guess that's why he wore the ski mask. I still don't understand why he attacked me."

"Well, he's also been in and out of the hospital for psychotic episodes." The officer kept her tone even.

"Oh." I shifted on the table, the paper crinkling with my movement.

"It isn't uncommon when a long-term drug user goes without a fix to act out violently, especially with a background of delusions. We won't know for certain his intentions until he wakes up. Charles Hammond clocked him pretty good. And then, after he attempted to knife the arresting officers, things got ugly. One of the officers had to have twelve stitches on his forearm."

"Oh my God. The man *must* be a lunatic to go after the police that way."

"Yeah. Well, the perp's not in good shape." She took a step closer to me. "I'm sorry for what happened to you. But don't you worry: this guy will get time. The Chief gave us your contact information, and we'll be in touch *if* he wakes up."

That sounds ominous. I felt better knowing he would do time and not be out there tasing or stabbing people.

"We also thought that once you're discharged, we'd coordinate your exit."

"Oh." I hadn't expected that. "I hadn't really given that any thought. With the press outside, that'd be kind. Thank you." I smiled at her and she nodded, handing me a card.

"Just hit up that number when you're ready to leave. Mr. Cousins—I believe that's your uncle." When I nodded, she continued, "He'll be picking you up."

I thanked the officer again before she ducked out of the room.

"Calvin's reach is vast." Quinn didn't sound as if he resented the fact, just that he recognized how plugged in Calvin was.

"Lyla, I . . ." Quinn got an odd expression on his face after the officer left. He rubbed the back of his neck and kept glancing over at me. He appeared to be struggling with finding the right words. One of the things I'd learned from my uncle, since the conception of our business relationship, was never to rush to speak. To always listen and listen not only with your ears; body language spoke as loudly as a verbal communication. Quinn's brows were drawn, his face taut with emotion.

A different kind of anxiety settled in my gut like a stone.

"It scared me." The words came off soft and thick. The strong, reassuring chief was showing vulnerability.

My pulse sped up. For all we'd been through together, and even though we hadn't worked out and Quinn could be a consummate ass at times, I could see he cared about me, and I didn't want to be rude to him. "It scared me too."

"Seeing that asshole charge toward you like the grim reaper and knowing I couldn't get to you in time. I thought he—"

"Quinn—"

He raised a hand and leaned forward. "No. Let me finish." He softened his tone. "Please."

I waved my hand as if to say "Continue," while I shifted on the table, dreading where this dialogue might lead.

Quinn ran his hand over the goatee on his chin. "I know we butt heads."

I raised my brows as if to say, *Can't argue with you there.*

"What happened last year with Carol Timms was eye-opening."

I pursed my lips.

He put his hand on his chest with a thud. "For me. It was eye-opening for me. What I'm trying to say is, the case showed me how capable you are. You have every right to choose the investigative line of work. And you have a nose for it. I'm admitting that. It was wrong of me to attempt to sway you."

I let out a long breath. Quinn had done his best to discourage my career choice. Before, he'd agreed with my mother about where she saw my life heading. Well, not precisely, but close enough for me to be turned off to his affections. I'd also learned a lot about Quinn during that time.

"This is an odd time to have this discussion," I said. Quinn and I would never be an item again. And I thought he knew where I stood.

"I know. I just . . . just needed to clear the air." I caught his meaning. In case I hadn't made it, it would have been on his conscience. *God.*

Fine. We'd do this then. One and done. "I won't lie. I learned a lot about you as well during the investigation."

"Right. My past. I explained it." Last year, he and I had agreed to put our past behind us. He'd done some things, exchanging favors, that, although not technically unethical, were close enough to being so for me to be put off. We both had to live and work in our small town, and in my chosen profession, our paths would cross from time to time.

I moved the pack to my forehead. "You did."

"And what I'm getting at is, I want us to be able to work together."

"Me too."

He smiled hopefully. "And maybe become closer friends."

"Friends." I tested the word. Friends would be good, just not *close* friends. That was stretching the limits too far. "Does that mean as friends we trust each other? Help each other professionally when needed."

To his credit, he didn't shy away. "Yes. When I can." He shook his head, a small smile playing on his lips. "Everything is about work with you. You were just attacked, and you're still focused on your job."

"And you needed to clear your conscience right after my attack." I lifted my shoulders.

His face flushed slightly. "Okay, and I'm sorry and I accept your terms. I should let you get some rest."

"Wait. Tell me about Harper first."

He hesitated. "We aren't exactly working together on the Richardson case. And I do wonder how you found out about her transport to the hospital."

"How did the crowd of reporters find out?" I gave him a level look. He would never know that Rosa had been the first one to inform me of the incident. Thinking about work and my friend would help me get over the trauma of my attack. I'd rather concentrate on something I could affect.

"That doesn't explain why you came here. Why would you think they'd allow you to see her?"

"Harper's attorney called Calvin. We've been asked to consult. I'm here because I want to help."

He studied me. "Help how?"

"Come on, Quinn. Just give me something." If things went the way I believed they would, he and I would be working on opposite sides of this case. If he told me anything, it would be because he wanted to prove his previous point of having a trusting friendship.

"She's alive. She took something before her arrest. She nearly overdosed." He leaned against the wall, looking tired. "They rushed her here straight after processing."

"Oh my God." I glanced up at him a little too quickly, and my head spun again.

"The doctors pumped her stomach just in time. The doctors said maybe thirty minutes later she'd have been dead."

Harper had seemed depressed when we were with her, but she'd begged for my help finding her aunt. If she'd meant to kill herself, why would she bother asking? Then I thought of the Richardsons all standing by idly without a care that she was being arrested, and shivered. Could they be that callous? Did they all hate her that much? Enough to poison her?

"It isn't unheard of for a suspect to decide to end it once they're caught. Her attorney is on his way here, I believe." He glanced at his watch. "Well, given the time lapse since your attack, I bet he's been here and gone."

I chewed on my bottom lip. Or maybe he'd heard of my attack and stuck around. One could hope.

Quinn's phone chirped, and he dug it out from his pocket. He tapped forcefully on the screen before sliding it into his pocket in an agitated fashion.

"Things a bit rough at the police station? This case becoming difficult?"

He raised his brows at me.

I put the pack down on my lap. "You looked upset. I'm not asking for you to break any rules. We're just two friends chatting."

"This is Detective Battle's case." Quinn rubbed his neck. "I'm sure the DA will need you to testify when it goes to trial. A friendly chat isn't something we're going to engage in. I shouldn't have said anything about Harper's condition." Quinn set his jaw. There would be no pushing him further.

"Okay."

"It's a solid case, Lyla. And if you have any pull with Harper, I'd suggest she cut a deal."

A deal would certainly require a jail sentence. Harper *needed* time. *We* needed time to build a case of reasonable doubt. "They'll be getting a psych eval, especially after the alleged attempted suicide, right? And I wouldn't be so sure about her guilt. Her home life is odd, and Leonard had some serious issues."

His eyes narrowed. "We don't arrest people without concrete evidence."

"The psych evaluation?" If Harper had battered wife syndrome or something, and I was wrong about her doing something this drastic out of despair, we needed to know that too. This was my first time working for an attorney on a case. It was doubly difficult because it was a clear possibility that I might be called to testify on the discovery.

"Yes, to my understanding, there will be a psych evaluation"

"Good. I'm glad to hear it."

Quinn studied me. "Right now, you should be worried about resting. You *were* just attacked."

My phone began ringing in my purse, and I started to rise. Quinn held out his hand, signaling I should wait.

"I'll get it." He stared at me for a minute but didn't make a move for my purse. His phone chirped again, and he gave a groan of irritation and put it to his ear. "Chief Daniels." His eyes narrowed. "She's here. Got it." He disconnected the call and pursed his lips. Annoyance radiated off him. "Harper's lawyer is waiting for you upstairs. *Just two friends chatting.*"

I held up my finger. "I did not lie. I told you we were going to consult on the case. And I didn't ask you to divulge anything that would damage your reputation or put your position in jeopardy. Mr. Jenkins will inform me of what happened with his client anyway."

Now, I detected a little more respect in Quinn's gaze as he regarded me.

"Hello." A nurse came in with a wheelchair. "I'm here to take you for your scan, Miss Moody."

Willing my legs to move, I hurried off the table, the paper scrunching up as I slid down. Quinn took my arm, and I let him help me into the chair. The petite nurse, with copper-colored hair similar to mine, smiled, appearing grateful for his help.

"Thanks." I settled into the chair as the nurse folded down the footrests, and I put my feet up.

Chapter Fifteen

Quinn and I parted after my discharge. I could tell by how he looked at me that, moving forward, he'd be more guarded about the case. From my perspective, that was sort of a compliment. My uncle and I spoke briefly, and I made arrangements with the officer by calling the number on the card. They'd be waiting to escort me out when I was ready.

I stood on the elevator, feeling a bit anxious. Before boarding, I'd smoothed my hair out and checked my reflection in the restroom mirror. I'd applied a little powder to smooth out my sweaty and tear-streaked face. I touched up my mascara, and as I stared at my blue eyes in the mirror and applied passion-rose lipstick to my lips, I thought of Mother. I could almost hear her say, "You look pale, dear. A little lipstick could help."

And it did. I felt more presentable and prepared for this meeting. When my uncle told me that Harper had requested a private audience with me, I'd become more nervous. Mr. Jenkins would be waiting for me in Harper's room, or so I'd been told. She'd requested to see me, and he'd managed to rearrange his schedule after news of my attack surfaced.

The elevator door started to close when a couple rushed toward me, waving. "Hold the elevator, please!"

Smiling, I held the door for them as they wrangled the massive bouquet of "It's a boy!" balloons inside. A set of grandparents, I presumed, their excitement palpable.

They didn't seem to notice anything off about me, and I nearly collapsed in relief. At least I didn't appear like I'd dragged myself in off the streets. "Congratulations. New grandparents?"

Heads bobbed gleefully. "Yes. Technically it's our fifth grandchild, but it never gets old."

"Nope, never gets old," the tall, older man agreed.

"We're over the moon," his sweet, round-faced wife said. "But I tell you what: there are so many people outside this hospital, we could hardly get by."

"Crazy." I kept my smile in place until they exited the appropriate floor.

"I can't stand knowing there is some maniac criminal in the same hospital as our daughter and grandson." The older man shook his head, his face reddening with irritation.

"Well, I'm sure the police have the person secured." The woman smiled and put her hand on her husband's arm. "And nothing can overshadow this beautiful day."

The man's face smoothed and softened as he covered his wife's hand with his own. "You're right, dear. This is a day nothing can detract from. Being a grandparent is God's greatest blessing." The doors opened, and the two exited, wishing me a good evening as they left.

I smiled as the doors closed. I couldn't help my mind from wandering back to Mother and how happy my parents would be in the couple's place if I had just given birth. It's what my mother had wished for most of my adult life. A pang of guilt took over before the doors opened onto the floor Quinn directed me to.

With my hair tucked behind my ears, I smoothed out my skirt, ignoring the stubborn wrinkles, and stepped off the elevator. A man wheeling a cart of flowers, stuffed bears, and other small items came down the corridor. I waved a hand toward him and began digging through my bag for my wallet. "Do you take credit cards?"

"Yes, ma'am." He presented an iPad with an attached card reader.

"Great." I scanned his offerings, which I had no doubt were way overpriced even before inquiring. "Can I get those pink roses in that green vase?"

He nodded, stuck a card reading "Get Well Soon" on one of his plastic picks, and placed it in the vase with the flowers, as I presented my Visa.

"Have a nice day." The man smiled at me, his eyes crinkling in a charming way as we completed the transaction and he handed me my purchase.

"You too." I traveled down the hallway. A couple of people were walking up and down it with walkers, in gowns and wearing yellow slipper socks. One woman carried a red heart pillow. Could this be the cardiac wing? Did Harper have a heart condition aggravated by the overdose? Surely she would have mentioned her illness to someone. Or perhaps this was the wrong floor. I rounded the corner and when I passed a sitting area by the massive wall of windows overlooking the drab parking garage, my suspicions were put to rest. A uniformed officer stood outside the last room on the left. Not the wrong floor.

On the opposite side of the room stood a stalky man of average height, peering at his phone. He looked up when the sound of my boots against the tile caught his attention.

"Miss Moody." He waved a hand in my direction.

I must've looked lost. "Mr. Jenkins."

He nodded and shook my extended hand. He frowned at my flowers and cards. "Harper won't be able to receive those."

"Oh." It had merely been my instinct to bring flowers to a patient in the hospital. "I'll just leave them at the nurses' station or something."

He gave his head a shake, and I wondered what he thought of me. "Never mind. Awful business what happened to you. I heard from the chief that they caught the man."

"Yes."

"And no serious injuries?"

"No. I'm fine." I smiled, despite the throbbing in my head.

"Good. I was surprised you still felt up to this, but here we are. I spoke with Mr. Cousins a little while ago, down in the cafeteria. We had an interruption from another of his clients he needed to tend to. I haven't much time now, but I'm obligated to accommodate this meeting Harper requested." This way. I followed him down the corridor and into an empty room. "This is normally reserved for the doctors and family consultations. I've arranged for us to use it."

"Okay." I nodded a little. He sat and motioned to the plaid bucket chair opposite him. "A man on a mission" is how I would have described the person before me. He was younger than I'd thought he'd be. He looked to be mid-forties, not late sixties like Mr. Greene. He had short hair and a closely cut beard, with deep brown eyes that matched his hair color, and round tortoiseshell-rimmed glasses. I sat and then placed the flowers on the table and decided to leave them there. Perhaps they'd cheer up someone else's day.

"Let's get to it. It appears Harper overdosed on"—Mr. Jenkins tapped on his phone—"haloperidol. When I questioned her after she woke, she seemed confused and disoriented, which the doctors told me to expect. She vehemently denied taking the medication."

"Haldol," I said, using the brand name. I leaned forward. I'd heard my father speak of the drug. Doctors prescribed it to treat bipolar disorder and schizophrenia. "Is Harper on the medication?"

"Harper says she wasn't, and there isn't any record of it in her charts."

I shifted in my seat. "What about Leonard?"

"We're still trying to ascertain whether Mr. Richardson was seeing a psychiatrist who prescribed the medication without Harper's knowledge." He put his phone into the pocket of his briefcase.

"Then she didn't try to kill herself. I suspected she hadn't. When I sat down with her the other day, she didn't seemed suicidal to me. Which begs the question: Did someone try to poison her?"

"It begs more than the one question." Mr. Jenkins folded his hands atop the small, round table. "The problem we're facing is her husband also died of an overdose of the same drug."

I felt the blood drain from my face. When Calvin told me Leonard had been poisoned, I'd never considered that someone used the same drug on Harper. "What about the injuries he sustained to his head?"

Mr. Jenkins inclined his head. "He did have a fractured skull, but the high levels of Haldol in his bloodstream would have killed him before the fracture."

Inconsequential then. "That's why Leonard was getting sick everywhere. His body tried to rid itself of the Haldol." Not from the head trauma I had initially assumed.

He nodded. "Exactly. I'm not going to sugarcoat this, Miss Moody. Your friend is in a heap of trouble. The victim's brother turned over Harper's torn purse. It contained traces of the victim's blood on it as well a few loose pills of Haldol in a small bag that also had Harper's fingerprints on."

I felt ill.

He pulled an iPad from his bag and scrolled down what appeared to be a list of notes. "Since you discovered the body, I need to ask: Do you recall seeing the strap in Leonard's hand that night?"

"I recall seeing what I thought was a rope or jacket tie. In hindsight, it could have been the strap to a purse."

He didn't like that. His brows furrowed. "Did you mention it to the police?"

"I told them what I believed it to be." I scooted to the edge of my chair. "But Harper carried a clutch with her that night. I saw it."

He sighed. "Even if other people did as well, it doesn't really help us. She could have brought both purses with her. Or had an accomplice who switched bags with her after the incident. It won't be difficult for the DA to discount something like that." I guessed not.

"The instrument used to inflict the head wound hasn't been found. Though again, the DA could spin a tale about two crimes, and if the weapon wasn't the actual murder weapon, does it even matter?" He sounded as if he didn't want to take this trial. It sounded like he would attempt to persuade Harper to take a plea, and that worried me.

What also worried me was the idea that the second weapon used, the candlestick, had been described by me to the detective but still hadn't been recovered. Where had it gone? Who would have taken it? And if the person who used it to ensure Leonard's demise didn't grab it when they fled the scene, did that person have an accomplice? Someone who might believe they were enacting a kindness. A lump formed in my throat.

Mr. Jenkins removed his glasses and began cleaning them with a cloth from his pocket. "It still would be good to have it. We might be able to establish reasonable doubt if another set of fingerprints were on it. Because if the DA argues Harper poisoned her husband and used a hammer or something to finish the job, it wouldn't explain why her clothes were clean. And there would be no way that would be possible."

"Still a long shot." I sighed, unsure if I wanted the weapon recovered. When he studied me, I added, "But it's a shot. And if we find out who poisoned Harper, I bet we'll find the person who killed Leonard. We need to discover where said person got their hands on a drug like that. Is anyone in the Richardson household taking it?"

"We don't know. And we don't know if someone even poisoned Mrs. Richardson in the first place. We'll know more as to what we're dealing with after a psych eval."

I studied him. "You're thinking an insanity plea?"

"I think this woman could end up on death row. If she's locked up in a psychiatric hospital for a few years, she might have a shot at a normal life again." He put his glasses back on his face.

"You don't believe her then? That she's innocent?"

Mr. Jenkins sat forward, fixing me with a piercing stare. "I don't know, and I don't care. My job is to get her the best deal I can. To provide her legal representation and do my best to see that she has a fair judicial process. I've never argued a case like this before, and the DA is out for blood. He has the means for murder—the drugs were in her purse. The purse was torn in the struggle and has the victim's blood on it. Harper's fingerprints were easily obtained. Harper overdosed on the same drug that killed her husband. He has testimony from family members who believe Harper is guilty."

With a deep intake of breath, I asked, "Why am I even here, then?"

"Because Harper insists she can fight this, that she's been framed. I'm just being realistic here. If Harper goes to trial without solid evidence and the DA seeks the death penalty—well, with what we have right now"—he let out a bark of bitter laughter—"we'll lose. If she can't plead insanity, maybe I could plea this down to second-degree murder. Perhaps with a sentence of fifteen to thirty years, ten with good behavior—but she'd be alive."

I closed my eyes and rubbed my forehead. If Mr. Jenkins presented all this to Calvin, he would see the case as a lost cause too. "So what's next?"

"We go see Harper. Wait for the psych evaluation, and I'll focus on trying to get her bail. If you can find hard evidence, and I can use it to do better for her, great."

I rose to my feet, blowing out a breath of frustration. The room spun a little, but I fought the sensation.

Mr. Jenkins glanced down at his watch as he stood. "We only have a few minutes with Harper before I have to leave."

The weight of this case landed heavily on my chest. Harper depended on me to help her. The thought of Harper spending ten to fifteen years in jail—unbearable. I'd get Mr. Jenkins the hard evidence he needed to fight this. I followed him across the hall, and the officer opened the door. Although I'd wanted to take this case and had insisted I was fine and able, I'd never fathomed I'd succumb to such a bout of nerves. Harper's life was literally in our hands.

"Miss Moody, are you coming?" Mr. Jenkins kept his tone low as he turned to me from inside the room; I hadn't realized I'd frozen outside the door.

"Yes," I whispered, and walked inside. The door closed behind me.

Chapter Sixteen

Staring down at Harper's small frame lying under the knit pink hospital blanket broke my heart. IV lines were running to her free arm. Soft snoring sounds came through her thin, parted lips. She appeared so young, frail, and fragile. How could anyone suspect her of such a horrific crime?

Mr. Jenkins neared the side of the bed.

I gripped my bag. "Wait." I kept my tone low. "Shouldn't we let her sleep?"

Mr. Jenkins appeared to be losing patience with me as he frowned. "I have to be somewhere." Harper's eyes went wide, and a little gasp left her lips as she glanced up at Mr. Jenkins and attempted to scoot away. The metal bracelet attached to her wrist clanged against the bar, restricting her movement.

An overwhelming need to protect her came over me. "It's okay, Harper." I stepped toward the foot of the bed. "You're okay."

"Lyla?" Her voice sounded thin and thready.

"I'm here." I forced my lips into a reassuring smile.

Her tense frame marginally relaxed. She swallowed and glanced around. She seemed to gain her bearings. "I apologize, Mr. Jenkins. I forgot where I was for a moment."

"Are you thirsty?" I reached for the paper cup on her tray. "Would you like some water?"

She cleared her throat. "Yes. Please." With her free hand, she moved the tangles of hair away from the face. "What happened to you?"

I guess my quick makeup job hadn't been as effective as I'd hoped. "I had a fall. I'm okay." I filled the paper cup with water from the plastic pitcher on her stand and handed it to her. "You gave us all a scare. We were so worried about you."

"I feel like I'm in a living nightmare." She greedily sipped from the straw, audibly draining the cup. "One minute I'm watching a movie, and the next the cops are bursting into my home and arresting me. I felt ill in the car on the way to jail. By the time they were booking me in, I could barely see straight. My heart started beating out of my chest. Way worse than when they slapped the cuffs on me. Then my head felt like someone put it in a vise. I told the officers. Begged them to help me. When the cell doors closed, I . . . I blacked out."

"You didn't take anything?" I pulled a chair closer to the bed and sat. "You're sure?"

She shook her head; her eyes were wide. "I did not. They said I tried to kill myself. I didn't. I didn't even know what Haldol was."

"Did Leonard take prescription drugs for anything?"

"Yes. He took several medications for his blood pressure and angina. I didn't ever see a prescription for Haldol, though."

"Tell me what happened before the police came."

"LJ and I were in my sitting room upstairs, watching a movie. We escaped from the others when Felix started in on me after we heard from the lawyer handling Leonard's will."

"Who's the lawyer handling the will?" Mr. Jenkins asked.

"Zeb Stanley."

Mr. Jenkins took the name down.

"What was Felix angry about?" I crossed my legs.

She rolled her eyes. "Felix is always angry about something. He was mad before the lawyer phoned. LJ told Janice and Kenneth they had to move out. They'd mooched off us for too long. That started things off, but it really hit the fan when Mr. Stanley said that neither Kenneth nor Janice would need to be present during the reading of the will."

I bet it did.

"Leonard excluded them," Harper said.

I nodded my encouragement for her to continue.

"Felix was livid. Blamed me for Leonard cutting them out of his will. He smashed the phone against the wall while Mr. Stanley was still on the line."

I found it hard to picture the feeble older man behaving in such a way.

"Felix ranted about some nonsense. How this must all be my doing and how I'd never get away with it. I never even spoke with Mr. Stanley. I have no idea what the will says. The last I heard, we were all to sit down with him after all parties were notified."

My heart broke for her.

"Then the cops showed up with a search warrant. LJ called you, and you saw what happened after."

"Did you eat or drink anything you didn't prepare for yourself? Perhaps while you were watching the movie?"

She sucked in her bottom lip. "Oh. I did have some tea Bea brought upstairs to me. It smelled odd, so I didn't even finish it all."

Beatrice? Leonard's youngest in the flapper dress.

I leaned in. "It smelled odd?"

She nodded, and I thought of Amelia and her god-awful smelling Valerian tea she'd taken over there. But I distinctly remembered LJ taking it out with the trash. Or maybe he pretended to. There was something strange about all these coincidences with LJ. He would undoubtedly benefit from his father's demise and getting Harper out of the way. "This tea. Was it Valerian?"

"I don't know. I usually drink chamomile. Bea said it would calm me—" Harper's bloodshot eyes filled with tears. "You think Bea tried to poison me?"

"We not accusing anyone of anything. Yet," Mr. Jenkins said. He didn't want her getting her hopes up and kept shaking his head. "We need to take this one step at a time."

"We should get the cup and test it for residue." I stared up at the attorney.

"There won't be any." Harper sighed. "Edna came and took it. She washes all the china by hand every night."

"Oh." I sighed.

"Why would Bea do such a thing? And if she did, doesn't that prove I didn't kill Leonard?" She bit her bottom lip, and her eyes were downcast. "No," she said after a moment. "As much as I want to prove my innocence, she couldn't have. Bea acted out not because she hated her father; she did it to get his attention. I, um, I just don't know."

"Harper, I have to ask you. Are you and LJ involved?"

Tears streamed down her cheeks as she closed her eyes. "You have no idea what it was like for me. LJ and I are kindred spirits. He gets me. I never intended this to happen. Please don't think me a horrible person."

When I glanced over at Mr. Jenkins, his lips were thinned into a white line.

"No. I don't." I squeezed Harper's hand. "I'm going to get to the bottom of this. You stay calm and try to rest."

She gripped my hand tightly. "I can't go back there." I didn't have to ask. I knew she meant jail.

"Harper, I'm going to do everything I can to get you bail at arraignment." Mr. Jenkins grabbed his briefcase from the chair next to him. "I'm going to see you in a couple of days. We discussed this. You need to stay strong and let us do the hard work."

"Yes. I'll be strong." Harper sniffed.

Mr. Jenkins pulled his phone, which had begun buzzing, from his bag. "Excuse me."

When he stepped out the door, Harper pulled me closer, surprising me with her strength. "Talk to Charlie."

"Charlie?" Janice had mentioned a Charlie too. "Wait. You mean Charles Hammond?"

She nodded. "He's—"

"Miss Moody. We really need to go." Mr. Jenkins called, and Harper released me.

"Just a sec. What were you saying?"

Harper appeared weak once again. "I said I'd be strong."

What in the world? Did she not trust her attorney?

On my way out, I mentioned seeing LJ outside the hospital that morning and asked if he'd tried to see Harper. Mr. Jenkins said he didn't know and dismissed me before rushing out to God knows where. He didn't seem as invested as I wanted him to be. However, my relationship with Harper might be skewing my view. I expected him to jump through hoops for my friend. Hoops he couldn't even see.

Chapter Seventeen

Uncle Calvin was waiting for me when I emerged from the back exit of the hospital. A couple of uniformed officers had taken me out the back way to avoid the press, which I'd greatly appreciated. After the day I'd had and my short time with Harper and her news about Beatrice, as well as her confirmation of the affair, I couldn't handle anything else. I'd managed to push the pain in my head aside, but now felt I could collapse at any second.

I climbed into his black Ford pickup and secured my seat belt. I was thankful to be going home, but I had no interest in driving myself. When Quinn had offered to have a uniform officer drive my car back to my place, I'd gladly handed over my keys.

My uncle fired the engine to life. "Wow, you don't look so good. You should have skipped the meeting with Harper and Jenkins. I knew I should have insisted he reschedule when she wouldn't agree to speak to me instead of you."

I hadn't known Harper refused to speak with my uncle, just that she'd wanted to talk with me privately.

"I tried to handle everything so you could rest." Uncle Calvin scratched his chin.

"I appreciate the sentiment, but I needed to speak with her while her memories were fresh. I'm fine. Stop being like Mother."

He gave a bark of sarcastic laughter, but I knew that'd shut him up. "Jenkins informed you of her situation?"

"Yes. But I'm not ready to give up on Harper's defense."

"He's not giving up on her defense, Lyla. He's just realistic. Did you get anything from Harper?"

I smiled in the darkness, glad he at least remained interested in the case. "Harper said Beatrice served her some funky tea before the cops arrived. She had no idea what Haldol even was."

"Funky tea?"

I explained about the tea Amelia called nature's valium.

"Huh. You need me to stop off anywhere before I take you home? They give you a prescription to pick up or something?"

"Yeah, they called one in. It'd be nice if you could run me through to pick it up. The CVS on Flint Street should have it ready by now." I pulled out the second ice pack the nurse had given me and cracked it like she'd showed me how to do to activate the cooling beads, before pressing it to my head. I winced on contact.

"Pretty significant knot there, huh?" Uncle Calvin took a left out of the lot after paying the attendant.

"Gran would call it a goose egg, so yeah. But I'll be fine."

"Drug-dealing nutcase. This crazy city, I swear." He gripped the wheel. "A coma is too good for him." Calvin was one of the best men I knew. He was solid. You could always count on him, and he was the driving force behind my PI career. He's also headstrong, and his opinion is immovable. His love for his family and me is immense. But sometimes, I get a glimpse of the man he used to be. The Navy Seal he still is deep down. That man is terrifying.

"Listen, if you're too worn out to discuss the Richardson case, we can—"

"No. It's okay. I want to discuss it. Harper is counting on us." I gave him the condensed version of what had transpired and my impression of Mr. Jenkins. Even after the events of the day, I had no intentions of getting behind. "What we need to find out is who benefits most from Leonard's death and with Harper out of the way. Maybe even dead. She asked me to speak to Charles."

"Who is Charles?"

I explained what I knew about the writer, which wasn't much.

"Not sure how some nosy writer can help us. Listen. I know you're invested in this case. And I won't try to dissuade you. I'll do what I can, but I cannot put off other well-paying cases."

"I understand that, and I won't let this get in the way of my job." I shifted and rushed to add, "If the money isn't sufficient to cover the time, that is."

We sat in silence for a few minutes.

Calvin cleared his throat. "The ones most likely to profit would be the daughter and son. Especially since the daughter brought her the tea." I could almost detect the wheels of his brain turning. "Mr. Jenkins mentioned sitting down with the family. It would be a good idea to be there with him when he does."

"Yes, it would." I yawned, trying to stay focused. Fatigue began to set in. "The Richardsons are a strange bunch. They all live under one roof. And I'm talking aunts, uncles, cousins, son and a daughter—the whole nine yards. The vibe in the place creeped Amelia and Mel out. Harper told us some odd stories about pooling of family funds." I shivered and looked out the window. "And the rumors about Harper and LJ are true. I found that out from Harper tonight."

He grumbled.

"I know it looks bad. But it still doesn't make her a murderer. Leonard was a total nutcase, and she told me tonight that LJ kicked the cousins out of the house."

"You went to their house, met the family, when?" He stopped at the intersection. The traffic light was out, and the yellow light blinked rapidly.

"The other day, Amelia, Melanie, and I took food over there. We had no idea how Harper was living until we got there. Her husband was so controlling. He told her how to dress, where she could work, and who she could befriend. She even believes he had something to do with her aunt going missing. She'd had enough. You can't blame her for seeking comfort wherever she could get it."

I could see his shoulders tense. "All that and the evidence the police collected is considerably damning."

"I know. But let's just say someone framed her. How would we go about proving something like that? Where would you start."

"Lyla."

"Come on, Calvin."

Uncle Calvin shifted in his seat. "We'd have to come up with a solid theory for reasonable doubt. And even if it was a good one, a jury might still convict."

"Staying with the theory, Harper said there was a fight about the will before the police arrested her." I planned to find out the truth. I wanted to put the person responsible behind bars, not just to get Harper out of a bind. If we didn't, who's to say they'd leave her alone?

I focused on my uncle while he focused on the road and said, "When they read the will, we'll get some idea where Leonard Richardson's head was concerning his family. I'll get in touch with the attorney and find out the plans for the reading. They may be postponing it, after the arrest. I wouldn't be surprised if Leonard's assets are frozen during the investigation. And even after the reading, the family can contest it."

I'd thought about the possibility of frozen assets. I feared Harper wouldn't have funds to retain legal representation. Still, I'd do what I could to help her. I felt responsible now.

"We also need to know if Harper was involved."

"Cal—"

"No, Lyla, this is the way investigations work."

"We are working for the defense."

"We still need to know."

"Her attorney said he didn't care if she was guilty or not."

He cast a stern glance in my direction. "We care."

"You're right." We rode in silence for a while. Someone in that house knew something. They had to. My head ached, and I did not want to believe Harper could be guilty. "Let's put a pin in this."

"Wise. I spoke to your mother earlier when she had a hard time reaching you."

"I completely forgot to call them. Everything happened so fast, and I was trying to make heads or tails of my attack, and then I focused on Harper." I put my hand over my mouth, feeling rotten.

"It's all right. I reassured Frances, told her you were fine. She's pretty shaken up."

"I'm sure she is. I'll call her." I readjusted the pack against my head. "I'm grateful you reassured her." A lump developed in my throat when I thought about my mother and then of Leonard Richardson lying there inside her library. I turned in my seat, watching Calvin's profile in the darkness of the cab.

"I have to tell you something." I took a deep breath. "I should have told you earlier today."

He gripped the steering wheel, and I watched his knuckles turn white before he loosened his grip. "Why don't I like the sound of that?"

I told him about my statement to Detective Battle, how I'd described the scene and the body. And about the candlestick that magically vanished. I explained seeing Harper and Mother together and how my mother appeared to be consoling her; how Harper later confirmed my suspicions. I focused on the red taillights in front of us. "And before I sat down with the detective for a recorded interview"—I cleared my throat—"Mother said some strange things."

"Okay." He scratched the back of his toffee-colored head.

"Well, Mother pulled me aside before I sat down with the detective. She impressed on me very strongly the importance of not mentioning to the police Harper's request to locate her aunt. I took a breath. "And she said Leonard did not deserve our sympathy. She more or less said he deserved to die."

He turned sharply in my direction. Bright red taillights greeted us.

"Calvin!"

He hit his brakes so forcefully that I was flung forward, the seatbelt cutting into my chest.

"Ow!" I held my head with both hands.

"Sorry. I'm so sorry, sweetheart." He reached over and touched my shoulder. The light changed, and he maneuvered the truck into the drive-through of the pharmacy.

"I tried to convince myself Mother was probably just upset when she asked me, because she seemed to like Harper. And Harper later confessed to having confided in Mother about her situation. Now I don't know what to think."

Calvin stared off for a few long moments before he pulled forward. He cleared his throat. "You can't possibly believe your mother would remove the bloody candlestick from the scene?"

I gave my shoulders a small shrug.

"Lyla." He shook his head. "Frances probably heard rumors and reached out to the girl. Maybe she feared abuse. You know how your mother does all that work for the battered women's shelter. She's an empathetic person. And when the girl confided to her about the hell she was living in, your mother just spoke out of anger."

"Maybe. What worries me was the way she looked when she spoke to me. I'd never seen her like that before. It wasn't just lashing out. I've seen plenty of that. This was a cold and calculated response." I battled nausea from the jolt forward. "I need a ginger ale or Sprite or something fizzy. My stomach is threatening a revolt." I moved the ice pack to the back of my neck and rolled down the window—the cold fall night air rushed inside the cab. I could smell rain in the air. A storm must be brewing.

"I'll get you one." Calvin pulled up to the window and asked for my prescription and a Sprite.

I handed him my driver's license, and he slid it into the open drawer for the attendant. The little metal drawer closed. "In the spirit of full disclosure, I had to tell you. But Calvin, I would have taken it to my grave otherwise."

"I understand." His nodded and his green eyes, the exact shade of Mother's, gave me a pointed stare. He understood I would never betray my mother or any member of my family. I could read that in his eyes. Nodding again, he said, "You leave this with me."

"Okay."

He handed me my prescription and pulled out onto the street. "With all the publicity and the oddities surrounding the family and where the murder took place," he said, shaking his head, "this will rock Sweet Mountain. We have to be discreet in our work."

"Are you saying we're working the case?" I took one of the pills from the bottle and washed it down with Sprite. It wasn't long before my eyes began to grow heavy.

"We are." My uncle shrugged out of his coat and handed it over to me, saying, "Here."

"Thank you. I'll just close my eyes for a second. We should keep talking about this." I folded the corduroy sports coat into a makeshift pillow and leaned against the window.

"We will. Just rest your eyes for a minute."

The expressway sounds lulled me into sleep.

Chapter Eighteen

Uncle Calvin encouraged me to take the day off, but I decided that I couldn't afford to take the day with so much to do for Harper. I'd had a decent night's sleep. I got myself a cup of coffee, dug out my phone and set it on the coffee table, and opened my laptop. I'd left LJ a message asking if I could come by and have a chat with the family. I figured I needed to have a conversation with Charles Hammond at some point as well. I agreed with Calvin that he probably wouldn't be much help. I'd lost the card he'd given me during the scuffle; I'd have to ask LJ if he knew what Charles's number was. If he didn't have it, I'd have to call Piper.

My messages began syncing after I booted up. I had a total of fifteen messages and voicemails. I grabbed my phone.

Quinn must have set it to silent when I'd gone to get my scan, and I'd been so out of it last night that, after I left a message for Brad, I'd fallen into bed and neglected to check messages.

My finger hovered over the text from Melanie:

Oh my God. Your attack is on the news! Call me! xoxo

Melanie had sent me links to the coverage of my attack. I cringed as I hit "Play." People were scattering as the camera panned the crowd. *Oh no!* My hands went involuntarily to my face, and I continued watching through my fingers. The cameraman had managed a close-up of my face. The terror on my face as the masked man grabbed me made me shiver. I'd crumpled to the ground mere seconds later. My skirt rode up as my body gyrated and jerked on the pavement.

Super embarrassing and horrifying. Charles flew at the man. I watched as he reared back and cleaned the perp's clock. Wow. Charles looked furious. His teeth bared. His eyes were fiery.

Chills erupted across my skin, and I suddenly felt queasy while I eerily watched Charles cradle me in his arms. He shouted for the press to get back as he lifted my head and began stroking my face. I zoomed in. The act seemed almost intimate, and I swallowed. Why did I feel a bit violated?

I took a sip of coffee and closed the window. I needed a break. Sighing, I checked my phone—nothing from LJ. I needed to speak with him ASAP. I listened to the long-winded, ranting messages from my friends and parents, who sounded worried. Each said they'd talked to Rosa, who'd relayed what she knew. Poor Rosa had left a message too. I' shot off a group text to my friends.

I'm fine. Thanks for checking in. Speak with y'all soon. I added a heart emoji.

Then I scrolled through my voicemails and decided to listen to Brad's first. He'd left three. By the third message, he sounded on the verge of murder himself; my finger hovered over the "Callback" button when I noticed a news alert from *Sweet Mountain Gazette* on my laptop. Tossing my phone aside, I clicked on the link, which showed the attack from a different angle.

I steeled myself for viewing. As I watched the commotion, LJ had moved closer to Charles before he launched himself my way. LJ attempted to grab Charles's jacket. Almost like he tried to discourage Charles from coming to my aid. *What?* I rewound the footage and zoomed in on the frame; then I watched as LJ trotted toward the writer instead of scattering like most everyone else. His head was lowered, and he appeared to say something to Charles, who shrugged him off, reacting like a cat with excellent reflexes. He sprang to the left, leaping atop the attacker right after I dropped to the ground. They grappled, and the masked man got away. The cops chased after him in pursuit.

Wow. I sat back. LJ had stayed cemented to the sidewalk. Charles participated in several interviews. In the first one with Piper, he appeared camera shy as he said, "I just did what anyone would do. Miss Moody needed help"—he shrugged—"so I helped."

Clearly, from the video footage, it was not what *anyone* would do. "Thanks for nothing, LJ," I grumbled at the screen.

I thought back to the perp's stale breath, the aggression that had thrummed through his body and vibrated as he grabbed me, the violence that radiated off him when he hit me with the taser. I shut my eyes and rubbed them. Maybe Calvin was right. A coma was too good for that man. No, ugh. Enough of this. I didn't want that in my head. Those thoughts. That emotion.

Closing the laptop, I rubbed my arms and decided I need a long hot shower. I'd taken one last night before bed, but for some reason I just felt I couldn't get clean enough. As much as I wanted to put the incident out of my mind, I recalled his low menacing voice in my ear as soon as I got still: *"Strike at the shepherd."*

After I'd thoroughly scrubbed myself down, I stood under the hot spray. The spot on my head was still tender; I hoped the warmth would soothe the ache. The steam was a warm, comforting cloak around me.

My trust in humanity would be jaded for a time—some random drug-addicted man targeting me out of the crowd, probably excited by the media presence and deciding it would be the perfect time to make his deluded statement. *I'm fine. Safe. No serious harm done.*

I concentrated on creating a visual criminal profile for Leonard's murderer. I'd studied psychology and had always been fascinated with the workings of the criminal mind. I'd even considered going back to school and furthering my education. Not only would a profiler be a great addition to the services Cousins offered, but I could potentially seek to further my career in the years to come. It certainly could have come in handy with this case. The murder didn't look premeditated by the crime scene photos. But then, because Leonard had been poisoned, it must've been. Harper had made it known to her close friends and my mother that she wasn't happy in her marriage. My body chilled even under the hot spray. If she'd told anyone or if anyone saw, as I had, the connection between Harper and my mother at the charity event, Mother could be called to testify, questioned thoroughly at the very least. The way Calvin had looked at me when I posed the question about the candlestick made me feel like a traitor. But in my opinion, just as he'd said, we needed to know if Harper was guilty in any capacity; I needed to know Mother's culpability, whatever it might be.

Someone might have witnessed it. *Charles.* Perhaps he'd used this leverage to set up that meeting at the deli. Had he verbally twisted Mother's arm so she'd cooperate? Blackmail for a story? Reprehensible. But he hadn't seemed like that sort of man to me. And she'd made the statement that he understood everything.

I let out a groan of frustration. My thoughts were in a tumult. Mel, Amelia, and I had joked about the similarities the Richardsons had with the Leonideses in *Crooked House*. But now I wondered. The family did seem to stick together, even though they appeared to have a deep disdain for one another.

I shut off the water, bundled up in my terrycloth robe, and toweled off my hair, then called my mother. Gran said she'd had a bad night and decided to take a nap.

"Are you sure you're okay, sugar?" Gran cared so deeply.

"Fine. Don't worry. They ran all the appropriate tests and released me to rest at home."

"That sure was scary to watch. Your whole body twitched on the ground."

My already flushed cheeks heated more. "I know." I groaned in mortification. "I saw it."

"Don't be embarrassed. You are as tough as nails. I don't know anyone who's ever been attacked like that and lived to tell about it. It sort of makes you a hero, I'd say."

"I wouldn't say that."

185

"I would. My phone has been ringing off the hook. Sally Anne at the beauty parlor said she'd never seen anything like it in her life. I told her, 'And you probably won't ever see it again. My little Lyla is a force. She can survive anything.'" *Oh Lord.* "How many people can say they've been stunned by a taser gun? And that guy they caught, he looked scary. Like a—what do they call 'em?" Her voice trailed off for a few seconds.

I had no idea.

"Oh, I know. A tweaker."

I let out a little chuckle. Leave it to Gran to improve my mood by her regurgitation of cop shows. "I've got to run. I have a lot of work today. Love you."

"Okay, sugar. I'll tell you about the forensic team later."

I sat up. "Wait. What? Why didn't you tell me that first thing?"

"There's been so much drama to talk about, and it's hard to get it all in. Exciting times we're living in. And just think, we're the ones who discovered the dead man, and the cops scoured the house, hunting for something."

"Hold on! Scoured the house for what? Did they have a warrant?" My heart dropped to the floor before it started beating rapidly. I knew exactly what the police hoped they'd find. Why they were still looking for it after the poison discovery, I hadn't a clue. Unless they believed someone in the house was Harper's accomplice. It was unthinkable.

"No warrant. Your father called William, and after he showed up, they gave the police permission to conduct a gentle search."

"Of course. Daddy wouldn't want them tearing the house apart."

"I nosed around to see what they were up to. And the police left empty-handed. What do you suppose they were hunting? Who do you think killed him? I still can't believe they think that sweet young thing killed her old, shriveled-up husband."

"All good questions and observations. I wish I had the answers." I let out a slow controlled breath.

"Well, you will. Sally Anne and the ladies at bingo were riveted. Sally Anne is always talking about her granddaughter Piper as if she hung the moon. I told them *my* PI granddaughter would bust this case wide open. She always gets her man."

"Oh, Gran. You didn't." I put my hand over my face. That's how Piper found out about my involvement.

"Oh . . , I didn't say anything wrong, did I?" Gran sounded a little upset.

"No. It's okay, but let's not talk about the case anymore, all right?"

"I'll keep it hush-hush."

She went on to tell me about how the forensic team had been out to the house again yesterday. And she'd seen on the news a nice big shot of the house.

"If I'd had known they were filming, I'd have stuck my head out and waved. Your mother was horrified, though. I told her not to worry. We didn't do anything wrong."

Sadly, my mother would need to buck up and brace herself for what was coming. Unbeknownst to her, when she opened herself up to Harper, she'd opened herself up to the police, the media, and those like me who were investigating the murder. And although she believed that most decent folks didn't want to gossip about their problems, a whole faction of the world did and would gladly spread rumors for ratings. For confirmation, all she had to do was go onto social media. Sweet Mountain's murder at the elite Moody house was big news. And a criminal named Spider who attacked their daughter outside of an Atlanta hospital would only fan the flames.

"What a mess."

"Yes, indeed." Gran didn't sound all that bothered. She seemed to enjoy the drama. "I'll tell your mother you called."

"Thanks, and remember no more gossip about the case."

"Ten-four."

Chapter Nineteen

An hour later, I leaned back on the sofa, feeling deflated. I'd put another call into LJ, eager to sit down with the family, and had gotten his voicemail again. If he didn't call me back by the end of the day, I'd take a ride over there. After watching my attack coverage, I had an odd feeling about Charles and did another search, this time using our encrypted software. I wondered where exactly he fit into all of this. What had made him show up to Sweet Mountain when he had, and how had he gotten cozy with Harper and LJ so quickly?

I came up empty. How in this modern world could so many people have stayed off the grid? Charles Hammond didn't have a Facebook profile or any other social media presence. He didn't turn up in my usual databases either. Perhaps Charles Hammond *was* a pseudonym he'd decided to go by since working on his novel. Gran's mention of the "tweaker" caused me to search on the drug Haldol. I wondered how easy if it would be to obtain, and decided to make a point to ask my father about the specifics of the medication.

I rechecked my watch, decided I was done waiting on LJ, and began throwing my things into my bag. I'd take a ride over to the Richardson house now. An odd thought came to me: in the novel *Crooked House*, the granddaughter of Aristide Leonides tells Charles Hayward she won't marry him until the murderer is found. Funny, while reading the book, I'd never imagined myself as the character Charles. Yet here I was in the role, with the exception of the betrothal part.

I shook myself. Still, the answers to the crime would probably reside within the walls of the Richardson home. Maybe Bea would speak to me, and I could determine whether a doctor had prescribed the drug Haldol to anyone in the house.

My phone rang as I was on my way out the door, and my father's face came up on the screen. *Oh boy.* I placed my bag down. "Hey, Daddy."

"Hey? Hey? That's how you greet your father after some low-life attacked you in broad daylight?" *Here we go.* I needed more coffee. "I came by your place last night. I knocked and knocked on your door."

"You did? I'm so sorry. I must've been out cold." I fiddled with the strap on my satchel.

"Calvin said he dropped you off, and you were fine. But I wanted to lay eyes on you myself. To look you over." Daddy, the family doctor, always liked to give us the once-over. It didn't matter whether his field of medicine differed from whatever illness we were battling.

"I'm good. Daddy, I—" I heard voices in the background. Lots of urgencies.

"Hold on a sec." He put me on mute, then came back. "Listen, Lyla, I have an emergency I have to deal with. But can you come by the house for a chat tonight? We need to talk." That sounded ominous. I'd planned on stopping by to check out the crime scene again anyway. Having my father's invitation just made things easier.

"I'll be by—if not tonight, tomorrow. Go take care of your emergency."

"Lyla. Make sure you take some time to ensure you are indeed okay. Sometimes we get overwhelmed with trauma; we neglect to see our struggles. Do you hear what I'm saying?"

"I hear you. Stop worrying. Bye." I disconnected the call and looked myself over. I was fine—no visceral aftereffects. Then I noticed my right boot wasn't zipped up, and there was a stain on my sleeve. As I raised the zipper the rest of the way and used dish soap to clean my sleeve, I considered what I might be walking in on in the Richardson house. The file on Harper was pretty sparse. We didn't have much background on her. I'd found the last known residence before she married, where she'd lived with her aunt. Her maiden name was Carlson, different from last name of her aunt, who had raised her. I guessed Phyllis Johnson never formally adopted her. I found some school records and one juvenile charge, petty theft. She'd served community service and cleaned up her act. Nothing else was out of the ordinary.

I'd been able to find a little on Leonard. I'd built a sufficient background on him. But nothing before 1970. Not unusual. Still, the lack of records bothered me.

The doorbell rang just as I finished running a brush through my hair for good measure; I checked my reflection in the mirror. My eyes had dark circles under them, and the bump on my temple had started to bruise. Carefully I placed the comb aside and fingered-combed my hair into place to cover it. My fingers were far gentler to my injury than the comb. I hesitated a second as I reached for the doorknob. *Stop it, Lyla.* For safety, I checked the peephole, a little shocked to see Quinn on the other side of the door.

"Quinn. Hey. I'm surprised to see you.," I said in greeting as I opened the door.

"Hey. Calvin said you were working from home." He dangled my keys. "I brought your car back."

Ah. "Thanks." I took the keys from him and leaned against the door. "I'm heading out. You got a ride back?"

He nodded. "Yes. A patrol officer is on his way to pick me up. He should be here any minute."

"Oh well, come in and wait." I stepped aside so he could enter. I supposed I could wait a few minutes to leave. Anything less would be rude, and he had gone out of his way to return my vehicle. "Want some coffee or a cup of tea?"

"No, thanks. How are you feeling."

"I'm fine." I waved my hand toward the living room. "Let's sit on something softer." We went into the living room, and I moved my favorite baby-blue, chunky chenille throw Mother had given me for Christmas last year to make room for him.

He settled on the chaise lounge side while I folded the throw.

He glanced at my bag, where my laptop peeked out. "Where you headed?"

"Just to work." I had no intention of sharing anything.

"How'd Harper seem when you saw her?"

"Quinn." I pursed my lips.

He folded his hands. "Fair enough. I do have something I need to discuss with you. And I don't want you to get upset or to jump to any conclusions. Atlanta PD is still investigating, and we can't be positive about anything yet. But if you'd like me to wait—"

"My God, Quinn, just spit it out."

He gave me a single nod. "The perp that attacked you is still unconscious, but beat cops scooped up one of his gang members on another charge and leaned on him a little. What came out concerned your attack. The guy claims Spider was paid to attack you."

I sat up straight. "Paid? By whom?"

He shook his head. "He says some guy came into the bar the night before and offered up a thousand dollars to for one of his gang to trail you and enact the attack. Spider took him up on it. The man gave him five hundred up front, plus the taser and ski mask."

"Oh." I felt the blood drain from my face as I sat down on the sofa. I thought of the black car I'd seen outside my townhouse and again at the hospital. Had that person been the one to enlist the gang to attack me?

"What?" Quinn leaned forward, his eyes intense.

I told him about what I'd seen and the flashing lights and how I suspected the car followed me to the hospital as well.

"Why didn't you say something before?'

I shook my head and lifted my shoulders. "The car just flashed the lights, and by the time I got back outside with my phone, it was gone. And at the hospital, I couldn't be sure it was the same vehicle. I had a lot going on."

"Describe the vehicle."

I did, and Quinn took notes.

"Did the gang member describe the man who offered to pay them?"

Quinn snorted. "He tried. He claims he was under the influence at the time of the encounter, and no one else at the bar talked. The bartender says too many people came in that night. He hasn't a clue. And his security cameras haven't worked in months."

I narrowed my eyes. "Because he gets kickbacks from the drug being distributed freely in his bar?"

"That's what Atlanta PD suspects."

My thoughts whirled, and I wondered about the only person I knew who had acted oddly both around me and at the time of my attack. I wasn't big into believing in coincidences. I grabbed my laptop from my bag and pulled up the recording.

"What are you thinking?"

I explained about LJ being at the hospital, how he'd seemed so concerned about Harper but how convenient it would be for him to remove her from the picture now that his father was deceased. I turned the laptop around when I had the clip ready.

Quinn moved closer and zoomed in, watching as LJ attempted to prevent Charles from helping me. His jaw clenched.

"It makes me wonder why he'd do something like that," I said. "My first thought now is that perhaps he doesn't want Cousins helping Harper with the case. Perhaps he orchestrated the attack to dissuade me?" As I said it out loud, I realized that I had no evidence of my claim. "I have nothing concrete to back that up. I don't know." I rubbed my forehead. "Perhaps he simply doesn't like me." I shrugged. "He drives a newer Lexus." I dropped my hand. "I guess I'm stumped."

"Are you? Why?"

I shook my head. "I don't know. Harper seems to trust LJ, and he did contact me when she was arrested." I couldn't go into it further without perhaps leading the cops to Charles. If he indeed had information to help her case, I wanted to get to him before the prosecution did. If anything, my insinuations about LJ might lead the police to investigate him. That could be good for Harper.

Quinn locked his eyes on me. I could see he'd begun to have his doubts about Harper's guilt. Or maybe I simply hoped that was true. "I'll have a word with young Mr. Richardson. I'll also speak to Calvin about combing your company accounts. Perhaps you pissed someone off. I can imagine you aren't the most popular with client's husbands or ex–business partners." He closed the laptop.

"No, I guess not."

"I told the officer in charge of the investigation I'd liaise with him. Save him the trip out here when I can. They'll be sending over the sketch, and I'll have them send over a mugshot of the gang member in custody."

"Good."

"Anyone off the top of your head stand out? Any profiles?" He leaned forward, resting his forearms on his knees, staring at my laptop sitting on the table in front of him.

"Hmm. The 'unhappy enough to attack me' profile?" I shook my head. "Can't say that anyone does."

He pushed the laptop over to me, and I pulled it into my lap, guarding the screen against Quinn's prying eyes. I did a quick scroll through the client database to see if something stood out to me, feeling a tad guilty that I'd used my attack to steer the prosecution toward another potential suspect in the Richardson investigation. I wracked my brain, trying to think of any blatantly unhappy people.

A few clients had some disgruntled exes, but nothing that would cause such an extreme reaction. I closed my laptop. And certainty began to resonate about my suspicions of LJ and how they seemed the most relevant. Perhaps the cases were linked. I trusted my gut instincts, so I replied, "Nope. Nothing stands out. I'll have to speak to Calvin. Maybe he remembers something I don't."

"Okay. But if something comes to you later, give me a call. Anyone that gives you pause, we'll check out." Quinn rubbed the back of his neck; his telltale sign that he warred with what to believe.

"If the perp doesn't wake up or dies, then what happens next?" I feared that even if he didn't wake up, that might not be the end of this.

Quinn dropped his hand. "We'll have to see where the case takes us. He attacked you, and Charles's punch wasn't fatal, so he's in the clear. It was when the perp pulled a knife on the arresting officer that he sustained serious injury. It was justified. No one is raising a stink about his condition. I suspect nothing will happen in that respect."

"I guess I owe Charles many thanks. If he hadn't attacked the guy, he might not have stopped with just the taser." A full body shudder overtook me at the thought Spider might have begun working on me with a knife. My stomach started to revolt against the coffee and bagel I'd had a little while ago.

"You look a little green. Want a washcloth, or do you need to dash to the bathroom?" Quinn looked unsure of what to do for me.

"Maybe just hand me the ice pack over there." I pointed to the bar, when a knock came from the front door. "I wonder who that is." I began to rise.

"You stay put. Maybe you shouldn't go out just yet today. Did the doctor give you any discharge instructions from the hospital?"

"Just to take ibuprofen, I'm not taking the prescription anymore. It knocks me out cold. They did provide me with the glorious ice packs."

Quinn grabbed the pack off the counter and brought it to me just as the knock came with more urgency. "Here. I'll get the door."

I guess my furrowed brow alluded to the intensely dull ache that began inside my confused brain. "Thank you." The coolness soothed my brow, and my lids closed. I heard the door open and a deep voice say, "What are you doing here? Where's Lyla?"

"She's resting."

Low rumbling noises—words that I couldn't make out—came next.

I moved the pack and shifted higher on the sofa to see Brad and Quinn inches from each other. *Oh boy!*

"Hey fellas, let's not do anything we'll regret, okay. We're all on the same side."

Brad moved past Quinn; his eyes were heated. The words they'd exchanged hadn't been kind ones. They softened when they landed on me. I adored my no-nonsense man. He didn't mince words, nor did he care for people who did. He crossed the room toward me and knelt beside the sofa, leaning in to kiss me lightly, briefly, on the cheek. "Are you okay?"

"Fine." I lifted the pack from my head and showed him my ugly yellow and purple knot.

He winced. "Ouch. I called your cell a dozen or more times."

"I called you back and left you a voicemail last night."

"That was last night." Brad wasn't happy.

"I was about to call you again today but got distracted with the case. I'm sorry." I smiled sweetly and hoped he'd understand.

Quinn cleared his throat. "The missed calls would have been my fault. I didn't want it ringing off the hook while she was in the ER. She had enough to deal with, so I switched it to silent mode."

Brad cast an irritated glance in Quinn's direction, and I put the pack down and got up.

Brad took me by the shoulders. "No concussions or any other injuries?" *Aww. He cares.*

"No. I told you I was fine in the voicemail. Don't start fussing. All I have is this bump. And after seeing the footage of the attack, I'm more humiliated than anything else."

"Who's handling the case?"

Quinn answered for me, giving Brad the name and that he was liaising for the Atlanta PD.

"I know a couple of guys in that department. I'll give them a call."

"No need. I'm handling it." Quinn leaned against the counter, and his phone chirped.

Brad studied Quinn. His face took on a serious expression, his little too-close-together eyes narrowing just slightly. Rugged and unique was something I hadn't known I'd be attracted to until I'd met him during the Dumping Grounds investigation last year. Yes, he was so different from the other men I'd dated. Unlike the other men who had been in my life, Brad didn't concern himself with the idea that I was too fragile to deal with the criminal justice system's nitty-gritty details.

"They think someone paid the Spider guy to attack me," I told Brad, and then relayed what I'd told Quinn earlier regarding the black sedan. Quinn showed Brad the mugshot. "His street name is Spider."

While Brad stared at the image on the screen, he asked, "What did he shout? I couldn't make that out from the video."

Oh, I couldn't believe I'd left that out of the voicemail. I'd been really out of it. "'*Strike at the shepherd.*'" It still made no sense to me, and I wondered if it had been a statement to throw me off the correct trail.

The two men stared at each other, and I rose and crossed the room.

Brad handed the phone back to Quinn. "The shepherd as in the religious meaning?"

"We're not sure. Lyla and her uncle have ruffled a few feathers. The thousand dollars isn't steep and—"

"Yeah, I get it—not hit money, but it's the right price for street grunt work."

"Exactly. I'll keep you in the loop." Quinn stared me straight in the face, aware that Brad watched intently. "Lyla, I've got to run. I'll call you when I have something more. Be careful until we know for sure what we're dealing with. Call me if you think of anything." He lowered his tone, softening his gaze as if Brad weren't even in the room. "And take care of yourself."

Oh Lord. I frowned at him, showing my disproval as I moved toward Brad. "I will."

Brad wrapped a protective arm across my shoulders and said in no uncertain terms, "Don't underestimate her, Daniels. She's a lot more capable than you give her credit for. I have complete confidence in her."

I gazed up at Brad, who pointed his glare at Quinn. *Swoon-worthy.*

Chapter Twenty

"I can't get anyone to open the door," I told Mr. Jenkins the next morning as I parked my car across the street from the office. I'd run by the Richardson home, but no one answered the door. People were home; I saw the cars in the driveway. They simply had no interest in speaking with me. I'd left my card.

"I'm not surprised. No one in the family, other than LJ, is interested in cooperating with the defense, and he's at work today. Besides, I have another matter to talk over with you."

"Okay."

"Mrs. Richardson's assets have been frozen by the courts as of this morning. I'm in discussions with a benefactor who has expressed interest in helping out with some of the costs. Until that is sorted out, Harper seemed to believe you would be able to accommodate. I'm hoping to have the funds before the retainer is depleted."

Pro bono work was something I'd prepared for and thought through. "This benefactor?" I cringed, thinking about the insinuation from the reporters involving Mother. Piper got her information somewhere, and she has been correct about me. "Is it someone from Sweet Mountain or her old hometown?" I watched as a single yellowish-red leaf danced across my windshield before wedging beneath the wiper.

"I'm not at liberty to divulge that information at this time. If it changes, I'll pass the information along. And in the spirit of full disclosure, I've encouraged Mrs. Richardson to consider a plea formally. It's up to you if you'd rather not do this. I'm doing my job. I work for Mrs. Richardson."

Uncle Calvin would not be happy about pro bono work. Especially with what had transpired in front of the hospital and the possible link between the cases. But it technically wasn't a pro bono case yet, and perhaps it wouldn't be. And if it did become such a case, I'd work it on my own time if I had to. The link only made me more determined. There shouldn't be any travel costs, except maybe if the case took us to North Carolina—though I did believe most work could be enacted online and over the phone. And I could stretch the retainer if we needed to send Stephen, our part-time man.

"As I said at the hospital, I'm invested in helping Harper clear her name. I'm surprised you're going the extra mile, especially after your insistence that she take a plea deal."

"I'm out to do the very best for my client, whatever that looks like. I'll let Mrs. Richardson know of your decision."

"Okay, bye."

Mr. Jenkins confused me. He did seem more eager to fight for Harper than he had earlier. Perhaps the possibility of the influx of cash played a role in the change. I'd have to broach the subject with Calvin later today. Piper came darting around several parked cars the next morning as I waited to cross the street to my office. Wow, she must have dropped everything she had planned for the day and flown over here after I called. She called my name several times, but I ignored her, pretending not to hear her. I wanted her eager to speak to me, not thinking *I* needed her for information.

I had my key in the office door when she finally caught up to me. "Morning, Piper. I'm surprised to see you so early." I smiled. "Pleased, but surprised."

"Good morning. I was able to move some things around to accommodate your requested meeting." She smiled and tucked behind her ear a few strands of her dark shiny hair, styled straight as a board today but getting windblown. "How are you feeling?" Her perfume overwhelmed my senses, forcing me to stifle a cough.

I studied her for a second as I unlocked the door. She didn't seem to be holding a grudge. "I'm fine. Thank you for asking, and thank you for making time for me." I pushed open the door, flipped on the lights, and headed straight for the coffeepot.

"No problem. I also wanted to apologize for the other day at the police department. My editor was up my ass about getting the scoop before one of the larger media outlets did." She sighed. "I'm just like you. A woman who's trying to make a career out of what she loves to do."

"I'm sorry too. I didn't mean to behave so childishly." I held up a cup of coffee in offering. "Coffee?"

"Please." She made herself at home by taking a seat in front of my desk. She crossed her legs and smiled. "Tell me what I can do for you."

"Just thought we should clear the air."

"I'm all for clearing the air." Piper glanced around. "This is a nice office."

"Thanks." I adored the fifteen-hundred-foot functional space. We had exposed brick walls with painted tan columns. The ceiling, we'd painted black, to hide the exposed ductwork and beams. The floors were original hardwood, and we'd hired a feng shui consultant to help design the space when I came on board. I'd hung up some abstract art for color and added a couple of large floor plants to bring in life.

Usually, the energy in the office lifted my mood and made me more productive. Today, not so much. My mind continued to be haunted by the ghoulish sight of Leonard Richardson and of the man called Spider who'd attacked me. I was also still worried about who might be helping Harper as her benefactor. Not that I'd share any of that with Piper Sanchez.

She tapped her acrylic nails together. "Clearing the air could be healthy. And in doing so, maybe we could help each other."

I turned to face her. "How?"

She raised a shoulder. "I could offer some information that might help with your case, and you could allow an on-the-record interview." She raised her hands to stave off any objections. "Not about the Harper Richardson case, but about the attack on you in Atlanta. I'm thinking of a businesswoman's view of crime in the state. Tell your story of the attack."

A little quid pro quo was precisely what I wanted. Still, I didn't want to appear too eager to leap. "There's honestly no side to tell. I saw the footage; it's all there." I allowed a slight slump to my shoulders. "You were there, and I know you've watched the footage too. Everyone has." The Keurig finished brewing. "How do you take yours?"

She gave a sympathetic smile. "Black, please. There is a story. There's always a story. How did you feel when the man grabbed you? What did he say? How does the attack affect your day-to-day life? Why not get it on the record with me and your hometown paper rather than see some fabrication splattered all over the Atlanta papers."

"I don't know." I placed the mug on my desk's edge in front of her, then put another pod in the machine. "They caught the guy, and that's good."

"Yes, that is good. But . . ." Piper let the word linger for a few seconds. "I did see the footage and read the piece the *Atlanta Constitution* wrote, and it wasn't very flattering now, was it? There's a rumor that someone paid that guy to enact the crime. And what might have transpired if Charles hadn't intervened?" She took a sip from the mug as I settled behind my desk, and I realized she had a source in the Atlanta PD offices. "It painted you as a non-vigilant female, not as the competent businesswoman you are. Have they reached out to you?"

"The police or the paper?"

"The paper."

I shrugged a shoulder. I didn't think anyone had. But there could be voicemail waiting for me, and if that were true, a visit would soon follow. But I had no intention of revealing that I hadn't read the article Piper referenced. I simply waited. She wanted something from me badly, and the onus was on her to work for it, leaving me able to ask for whatever I wanted in return.

Piper cleared her throat and placed the mug on the desk. "Just consider it. I want people to get to know the real Lyla Moody. Private investigator Lyla Moody." Piper leaned forward. "The self-made, fearless woman who, by doing her job, rattled a few cages that landed her in the hot seat." She took her phone out of her brown leather bag. "We can take a few shots. What you're wearing is perfect today." She smiled approvingly at my designer brown pencil skirt, cream top, and brown jacket.

I sipped my coffee and stared over my mug at her. "I'm not agreeing to anything. Yet."

Piper made a noncommittal noise. "Is this about Quinn? Seriously, if you want him, you can totally have him."

"No," I said, narrowing my eyes. "This is not about Quinn." Gran's statement about Piper's discarded men rang true here. She was ready to dump Quinn for a story. *Wow.*

"What is it about then? I know you and I haven't been the best of friends lately, but we were really good friends once." *In middle school.* "But I thought we shared a mutual respect. I realized when you were rude to me at the police department, you were stressed out, and I got it." *Oh, cue the guilt.* "We were always friendly up till then. And we're both businesswomen working to make a name for ourselves here in our little town. I've even offered to share my scoops."

I kept my eyes trained on her dark brown irises as I sipped from my cup. We had been friends once. I had admired her tenacity in her work. Respected her for going after what she wanted in life—though not a fan of her desire to use Quinn as a bargaining chip. It certainly wouldn't be a method I'd use. But I'm sure other people wouldn't approve of some of my methods either.

"You're right. And again, I was out of line the other day. You have a gorgeous figure and a perfect ass." I gave her the "I hate you" look women gave their friends, which everyone understood was a compliment.

She smiled. "I better have. My grueling daily squat routine isn't for fun. And like I said, I completely overlooked what you said. Come on." She placed the mug on the desk with a thud. "I *need* this." I could tell she meant it. "And let's face it, so do you. Plus, I'll owe you one," Piper dangled at the end.

"Okay. I'll do it. But"—I smoothed out my fashion ponytail and gave Piper a point-blank stare—"I will not discuss anything about Harper or the incident at my parents' house."

"Fine," she said, nodding eagerly. "No problem."

"And I want the contact info for Charles Hammond. I want to get his take on what happened at the hospital."

"Sure thing." She dug through her bag and took out her phone. Within a few seconds, my phone pinged with a shared contact. One thing I could say was positive about Piper Sanchez. She took her work seriously and gave it everything she had. Her work was her life, and I could relate to that.

I decided to push, just a little. "And speaking of owing me—"

"What?" She pursed her lips.

"If anything about Harper crosses your desk, I get it first."

"Oh my God!" Piper rolled her eyes. "You know I can't promise that."

"I'm not asking for that. All I'm asking is for a heads-up. No one will ever know where it came from. And I'm not saying you can't run it. And"—I leaned forward—"if we see this works out, we might be able to help each other moving forward. I could send tidbits your way."

I could see her contemplating the possibilities of a working relationship. "You know this could be brilliant. Two powerful women running this town behind the scenes."

I smiled and nodded. "Exactly. Women helping women."

She nodded. "Girl power." She held up her pinky as she had in junior high.

I laughed and linked my pinky with hers. "Girl power."

Chapter
Twenty-One

Piper took several shots of me at my desk and in front of the office before she left. I had to give her credit; she came across as an excellent journalist and extremely professional. I actually felt pleased about the article now. Who knew? It might even bring in some business.

Speaking of business, I needed to find out who "Charles," or Charlie, as Harper had referred to him, was and what his role was in all of this. When I called him, he answered on the first ring and sounded downright gleeful to meet with me, which gave me the strange jumpy sensation in my stomach again. I had to get a grip on that.

I decided that I'd get us some refreshments before he arrived at the office. I'd intended on buying scones and perhaps some granola when the smell of pumpkin spice lattes convinced me to add them to my order. They would be better than the pods in the office. I was on my way back from the coffee shop, with a carrier containing two lattes and two ginger scones, when I spotted LJ coming out of Smart Cookie. He crossed the street, chewing on a large black and white cookie. I wondered why he hadn't returned my calls. The behavior was unacceptable.

Determined to catch him before he went MIA again, I intended to charge across the street and demand an audience. He'd claimed to be willing to do anything to help Harper. Time to put up or shut up. I was sick of chasing him down, and besides, I might still harbor a little irritation that he'd not lifted a finger to come to my aid, or even shouted for help, at the hospital.

I tapped my foot impatiently, waiting for a break in the traffic, when I noticed him opening the door of a big white van. Something inside me went still. Moving down the opposite side of the street, I stood behind the bed of a large four-by-four truck just as the van pulled out and slowly rolled down the road. "Hewitt Electric," written in big, bold blue lettering down the side of the van, caused my heart to race. The same company that Gran and I had spied leaving Ross's house the night of the charity event. The night someone killed Leonard Richardson.

Amelia called just as I crossed the street, heading back to my office. My heart hammered in my ribcage as my mind reeled with what I'd just witnessed. "Hey."

"You sound out of breath. Ah, I hear street noise. I thought you'd be home taking it easy."

"Nope. Back at work today." I waved and smiled at Mr. Newsom, who owned the hardware store, as I passed by. He'd been staring, and I didn't want to add any more grist to the rumor mill.

He grinned broadly, waving as he adjusted his orange and brown plaid hat, his hand on the door as he got ready to open up. "You all right?"

"Yes, sir." I paused. "Thanks for asking."

"How's ya mom and them? A shame all this mess your family is going through." His rosy cheeks shook in time with his head.

"They're hanging in there."

"And you are too, I guess. Bless your heart. My wife and I saw the horrible attack on the news. Be careful, ya hear? A woman on her own is a scary scenario in this day and age."

My smile nearly faltered. "I appreciate your concern. I'll be careful, and I'll let my folks know you asked about them. Have a nice day!" I continued up the street.

"You poor thing," Amelia said. "I couldn't help but overhear all that. Everyone should mind their own business."

"Can't argue with you there. But then again"—I paused and let a couple pass me—"if everyone minded their own business, we wouldn't have eyewitnesses, and no one would have rushed to my aid the other day."

"Well, that's true, I guess. I never thought of it that way. Any news from the police?"

"They're still investigating. They said the guy might've been paid to attack me."

"Oh my God! Who would do that?"

"They're not sure if there is any truth to the allegation. One of his gang members rolled over when he got picked up on another charge. The member could be attempting to make a deal for leniency. I'm being careful just in case. But I refuse to alter my life because of some lowlife. I will not live in fear." I had my small sidearm in my shoulder bag, and after taking a safety course last year, plus all the time I'd spent at the firing range, I felt comfortable and confident with my piece. I decided to wait until we were all together before telling her about the black sedan I'd seen before the attack.

"Good for you! Guess who I just got a call from?" Before I could guess, she blurted, "LJ Richardson, and he's asked me to come over and do a formal walkthrough of the property. He wants to put it on the market. He thinks he might need the money for Harper's defense."

I froze in front of the office door. "Amelia, don't go over there by yourself. Promise me."

"It's my job, and like you, I refuse to live in fear too."

Maneuvering the bag atop the cupholder, I managed to get the door open. "Okay, listen." I placed the items on the desk. "The night of the charity event, when I was taking Gran home, we saw a man come out of a neighbor's house and get into a Hewitt Electric van."

"And?"

"And I just saw LJ get into a Hewitt Electric van."

"Oh my God."

"Look, don't freak out, and swear you'll keep this to yourself."

"You're scaring me. But I swear."

I perched on the edge of the desk and lowered my voice despite the fact I was alone. "I believe someone tried to poison Harper before the police took her into custody."

"What?"

"And that's not all. LJ was at the hospital when Spider attacked me and, from the footage I saw, attempted to stop Charles Hammond from helping me."

Amelia sucked in a sharp breath.

The office door opened, and in walked Charles Hammond. "Amelia, I've got to go. Are we on the same page?"

"Same sentence, same word."

"Good." I placed the phone on the desk, then turned, smiled, and extended my hand. "Mr. Hammond. It's nice to see you again." I gave him a saccharine-sweet smile and hoped my eyes didn't show my distrust in anyone who associated with the Richardson family—or the nerves I battled from the way he'd held me after my attack.

He took my hand in his. "I'm glad to see you've recovered from your injuries."

I released my hand from his. "I believe I owe you thanks."

He shook his head. "Not at all. Like I told you on the phone, I only did what anyone would have. I just wish I could have reacted sooner and saved you from such trauma."

"That's kind, but I don't think anyone saw that coming, and I believe you did save me from a worse fate. The perp had a knife that he tried to use on the police."

"I'd heard that." He shook his head.

I pulled one latte from the carrier and, taking a bag containing a ginger scone, handed them over and waved toward the small seating area by the coffee machine. "Please, have a seat."

After I retrieved my refreshments, I joined him, taking a seat opposite him. This felt more conversational than it would with me seated at my desk and him on the other side of it. "I'll get right to the point, Mr. Hammond."

"Call me Charles, please."

"Charles." I smiled. "I understand you are close with the Richardson family."

He nodded. "I am. I'm currently working on a mystery that's set in a small town much like this one, depicting a family much like theirs."

"That's exciting. My book club would love to sit down and chat with you. Do you have anything published I might be familiar with?"

He shook his head. "I've written a few short stories and a couple of anthologies. This will be my first novel."

I took a bite of my scone and washed it down with a sip of coffee. "Ah, so 'Charles' is a pen name then?"

He inclined his head. "No. It's my birth name. Why?" He held up a finger. "Right. You mentioned before that you googled me."

I waved my hand. "To see what you've written. It came up with no hits. I found several Charles Hammonds, but none of them were you."

"I've yet to create a social media presence. It's probably something I need to look into. Clearly." He took a sip of the coffee and smiled. "Future fans will be researching me."

We both shared a fake laugh, and I detected a slight nervous tremor to his. *Why?*

"Is your story also loosely based on the Richardson murder?"

"I'm not sure yet. But if I don't write about the murder and the family, someone else will." He pushed his square-framed black glasses up on his nose.

"Before my attack, I noticed you and LJ having a conversation outside the hospital." I wiped my hands on a napkin. "What do you think of him?"

"Ah." He flushed a little when he smirked. "LJ is an interesting sort. He hasn't decided whether he likes the idea of me writing the story or not. I found his disdain for his late father particularly interesting, along with his relationship with his, um, stepmother. And right now, he's no fan of mine."

"Care to elaborate?" I inclined my head as I crossed my legs, a motion he watched intently. I swallowed the uneasiness and tugged my skirt over my knee.

"Only that I'm not sure he's decided if he's a fan of yours or not. And obviously"—he lifted his brows—"I am."

I cleared my throat and decided not to touch that last remark. This was a business meeting, and I planned to keep things professional. "LJ seemed to be on board with Harper's desire to hire our company to help with the defense discovery and investigations. What changed?"

He shrugged. "The guy's fickle with trust issues."

"Okay." I thought it was more because he was afraid I might discover the secret he harbored and perhaps would swing the investigation his way. "After my accident, I managed to get up and speak briefly with Harper. She insisted that I speak with you."

His eyes grew more serious. "Did she?"

"Yes."

"She didn't say why?"

I gave my head a small shake.

"Not surprising. Harper is . . ." He paused and tapped his index finger against the paper cup. "Troubled. She battles with a lot. Her life hasn't been easy."

I shifted to angle my body more toward him and placed my arm across the back of the chair. "What are you saying exactly?"

"All families have secrets, Lyla." His light brown gaze locked with mine. "Some are benign, and others are dark and sinister. I wonder if you know which your family harbors."

"*My* family?" Had Harper wanted me to speak with Charles because of *my* family and not about the case?

"This town isn't as it seems. Secrets here are like wounds beginning to fester. And some folks won't be happy when they reach the light of day. I'd be careful if I were you. You don't want to get caught in the cross fire." He leaned back against the chair.

I studied him. "Are you threatening me, Charles?"

His brows went up. "No. I'm trying to warn you. Your own family isn't what they seem. All I'm aiming to do is help."

I picked my cup back up. There was something about the way he spoke that had me on edge. I let out a small chuckle to cover my nerves. "You shouldn't concern yourself with my family."

Something I couldn't discern flashed across his face before he smiled. "I concern myself with all families. Each family has a story to tell. One day, you may want to unearth yours. When that day comes, I'll help you."

I met his gaze and held it. "I wouldn't hold out hope for scandal there, if I were you. It doesn't get any more normal than the Moody family." Even as the words left my lips, I could tell I hadn't sold it, and the thought frightened me.

"Very well. We'll let it go for now." He took another sip of coffee. Irritation began to build within me. "The only thing I can imagine Harper Richardson was referring to is some notes I took while interviewing the family after the murder," Charles said. He crossed his right leg over his left and took another sip from his cup.

"Would you be willing to share the interview notes?"

"I can do better than that. I'll get you into the house to ask the questions yourself. Beatrice mentioned you came by earlier. Perhaps we can make a deal of sorts." My opinion of this man was rapidly deteriorating. I shook my head. "I don't think so. I'm working for the defense, and it wouldn't help my client's case having a writer looking over my shoulder to profit from her misfortune. I do have a reputation to uphold, Mr. Hammond. Plus, I worry I might be making a deal with the devil by agreeing."

His head fell back in time with his deep belly laugh. "My sources at the *Sweet Mountain Gazette* informed me that you've already made a deal with the she-devil willing to sell her very soul for a story. I have contacts everywhere."

"Yikes. Don't think much of Piper, do you? And there's no deal." I wondered if Piper knew he had eyes on her as well. She would if she didn't already. Or had I misjudged her, and she'd betrayed my confidence? Perhaps Charles had replaced Quinn as her boy toy. Somehow I doubted Piper would choose a man over her career. But what was done was done.

"What's that expression?" He raised his finger. "Ah. 'The juice isn't worth the squeeze.'"

"Ouch." I smirked. *Guess not an item or partner in any capacity. Good.*

He rose. "You're right to wonder about the family, on the right track there. Perhaps ask the question why. Why did the Richardsons move to Sweet Mountain? Why did Leonard want to control the household? Why did his family despise him? And if you want to be brave, ask yourself why your family has hidden so much from me? Do a little digging. What might you unearth?"

The gloves are coming off. "Perhaps *you* should ask the question why." I got to my feet and smiled, fighting my warring instincts to throttle him until he told me everything he knew and my annoyance that he dangled so-called knowledge about my own family. "Why am I such an impertinent blowhard? Why do I think so much of myself? What creds can I lean on for validation?"

A glint lit his eyes. He took a step toward me. He didn't seem angry; he seemed excited. "Ah. I see. You think a little too highly of your skill set. You've been doing this—how long? And yet you still don't know the most important facts?" he said.

I bared my teeth in a mock smile. "It's funny. I was having the same thoughts about you."

"Oh?" The fire in his eyes dared me to continue. He was enjoying this interlude, and strangely, though I hated to admit it, so was I. It was a battle of wits. He wasn't that much my senior—ten years, give or take. And we seemed equally matched.

My breathing sped up to match his. "Yes. I wouldn't concern yourself about my competency. You have enough on your plate, attempting to build a career. You, sir, are no Truman Capote, and this isn't the case to alter that fact."

I would not let this man have the upper hand. *Could not.*

He laughed. "Oh, this is going to be fun."

The door opened, and Uncle Calvin strolled in. He paused when he noticed Charles. "Hello."

The smile dropped from Charles's face as he extended his hand; his tone dripped with charisma as he said, "You must be Calvin Cousins."

"I am. And you would be?"

"Charles Hammond."

"Mr. Hammond is the man who helped with the apprehension of my attacker," I volunteered. "He's writing a novel about small towns and the secrets they keep."

Calvin shook his hand. "I see." Calvin hesitated before releasing his hand. "Have we met somewhere before?"

"I don't think so. But I do travel quite a bit." He turned toward me and smiled. "I was just having a nice chat with your niece here. She's something all right. Going through that awful attack and back in the muck on another case. A tough cookie, she is."

Calvin regarded him warily. "It's what we do here."

"Yes. I know." He bent down and picked up his cup and scone. "Thanks for this. You have my number." He winked at me and started for the door.

"You're welcome. Good luck with your novel," I said with a sarcastic half laugh, and then caught myself. Why was I so eager to antagonize Charles again? I'd never met anyone like him in my life.

He smiled and paused, turning back toward Calvin. "Come to think of it, you look a bit familiar to me too. Any relation to the Folsom family in the Plains—"

I'd never seen my uncle fight for control of his facial expression in my life like he did then. "No." His tone came out low and menacing as he cut Charles off. "Good day, Mr. Hammond. I trust this is the last we'll see of you."

My gaze darted between the men.

Charles smiled. "Funny thing, trust."

"What?" I asked.

Charles turned toward me. "Trust is a paradox. Sometimes it can be misplaced and—"

Calvin closed the distance to the door in a flash and shoved Charles out, slamming the door and locking it behind him.

Charles does know things about my family. "What was that about?" I gaped at my uncle. "The guy's a nut." I let out a nervous laugh. "Harmle . . ." I began, but the word died in my throat.

Calvin didn't laugh. His chest heaved. "Something is wrong with him." He pointed at me. "I don't want you anywhere near that man."

I raised both hands in a defensive posture. "I'm not planning on hanging out with the guy. I'm only interested in what he can do to help Harper."

"He intrigues you. I can see it all over your face. You were enjoying whatever banter the two of you had going before I got here."

"He's odd. But a lot of writers are." I tried desperately to read his strange reaction—hoping that he and Mother weren't hiding some awful secret. "Why did you freak out when he asked you about that family?"

"It's a long story, and I don't want to get into it."

He started toward his office.

"Was it about a job you did? Or . . ." Again my voice trailed off.

He turned and pointed toward the door. "He's looking for dirt. Dirt he can turn into a buck."

I made a face. "Yeah, I know that. But you're awfully rattled over it. Why?"

"This family needs some peace," he bit out, and his nostrils flared. "We're working on a case that now I see we probably shouldn't have taken. The Richardson family has caused nothing but trouble."

"Wow." I took a step back. "Perhaps *you* shouldn't be working this case."

"Don't patronize me, little girl."

"*What?*" I threw my hands in the air. "Patronize you? I simply asked a question. I'm not going to allow Harper to get locked up because we dislike the family. Let's overlook all these inconsistencies. Hell, why do we fight anything? We should just lie down and let everyone and everything roll over us."

"Enough!"

I jumped.

He ran his hand over his chin, which needed a shave, and blew out a breath. "I'm sorry. I shouldn't have raised my voice." He put his hand on my shoulder, and I fought the urge to cringe. "That's not what I meant. Lyla, I've done things in my life that I'm not proud of. Many of us have."

He sighed, and I waited for him to elaborate. When he dropped his hand, he pointed to the door. "I plan to find out everything I can about Charles Hammond. And if that asshole thinks he can blackmail us into helping him write his filth, we'll f—ing bury him."

My mouth fell open. He hadn't just said 'bury him.' He'd dropped the f-bomb through gritted teeth before the word 'bury.' Charles had no idea whom he was dealing with, and right now, neither did I.

Chapter Twenty-Two

Melanie, Amelia, and I sat in the corner booth at the Trail Head Grill. We'd just finished our meal, and I told Mel about LJ driving the Hewitt Electric van.

"Wow." Mel leaned back and pushed her plate away. "Do you really think it's dangerous for Amelia to go over to the Richardson house alone?"

"Yes." I shook my head. "No. I don't know." I turned to Amelia. "I may have overreacted. Seeing LJ in the van freaked me out, and I may be just a little overprotective. Just take someone with you to be on the safe side."

"Yeah, it doesn't hurt to be safe." Amelia seemed to be pondering. "I could take my assistant along. Yes. That's what I'll do."

"Good." I let out a little sigh. "Although—"

The waitress came by and took our plates, leaving the bill behind.

"What?" Amelia asked after we split the cost of the meal.

"I wonder if LJ is authorized to sell the property. Last I heard from Mr. Jenkins, the will hadn't been probated, and the bank accounts were frozen."

"Oh. I wouldn't know about that. But it's something I will ask when I go out to the property."

I took a deep breath. "I have one other thing to tell y'all." Their eyes were wide as I told them what had happened in the office. My conversation with Charles was a real point of interest, but they were both stunned into silence when I told them how my uncle had reacted.

"Wow. What's your read on the writer? Do you think Calvin is onto something about him? Or maybe he was lying?" Amelia asked as she took a sip from her glass.

I glanced off, considering her question. "Honestly, I think Charles told me the truth. He knows something about the Richardsons, and I think"—I took in a deep, shaky breath—"my family too."

Amelia reached out and took my hand, and Mel said, "You poor thing. Not only do you have to deal with Harper's case, but you've also had an attack on your life. You are my hero. How you're managing to stay upright is astounding."

"Mel's right, Lyla. You are as tough as nails."

Mother would be pleased.

I smiled. "Y'all, I appreciate the support and encouragement. Don't worry about me. I'm fine." I glanced down at my watch. "And I have to go in a minute. I'm planning on running by and seeing who exactly was the technician on the Ross job the night of the murder."

Amelia nodded. "Good idea. Maybe Mrs. Ross will let you see a copy of the work order."

"Exactly what I'm hoping for. That should be more inconspicuous than calling the company. If LJ is involved, I don't want to make him suspicious that we suspect him until I have something more solid to go on. Then I'll be lighting that company's phone lines up."

"I had a bad feeling about him from the get-go." Mel pushed up the sleeves of her pink sweater. "The whole family is whacko. Harper married a crazy man and moved into his insane asylum."

She'd get no arguments from me there.

"Since Rosa isn't here, I have to play devil's advocate." Amelia leaned closer, glancing around, and then whispered, "And please, don't hate me for bringing this up. What if Harper, in her desperation, perhaps let something slip to LJ that she wished Leonard dead?"

Mel opened her mouth to argue, but I held up my hand. "No, Mel. This case is going to be tried in open court. The prosecution has tons of evidence against her. Until we have something solid to present even a plausible case for reasonable doubt, she's up the creek."

Mel scrubbed her face with her hands. "Okay, okay. So if we consider her as the guilty party, just like the cases we look at in our club meetings, we can rule her out."

"Exactly."

"Okay." Mel dropped her hands. "That makes sense to me."

"Let's examine what we know. One, Harper was unhappy in her marriage. She was having an affair with her stepson."

Amelia shivered. "Sheesh, that sounds creepy."

"Stepson her age," I added.

Melanie nodded. "Yes, that sounds better."

"She asked me to locate an aunt who, by all accounts, seems to have vanished into thin air." I leaned over and grabbed my bag, pulling out my tablet and stylus. Everyone waited while I jotted down what we'd listed so far.

"And not to sound absurd," Amelia said, "but most of the time, someone close to the victim in a case like this is the guilty party. And just like in *Crooked House*, sometimes it's the most innocent-looking one in the family."

I nodded. "And Harper did say that Beatrice brought her the cup of tea, and it was the only thing Harper ingested before her arrest."

Mel pointed at me. "Lyla, didn't you say that Beatrice was at the charity event?"

I nodded.

"You saw her, Mel. How could she have pulled off something like that? She weighs eighty pounds soaking wet." Amelia shook her head.

"What does that have to do with anything? Leonard was poisoned," Melanie pointed out.

"But the candlestick is still missing." Amelia shifted in the booth.

"True, but it isn't the murder weapon." I scribbled on the tablet. "And Harper nearly died of an overdose of the drug. Leaving the cops to believe she couldn't handle the guilt of her crime. But to Amelia's point, and having seen the body first-hand, it looked like someone wanted to make sure he was dead. Even after he dropped from the overdose."

Mel leaned closer to the table. Amelia and I mirrored her as Mel said, "Maybe we should discuss this somewhere else or at a better time."

I glanced around and noticed that we'd started drawing attention. A couple at the table across from us were whispering and staring our way—time to go. The three of us hurried out of the booth and exited the restaurant, keeping how heads low.

"They added some extra decorations this year," Melanie commented as we stood by Amelia's car. "I'm glad things here still feel sane." The square was lit beautifully, and all the fall decorations were complete for the pub crawl this weekend. I loved our town so. I nodded and wrapped my arm around my friend's shoulder as she sniffed and dabbed at her eyes. She hurt deeply for Harper.

"Yeah. It is good to have a little peace to enjoy." Amelia opened her car door and tossed her purse inside.

"Yes." As I smiled at the sights before us and looked forward to the pub crawl, despite the tragedy that had befallen our friend and town, Charles's words came back to me: *All families have secrets. Some are benign, and others are dark and sinister. I wonder if you know which your family harbors.*

A car alarm went off, and Melanie giggled. "Talk about a jump scare."

We all laughed. It sounded high-pitched and nervous.

Amelia's phone rang. She glanced down at her smartwatch. "That's Ethan. I better run; he'll be worried."

We hugged her and waved as she pulled out of the parking lot.

Mel looped her arm through mine, and we crossed the street to our cars. "I know it sounds stupid, but I still can't get the story *Crooked House* out of my head whenever I think of that family. We have to do our best to get Harper off this ridiculous charge and out of that family for good."

"I'm doing my best, Mel."

"I know you are." She gave me a sad smile. "Have you thought about asking Rosa for help? I know you want to know more about Charles Hammond, not only about his connection to the Richardson family but also to yours. If she helps you, Calvin won't find out."

I nodded. "Yes. I plan to see if Rosa can help me do a little digging. But only if it won't hurt her position in the police department. And also because she might be beholden to the detective, and that man is hell-bent on putting Harper away for good."

"That's a good idea. What about this Spider fella? Any news on that front?" Melanie leaned against her car. I'd parked right next to her.

"No. Last I heard, he was still nonresponsive. Who knows if he'll ever wake up? The doctors say he will, and Quinn said a sketch of the man behind the money would be sent to me, but it hasn't been yet. I don't think Atlanta PD has any real leads other than hearsay and Spider or whatever his name is. Calvin and I went through our records today after things cooled down, and no one rang any bells. The cases we've handled lately haven't been the type to leave disgruntled exes seeking revenge." I shrugged. "No one has made another attempt, and I'm keeping my eyes peeled for anything out of the ordinary. I haven't seen the sedan again, but whoever is after me won't catch me unawares again."

"You're packin'?" Mel asked, her voice implying she hoped I'd gone there.

I patted my purse with a smile.

Chapter
Twenty-Three

"Lyla, why don't we go out for ice cream?" Mother smiled at and me and took my hand. The idea of delicious, cold, hand-dipped butter pecan ice-cream nearly had me drooling. I grinned up at her and squeezed her hand, nodding vigorously.

She buckled me into the passenger seat while I held my tablet and kept taking notes on Harper's case. Mother hummed and sang in time with the old song "Summer Days." It was a scorcher today, even with the windows down, and the breeze blowing the skirt of my pale blue sundress offered not much relief. Georgia summers could be like that.

I glanced up from my tablet to see Mother had driven off the road and was headed straight for the cliff. I screamed and shouted for her to stop!

Mother didn't seem to hear me. She turned to me, and her eyes were all white.

"Some family secrets are dark and sinister. It's better if they're buried with us." She floored the car, and we were airborne.

I woke in the darkness, sitting straight up in bed, panting. My damp hair stuck to my forehead and the side of my face. My God! Had I dreamed I lived in Agatha Christie's *Crooked House*? Mother had been Edith, driving me off the cliff. Wow. Charles's secrets and the similarities my club saw in the Richardson case sure had gotten to me. This case with Harper's twisted family living in their version of *Crooked House*.

My phone began ringing, and I nearly leaped out of my skin. A glance at my phone's screen showed me both Gran's smiling face and that it was roughly six thirty in the morning. I wiped my hair from my face and answered the phone. "Gran, is everything okay?"

"Hi, sweetie pie. I didn't wake you, did I?"

I blinked a few times before answering. "Uh, yeah. It's six thirty, and I worked late."

"Sorry about that. It's just, well, I thought I should call you. James said you were supposed to come by last night, but he didn't get off in time. For some reason, he seemed to think that you shouldn't come by if he wasn't here to, um, explain things."

"Yeah, I'd planned on coming by after dinner, but Daddy called and told me not to bother coming by because he'd be late." My hand went involuntarily to my heart. "Explain things. What is it? Everyone is okay, right? No one is ill?"

"No, no, nothing like that. Not physically ill anyway. It's Frances. She's been acting odd lately. And I don't mean the normal odd for your mother, but *really* odd." Gran did sound worried, but she tended to be a little dramatic at times. It was part of her charm.

"She's probably still shaken up about what happened to Leonard Richardson." I got up and padded down the steps and into the kitchen. I needed coffee.

"Maybe. It's just—well, I heard her whisperin' to herself in the pantry earlier today. She's been watching the local news and reading online incessantly."

"She's been through a lot. First, the murder, then forensics and cops coming and going at all hours. Add that to my attack that made local news, and I think she's holding up well." I got a mug out of the dishwasher. "I saw her out to eat with her ladies' group."

"I'm tellin' ya, honey. Somethin' is off about her. She was up in the attic for hours last night. I kept hearing her movin' around above my bedroom. She doesn't sleep anymore unless your daddy gives her a pill. I'm worried."

My hand stilled halfway to closing the dishwasher. Had Charles said something to her about family secrets that triggered what Gran was describing? I had a busy day ahead of me. Mr. Jenkins had called late yesterday to tell me about Harper's arraignment today. He apologized for the late notice. I'd already made the decision to go by Mrs. Ross's, so I'd have to squeeze everything in today. I could not leave Gran on her own.

"Okay, that does sound like unusual behavior. I'm going to hop in the shower, run by the bakery, and grab a really strong cup of coffee, and then I'll be over there."

"Good. I'll just feel better having a second opinion." I didn't even comment that our opinion paled compared to that of the psychiatrist, a leader in the field, in other words, Daddy. "Get me a few of those bear claws while you're there."

"You got it."

At seven thirty, I was on my way to my parents' house. I was downing my double shot macchiato as fast as I could without burning the roof of my mouth. I'd called Mrs. Ross, and she said she would be expecting me this morning, which made popping over and questioning her more straightforward than I had expected.

Gran's concerns had resonated a little more as I'd showered. I thought about the times I'd briefly spoken to my mother after the incident at the house. She'd been distant, which didn't surprise me after the ordeal, but she hadn't chastised me about my involvement or blamed my job for the attack. I was not complaining; it just wasn't like her to keep her opinions regarding my life to herself. I feared what Charles could have said to upset her. He'd sure done a number on Calvin.

I'd even run a detailed search on my mother and uncle last night, something I'd never done. While I wanted to respect their request for privacy about the past, I felt the time had come for the air to be cleared. Charles had shoved the secrecy directly in my face, and I needed answers. I'd not been able to find a single record of my maternal grandmother until her move to Sweet Mountain. And even more concerning, a couple of years after moving to our town, my mother and uncle were listed on adoption papers that I'd managed to locate. I had more questions than answers after my search.

When I pulled into the bricked driveway of Mother and Daddy's home, my anxiety reached new levels. Something was up. A sense of dread began to creep up my spine the closer I got to the house. I'd even started to eat one of the pastries from the box, but the more I thought about the situation, the more I just

Kate Young

couldn't stomach the sweetness. And that was unlike me. Sugar was my crutch. My own words inside my head failed to comfort me.

I took the brick steps two at a time, rushing through the massive white pillars of the front porch, then knocked twice on the large mahogany front doors before turning the knob. It didn't budge. Locked. Mother never locked the front doors.

I rang the doorbell. When no one came to the door, I rang again. After what felt like an eternity, Gran answered the door, wearing a robe. Her hair was wrapped in a towel, and her face was shiny from skin cream.

"Why's the door locked?" I hugged her before entering.

"It's so good to see you." She held my face in her bony hands, looking up into my face; her pale blue eyes looked tired. "You bring my bear claws?" Sugar was Gran's crutch too.

I held up the box with the little string. She smiled then and took it from me. "You okay, sweetie pie? You never said if those headaches went away."

"Don't go fussing over me too. I'm okay. See?" I smiled brightly at her. "No more headaches. Plus"—I patted my bag—"I'm ready for the next time."

Gran gave me a single head nod. "That's my girl." She chose the largest pastry from the box and took a big bite. "It's been a trying few days." She couldn't hide the weariness in her tone after she swallowed the bite.

A beep pulled our attention to the wall beside the front doors.

Gran punched the code into a security panel on the wall with a sugary, glaze-covered finger. With a sigh, she said, "Your mother insisted that every door stay locked and the alarm engaged."

Before I could comment on that strange news, I noticed the house's condition and gaped as I glanced around. My parents' entryway table usually boasted huge, fragrant bouquets that always greeted you upon your entrance. Today, they were wilted, and the water tinged a greenish-brown color.

Alarm shot through me. *Gran hadn't been exaggerating.* I moved down the hallway and into the empty kitchen at the back of the house. Another shock overtook me; there were dishes in the sink and plates on the large granite island. The six Provençal grape swivel barstools were not pushed in or spaced appropriately.

Glancing into the room adjacent to the kitchen, the great room, I expected to find Mother. It, too, was vacant. The light shining through the floor-to-ceiling windows made the fine layer of dust evident. My entire life, there'd never been a speck of dust in Mother's house, unlike my own townhome. She had a cleaning service come in three times a week. *"Cleanliness is next to godliness"* I'd heard all my life.

"I told you. Your mother is off her rocker. She canceled the cleaning service and flower delivery and wanted to cancel the yard service. Your father pushed back on that one. The home-owner's association would fine us if we allowed the leaves to pile up on the lawn. The only people she's permitted into the house are the police, and that's only because she hasn't had a choice in the matter." Gran continued to blend in the cream on her face with one hand and hold her bear claw with the other. "She's been on the phone a lot. I caught her sneaking out back and whispering with Mrs. Ross."

Uh-oh. I wondered if maybe that was the reason Mrs. Ross had seemed eager for me to come over. Perhaps she, too, worried for her friend.

My eyes went wide as Gran shoved half a bear claw into her mouth. She reached for my coffee. I handed it over and waited for her to wash down her pastry. Never in my life had I seen the house look in such disarray.

"Is this why Daddy called me and told me not to come?" I couldn't believe how, in a matter of a week, my entire life seemed to be crumbling around me.

Gran nodded slowly. "He didn't want to worry you. But"—she got closer and glanced around conspiratorially—"from what I could tell from Frances's body language, Mrs. Ross seemed to be all in on whatever it was she was saying. They've called a neighborhood watch meeting. I think they're scared that whoever whacked old man Richardson is coming for them. But it wasn't until Calvin called with news of something or another that he made the decision."

Oh God! I was right. This did have to do with Charles. "What did Calvin tell them?"

"I have no idea. But whatever it was sent your mother into a real tizzy. She got hysterical, shouting for James to go and pick you up. Shouting that she didn't want to start all over or have her entire life crash down around her."

I rubbed my forehead. *Oh my God.* Without a shadow of a doubt, I now firmly believed Charles. Whatever hidden secrets were out there about my family, he planned on unearthing and perhaps sharing them. Mother had always been secretive about her past. I'd trusted her and Calvin to know what was best. Though as much as they tried to safeguard me, the past still touched me. And they had been wrong to keep me in the dark!

I walked back through to the new library. The yellow crime scene tape had been stripped away, but the room still showed signs of the struggle. Stepping back, I shut the door. I couldn't handle this trauma and mother's too. Back in the kitchen, flashes from childhood came rushing back. For the most part, my childhood had been idyllic. But there were those occasional blips where my mother wouldn't "feel well." Gran would step in and see to my needs while daddy cared for Mother. He'd explain it as sometimes her past trauma bringing back ghosts she longed to forget.

The episodes would confuse me as a child. Seeing my proper mother walk around the house like a zombie with unwashed hair and in sweats always brought a bout of nerves, though these occasions were rare. I could even recall waking in the middle of the night to find her standing over my bed, watching me sleep. I gave myself a mental shake and focused back on Gran, who was still speaking.

"Your father was talking about sending her on vacation. Asked me to go with her. Frances says she won't go, but James can be mighty convincing when he wants to be. You should come with us." Gran pulled the towel from her hair and ran her fingers through her long gray locks.

I shook my head. "I've got a lot going on at the moment. With Harper's and my assault case—"

"Daisy! Who's here?" Mother's tremulous voice called down the staircase from the second floor.

"It's me, Mother!" Before I could move to the foyer, we heard the sound of footsteps running down the staircase.

Gran grabbed my arm, her gaze serious. "Prepare yourself."

A woman I didn't recognize came into the room. The sight was way worse than what I remembered from childhood. Her tangled hair was about her bare face. Her wrinkled terrycloth robe hung awkwardly off her shoulders and was half tied at her waist.

"Good morning, Mother." I attempted a smile.

"Lyla! What are you doing here so early? Not that we're not happy to have you." She smoothed her hair back from her face. "Daisy, did you fix Lyla some breakfast?"

"She brought pastries, Frances."

"Pastries aren't an adequate breakfast. Full of processed sugar and flour." She moved past us and started for the kitchen. "I'll prepare you something."

Gran and I exchanged an odd glance. Mother did not cook. *Ever.*

"Come along." Mother gave us a too-bright smile over her shoulder.

Gran and I slowly joined her in the kitchen, where she had a frying pan out, and she began rummaging through the refrigerator. "I don't know where Sandy is," she mumbled. I supposed she didn't think Gran knew she'd put a stop to her housekeeper's visits. She stood in front of the stove, holding a dozen eggs and some spinach.

"I'm not hungry. Really, Mother, you don't have to make anything."

She turned back around and stared at me. "Are you sure? It's no trouble."

Gran and I nodded in unison.

"Please, sit down." I pulled out the barstool next to me.

She just stared at it. "There's just so much to do."

She looked so lost. I rushed over to her and gave her a hug. "It's okay. Everything is going to be okay."

She rested her cheek on my shoulder and stroked the back of my hair. "Yes. It will because I will make it that way. He can't creep into this life. He. Can. Not."

"Who?" I whispered. "Charles Hammond?"

She pulled away, grabbing my forearms tightly. "If anyone approaches you and asks about your family, you tell your uncle."

She blinked at me, and somewhere deep down, something resonated. All these years, she'd only been trying to protect me from what she believed, I saw now, was danger. Yet in doing so, she'd sacrificed the beautiful relationship we could have had.

"Why not just tell me? Whatever it is, just get it out in the open, and I'll help. This is having an unhealthy effect on you."

She vehemently shook her head. "You have no idea what it was like for us. No idea. And I don't want you to." Her vacant stare worried me even more. Fear that Mother might be having some sort of breakdown made my eyes sting with unshed tears.

I thought about Mother's obsession with makeup. My entire life, she'd say, *You look pale, dear. A little lipstick could help.* In my desire to bring that woman back to the surface, I forced a smile. To remind her that whatever had transpired in her childhood could no longer control her here. "I know what will make you feel better. We'll go up, and you can take a nice long shower. I'll brush your hair, and you can put on some lipstick, and then we can have a nice chat."

She blinked at me again, then took a step backward. Her hand went to her hair. "I must look a fright."

"No," Gran and I said in unison.

The front door opened, and we heard Daddy punching in the code on the keypad.

"Who's there?" Mother wrapped her arms around me, cuddling me close and too tightly. It was almost as if she'd forgotten I was no longer a child, and she wanted to protect me from the boogie man.

Gran slowly shook her head. I could almost see the weariness settling over her. Her shoulders slumped forward, the corner of her mouth dipping down. "It's just James, Francis."

I stroked Mother's arms, hoping to soothe her. "It's Daddy. It's just Daddy."

Her breath heaved in her chest, and I couldn't stop the tears spilling over my cheeks. This woman was *not* my mother. Mother was strong, beautiful, opinionated to a fault, and always composed. She was the embodiment of old Southern grace.

My father came into the room. "Frances, dear, everything is okay. You're safe. Lyla is safe. The doors are locked, and the alarm is engaged. No one can get in."

His words seemed to settle my mother some. "No one can get in?"

"No, darling. No one can get in," he repeated.

I glanced from Gran to Daddy.

Daddy's eyes never left Mother's. "You're safe."

A sob overtook Mother, and Daddy opened his arms. She went, taking me with her. The three of us stood in the middle of the kitchen, Mother sobbing with what I hoped was a relief. I'd always been aware of the hellish childhood she and her brother had endured, but this behavior was on a whole new level. Mother had always said the past should stay buried, insisting it would only bring heartache.

Experiencing her pain on some minuscule level, I broke too. My sobs came in loud hiccups. And if she'd experienced such agony, that meant Uncle Calvin also had. No wonder he threatened to bury Charles. But I had news for everyone involved: if Charles dared to unearth secrets that would hurt my family, he'd have to come through me first. It was high time for the passing of the torch. The secrets buried in the red clay of Sweet Mountain, Georgia, were mine to dig up and guard.

Chapter Twenty-Four

"How is she?" I asked my father. He'd made a giant crackling fire in the large fireplace in the family room while I'd cleaned myself up and reapplied my makeup. I had to be at Mrs. Ross's by nine and at the courthouse for Harper's arraignment at eleven.

Daddy stood now, staring into the flames, with his hand braced on the mantle. "She's taking a shower. She seems to have pulled herself together after the emotional release. Your gran is sitting with her for a while, just in case she needs something." Gran was the best. She loved wholly and completely. "It was good of you to give her some space. I know you have questions."

"I don't want to push her." I sipped on a mug of coffee, staring into the flames that reflected on the Persian rug.

Daddy settled into his favorite leather armchair in the corner, a glass of scotch in hand. "Your mother claims to have an appointment this morning, but I'm going to talk her out of going."

"That's wise." Mother would not want anyone around town to see her have a meltdown.

"She'll hate that you saw her that way. She never wanted her past to affect you. Your mother is a strong woman and has managed herself with grace and dignity all these years. I can't remember a time that something triggered such a response." Daddy rubbed his finger around the rim of the glass.

"She is strong and controlled almost to the point of being extreme at times," I said. "I won't lie and say that I didn't feel like I needed to tiptoe around her at times. And still do. Not that it matters at the moment. Now, I need you to level with me."

"Level with you about . . .?"

"Don't. Please, just stop this. I'm tired of the charade. I've been through enough over the past few days. People lie to me all the time when I'm working cases. I'm becoming quite proficient at figuring out the reasons behind it too. My entire life, I've granted grace out of respect. Now, there's a writer in town kicking up a lot of dirt. He came by the office yesterday, asking me if I knew what secrets my family harbored. Uncle Calvin lost it. I mean, how telling is it for guarded, in-control Calvin not to be able to hold it together in front of me? And I know Calvin called here. Gran overhead the conversation."

Daddy leaned forward and pierced me with his intelligent ice-blue eyes. "You need to stay away from that man. The writer. He isn't what he seems to be. I'm not sure what his motives are or how he plans to blackmail this family, but I'm positive he will."

"Blackmail us about what? Who could this man possibly be to have the power to terrify everyone in our family?"

He sighed and ran his hand through his thinning brown hair. "I knew this day would come. I knew, when your mother made me swear to keep certain parts of her life secret, that one day you would insist on knowing about her childhood."

"What was so terrible? Were they running from something? I searched. I didn't find much except that Grandmother's second husband adopted Mother and Calvin."

Daddy looked tired as he took a deep sip from the glass. "Your mother is a remarkable woman. She's overcome so much, and we built a wonderful life. Still, trauma is like that. It's always there in the corner of the room, ready to rear its ugly head. I won't tell you secrets that aren't mine to share. But I do think you have a right to some explanation."

The look on my father's face had my heart beating like a drum. I was almost afraid to move, to breathe even, in case the sudden movement would make him change his mind. Living in the dark about your parents' past can be damaging. I couldn't speak for everyone. That'd been the experience for me.

"I'm not sure how much you remember your grandmother. She died when you were still so young."

"I remember seeing her at Christmas and Easter a time or two. One thing that stands out about her is that she favored Aunt Elizabeth to Mother." I put my cup down on the end table.

"Elizabeth represented a new beginning for her. A new life here in Georgia." *Mother hadn't always resided in Georgia.* I made a mental note. "Your grandmother had been in an extremely unhealthy relationship, and it affected your mother and uncle. He let out a big sigh. "She escaped in the middle of the night with her children and drove across the country and settled here. Your mother had lived a rigorous and constrained life before that. Her every move was monitored, and every decision was made for her."

My father's description of Mother's past sounded an awful lot like how Harper had described her marriage. Perhaps that's what linked the two. No wonder Mother hadn't wanted me to say anything that would paint Harper in a negative light.

"Were they abused?" I asked softly.

He glanced down at his hands. "Abuse was involved."

"That's why she took to Harper?"

He nodded his head. "Yes. I suppose she relates to the girl on some level. Once she's rested, we'll discuss it. I don't have all the answers, Lyla. I don't even know every detail of your mother and her brother's past. Some things she found too painful to discuss with anyone other than Calvin."

"How could you not know everything?" I asked incredulously.

His head lifted. "Honey, childhood trauma is unique for each individual. Some of it she's blocked out to preserve her sanity. Not everything comes out at once. And sometimes it's lost for good. Pushing her to recall every traumatic event is counterproductive. We deal with what we have to when it surfaces. This is about her mental health, not about my need to be told every sordid detail."

"Yeah, sorry." I massaged the area between my brows. "That makes sense."

"I'm going to try to convince your mother and your Gran to go on a cruise. The change of scenery will be good for both of them." He sipped the amber liquid. "I'm handing off the patients I can to other doctors and keeping my time away from home limited to hourly appointments."

"That's good. I heard a doctor in your practice evaluated Harper."

He nodded. "At the request of the lead detective."

With this new information, I wondered if Mother had confided in Harper a little as well. And with Charles befriending LJ and Harper, I wondered how much they were privy to about whatever he held over my family.

"So, Charles Hammond. Who is he to Mother and Calvin? One minute Mother was lunching with him and claiming the man understood her, and the next, Calvin was ready to rip his head clean off."

Daddy gave me a blank look. "I'm not sure he's anything to them. But I think he's asking questions around town under false pretenses. And he knows some things about your mother's past. How much, I'm not sure of, but anything at all is enough to send them on a downward spiral."

I nodded, thinking over what he'd said. It made sense. Maybe Charles had come across someone from wherever they lived before, and decided to come to Sweet Mountain to collect a payday. Now he sought something from me. I could use that. And I planned on digging into all angles, both for Mother and Harper. One thing I knew for sure: I did not want my mother anywhere near any of this while the dirt flew. Calvin once told me that digging into cases such as these, those that were buried deep, shined a great big spotlight on the one holding the shovel. Now, that would be me.

"Thank you for talking to me. I think you're right about Mother. She can have spa treatments and be waited on while soaking up some vitamin D. And by the time she returns, the police should have this case closed. And we'll find some way to get rid of Charles." I leaned back into the plush leather and then stood.

"Honey, how are you?" Daddy glanced up at me, his face flushed. "I should have asked about you and the assault case before dredging up the past."

I swatted the air and grabbed my bag. "I'm fine. You don't need to worry about me." I met his eyes directly, and for the first time in my life, I felt like the strongest person in the room.

"Are you sure you don't want to go on the trip with them? You've gone through an ordeal yourself. And it might give you and your mother time to talk."

"I appreciate the offer, and under different circumstances I would take you up on it. But not now." I shook my head. "I can't go with them. I have too much going on here."

"Just think about it. Calvin said your attacker still hasn't gained consciousness. And that poses a serious and dangerous question."

"What do you mean?"

"I mean, without questioning the man, we have no idea what his motives were."

I gave my father a small, sad smile. "I know. We're digging into our past cases just in case. I'm also not under the misconception that I'm safe now that he's been apprehended. This is the life I've chosen. I'm more than capable of dealing with the backlash from my choices. I'm prepared."

"It's amazing to see who you've become. You are maturing before my very eyes."

I almost cried when I spied respect in his gaze. "Daddy, I've got to go." He rose and embraced me. "Thank you," I said. I didn't have to say for what. My intelligent father would know how much his words meant to me.

"Anytime, Lyla bug. You stay safe."

I kissed him on the cheek. "Promise."

Chapter
Twenty-Five

Mrs. Ross stood out on the front porch with me. "I saw your car over at your parents' place. How's your mother today?"

I smiled. "She's doing just fine. Why do you ask?"

Mrs. Ross glanced around, looking uncomfortable. "Oh, you know, just understanding how all these rumors must be taking a toll on her." She lifted her gaze to meet my own. Her amber eyes filled with sincerity as she said, "Your mother is the strongest woman I know. You are blessed."

"Thank you. I believe I am too." I cast a glance backward. "Mrs. Ross, if you need to tell me something, you can trust me. I will forever protect my mother."

Mrs. Ross let out a nervous laugh. "Whatever could you mean, dear?" She shook her brown curly head. "I'm sure you're in a hurry, and you're here to find out about the company who did some work for me. They did a good job for me. I certainly would recommend them."

"Well, that's good to hear. We need some work done at the office and we're looking for a reputable company with time in their schedule to squeeze us in soon. Um, do you recall the technician who came out?" She wouldn't check with Calvin about my visit, but if she did, he'd probably think she got the dates mixed up since he'd already had an electrician out. I'd have to make a point to tell him about my visit. He wasn't returning my calls, and I had no idea if he had any interest in working on this case any longer.

She'd stared at me oddly. "I don't know if I recall the young man's name."

"That's okay if you can't remember. It just always makes me feel better to get a reference from someone as reputable as you are before I hire someone. I mean, I'm a woman who sometimes has to mind the office alone, and you know how dangerous it can be. Letting a strange man into your office when you're the only one there . . ." I made a pained face. "Perhaps I'm being a little ridiculous."

"No." Mrs. Ross placed a hand on my shoulder. "You can't be too careful. I completely understand. Let me go see if I can find that paperwork." She left the door open while she rummaged through the drawer of the entryway table. A car slowly rolled past the house, the black sedan with deeply tinted windows that I'd seen several times before my attack.

"Here it is." Mrs. Ross came back out onto the porch. "Who's that?"

"I have no idea." My pulse rate kicked up, and I pulled my phone from my bag. I held it up and began snapping off pics.

She glanced at the street just as the car drove away. "I'll make a note to bring up that black car at our neighborhood watch meeting." She gripped my forearm with her bony hand. "Hon, promise me you'll be careful. Things are beginning to unravel around here."

Wasn't that the truth. "Yes, ma'am. I will." We locked gazes, and it was almost as if she was about to confide something to me when she seemed to catch herself. "Here you go." Mrs. Ross handed over the work order. I flipped to the last page, where the tech had signed the order. Julio Gonzalez. I repressed a sigh.

After I bid Mrs. Ross a farewell, I took a look at my phone. I'd managed to make out GMP58 on the license plate before the car turned around the bend.

As I hightailed it over to the courthouse, I called Rosa.

"Hey, Lyla." She answered on the second ring.

"Hey, I need a quick favor." I explained about the car following me and how I'd managed to get a partial plate number.

"Has the person made physical contact with you? Do you think it might be related to your earlier attack?" My friend Rosa had vacated her desk job at the PD, and Sergeant Landry had resumed the position.

"No contact. I think whoever is doing this is just trying to scare me. But I'm about sick and tired of people thinking they have the right to intimidate me, with no repercussions."

"Damn straight. I'll run the partial and give you a call back with the most likely candidates."

"Thanks! You're the best."

"What are friends for?"

I made another call as I parked the car. I spoke to the appropriate person at Hewitt Electric, politely asked my question, and was put on hold. I placed my earbuds in as I locked my car and headed across the parking lot. When I left Mrs. Ross's house, a thought occurred that perhaps the technician might not sign his real name if he was attempting to cover his tracks. LJ would be intelligent enough to do something like that.

"Miss Moody?"

"I'm still here." I held my hand up to the car yielding to allow me to cross the street.

"Thank you for holding. Yes, Julio Gonzalez is indeed on the work order, but two technicians were sent out on the job. Julio Gonzalez and LJ Richardson." Bingo! I wanted to do a little happy dance. That's reasonable doubt. She seemed to pause. "Wasn't it LJ's father who was murdered on that same night?"

"Yes. Yes, it was. Did the police contact your offices to inquire?"

"No. Not to my knowledge."

I rushed up the front stone steps. "And what was your name again?"

"Farrah Rhodes."

"Thank you, Farrah. You've been most helpful."

After I went through the metal detectors, said hi to one of Calvin's retired officer buddies checking through my bag, my phone rang again. When I saw it was Rosa, I answered and blurted without preamble, "Whatcha got for me?"

"You're never going to believe this. From the partial I managed to narrow down to four vehicles in the area that matches the description you gave me. And out of those four, only one name stands out. "The car registered to Leonard Richardson."

I continued down the hall toward the courtroom. "My money is on LJ because we know Leonard's not driving it."

"Nope."

"Thanks, Rosa. I gotta go. I'm at the arraignment." I had my hand on door.

"Hey, Lyla. Be careful."

"Always."

I put my phone on silent, slid it into my bag and slipped between the heavy double doors of the courtroom. Reporters, friends, and relatives of people awaiting arraignment filled the seats. As quietly as I could manage, I moved down the aisle near the wall past Detective Battle and Quinn. I gave a single head nod and kept moving, trying not to draw too much attention to myself while the judge ruled on another case.

I froze at the second bench behind the defense table where Mr. Jenkins and Harper would soon be sitting. On the other side of the aisle, the entire Richardson family sat, including LJ, who turned to make direct eye contact with me. The other family members noticed and followed. Although I knew LJ couldn't have known that I made the phone call or had just spoken with the scheduler at his place of employment, still his gaze was cold and cruel.

I've got your number buddy. I would not be the first to look away. I held LJ's gaze as traveled down the aisle. Then even as the entire family turned to give me a murderous glare, including the elderly Felix at the end of the bench in his wheelchair. What had I ever done to that family? Other than stand up for Harper. I supposed from their perspective, protecting the murdering who stole their beloved patriarch was sufficient.

Then as I slid onto the bench next to Melanie, and Amelia, I noticed something. The rest of the family wasn't glaring at me; they were staring behind me. I could tell by their eye movement.

I glanced back over my shoulder to see Charles Hammond taking a seat two rows behind me. My blood began to boil, but I force it to a simmer. Charles nodded to the family, who looked like they might want to murder him next. LJ showed his colors by sitting with the family.

Charles sighed and glanced down at his hands.

The court clerk called several court cases while we waited. A tap on my shoulder caught my attention, and I turned to see Mr. Jenkins had kneeled beside the end of the bench. "Miss Moody."

"Oh, Mr. Jenkins." I scooted to the end of the bench. "I have some news. I just spoke to Hewitt Electric and," I lowered my voice to barely above a whisper, "LJ had been on the street the night of the murder. And even more damning, he been just next door. In the backyard where he could have easily crossed and entered the house through the construction site. The door was wide open when I got there. The library connects to the outdoor area."

The man's eyes narrowed. "You have confirmation of that fact? From his employer?"

I nodded.

"That's good. I'll need you to forward whatever you have over to me."

"Yes, sir." I said with a pleased nod. "This is good, right?"

"Yes. It could be." His face didn't show the enthusiasm I'd hoped for. "Um, unfortunately, I have some unwelcome news to share with you." He scratched his jawline.

I did not care for the sound of that.

"We are going to be terminating the agreement with Cousins Investigative Services."

"What?" My tone came out in a hoarse whisper.

"We've appreciated all that you've done and especially with this new information, but unfortunately, Mrs. Richardson's situation has changed, and we've decided to go a different route."

"If this is about the money?"

He held up a hand. "No, it's nothing like that. But it's all I'm at liberty to share with you. I informed Mr. Cousins an hour ago."

And Calvin had not called me.

The court clerk called Harper's name, and Mr. Jenkins rose to take his place at the front while I sat there stunned.

"What happened?" Mel mouthed and scooted closer with Amelia right beside her.

"I got fired," I whispered, and they both gaped. I shrugged.

Mr. Jenkins remained standing as Harper came in through the little door to the right located at the front of the courtroom. She came out in orange, shackled and chained.

My hand went to my heart. Mel let out a slight gasp, and Amelia's hands went to her lips. Harper's hair looked unwashed and stringy. And yes, from this advantage point, I could see how Mr. Jenkins would attempt an insanity plea. The woman did not even remotely look like our friend. Her eyes were vacant as Mr. Jenkins helped her into the appropriate place.

Amelia took Mel's hand, and Mel took mine as we listened to the judge read the charge. When the older white-haired judge asked Harper how she pleads to the charge of murder, she just stood there. Mr. Jenkins leaned over and whispered something to her.

"Not guilty." Harper's weak voice barely made to us, and when the judge bellowed, "Speak up, please," she jumped.

"Not guilty," Harper said, just slightly louder than before.

The three of us had to choke back tears as we listened to the two lawyers argue for bail. And when the judge finally found in favor of the defense, I could have sobbed with relief. He pointed to Mr. Jenkins and Harper. "The defendant will be on house arrest until the trial. She'll wear an ankle bracelet and not be allowed to leave her residence except for doctor appointments or other necessary travel."

The DA spoke up. "Judge, the Richardson family have been made aware that according to Leonard Richardson's will, Mrs. Richardson is disinherited if she is involved in any criminal proceedings. That being the case, the defendant doesn't have a place of residence and therefore cannot be released on house arrest."

Harper didn't move. Didn't react. Mel, Amelia, and I exchanged wide-eyed glances.

"Yes, we're aware of the clause stipulated in the will, and Mrs. Richardson will have other lodgings in Sweet Mountain." Mr. Jenkins turned and glanced to the back of the courtroom. Everyone else did too. The deputy opened the double doors, and in walked *my mother*, dressed in her power woman suit, her hair perfectly set, and her chin held high. She moved through the courtroom as if she owned the place. She inclined her head to the judge who had dined at our home on numerous occasions. "Mrs. Moody and her husband are prominent members of the community and have generously opened their home to this innocent woman."

Gasps went up in the courtroom, and I accidentally squeezed Mel's hand a little too tightly, and she squeaked. "Sorry. Sorry." I released her hand.

"What in the world?" Amelia whispered around Mel.

"I haven't a clue." *She* terminated my employment. I watched my mother take her place on the row next to Mr. Jenkins.

The judge cleared his throat and began speaking, but I couldn't hear anything. My heart hammered in my ears so loudly, I nearly fainted. This new development left no doubt to the town, the press, or the DA regarding Mother's involvement. She just shined a massive spotlight on herself. How had she gone from a broken woman to this in a matter of hours? Why hadn't my father told me they planned on stepping in to help Harper?

The gavel hit the bench, and I came back to the present, feeling numb and, for some reason, betrayed. I didn't mind if my family reached out to help Harper. That was precisely what I was doing. But to shut me out as they did hurt. Why did they always want me on the outside?

My mother rose and conferred with Mr. Jenkins; their heads were close together. She never even turned to acknowledge me. When they concluded whatever they were discussing, she walked right out of the courtroom, dragging my wounded heart behind her.

Chapter
Twenty-Six

A hand on my shoulder pulled me out of the abyss. I glanced around to see I sat alone on the bench. Melanie and Amelia had left, and I hadn't even noticed. I supposed Harper's case was the last one before the lunch break. I lifted my head and Charles's brown eyes latched on to mine. His brows pinched together. "Hey. You all right?"

I gave the obligatory answer with a nod, and for some odd reason, I wondered why we always felt as if we had to say yes when asked the question. And right now, I was anything but all right. "No, Charles. I'm not all right. I have no idea what just happened."

"I'm going to help you clear things up. Okay? Come on. There'll be press outside the courthouse if we don't hurry."

I rose, and I followed him toward the back of the courtroom, then stopped in my tracks. I didn't know this guy from Adam. I had no idea if he was the good guy or someone trying to blackmail my family, as my father had told me. My uncle indeed despised and questioned his motives.

Charles cast a glance over his shoulder and realized I'd stopped following. He backtracked the few steps to reach me. "We have to go."

"I have no idea who you are." I shook my head from side to side, studying him. "What are you doing here? What ulterior motives do you have lurking below the surface?" I gave out a soft bitter laugh. "Because I'll tell you. Right now, I don't know who to trust anymore."

He lowered his head close to mine. His breath brushed my cheeks. It smelled of wintergreen gum. "There is so much you don't know about your mother. She is not what she seems."

"Clearly!" My voice shook. And I lowered my head and whispered. "My always avoiding scandal mother flipped out this morning, and now she's opening up her house to a stranger and the most scandalous case this town has ever seen."

"I'm here to help you. To tell you who you are. That's why I've come to Sweet Mountain." His face grew grave, and his brown gaze bored holes through mine as he gently gripped my biceps. "For you." His hand moved down my arm and thrust something into my pocket. I jumped at the intimate contact. He bent, retrieved his bag from the floor. I slowly reached into my pocket and he raised his hand, his eyes deadly serious. "Wait until you're alone to look at the picture. Understand?" My head bobbed in response and he left me there.

It took a few minutes for his words to sink in. Picture. He'd given me a picture of something he found massively important to my current predicament. What did the image hold? Fear crept up my spine like cold fingertips. My whole life began crumbling around me. And as much as I fought them, tears began to make little tracks down my cheeks. I violently wiped them away. Melanie popped her head back in the courtroom and waved a hand for me to come with her. I rushed out the double doors of the courtroom and through the throngs of people milling around, avoiding all calls to my name. Thankfully flanked by Melanie and Amelia, no one could get directly at me. On the courthouse's front steps stood Mr. Jenkins and my mother facing the reporters with an air of both triumph and defiance. "Mrs. Richardson is innocent, and we plan to prove just that."

My, my, had his tune changed. Mother's bank account the motivator, I felt sure. He also seemed more composed than I believed him capable. Perhaps he also thought this case would make his career, and he'd be in higher demand.

Frances Moody stood with her hands clasped in front of her black and tan knit suit and said with authority I didn't believe she possessed under the circumstances, "The reprehensible injustice that has occurred in this town is appalling. The arrest and charge of a young, manipulated woman by an abusive and oppressive man and his family will not go unanswered. As a pillar of a community I love dearly, I must say, we *are* better than this." *Wow.*

"My God, your mom is a Rockstar! I thought I couldn't love her more. But now, I'm totally adopting her." Melanie beamed, her eyes full of admiration as she stared at my poised and collected mother. The flashes of cameras would have caught a completely different picture a couple of hours ago. How could she possibly manage to hold it together with Harper in the house?

"She's certainly something else." I hoped my statement was ambiguous enough. I didn't feel like answering questions right here out in the open.

"You okay? I have to go to work." Amelia took my hand, squeezing it.

I scrounged up a smile and hugged her. "I'm good. Go ahead."

"You good, Mel? You need me to drop you off or—"

"No, I'll catch a ride with Lyla." She hugged Amelia, and we watched her hurrying down the steps.

"It's not a problem for me to ride back with you, is it?"

Questions flew at Mr. Jenkins. I watched him evade with grace, and then finally, he waved, signally they had concluded. He took Mother's forearm, leading her down the steps. She never saw me. Never looked in my direction or around as I expected her to. I understood her vehemence toward injustice, not how she managed to wield it *now*.

"Hey." Mel touched my arm, and I jumped.

"Oh yeah, sure. No problem. I'm in lot D, in the back. Come on."

Before the reporters could notice me—the fired investigator for the defense and daughter of Harper's guardian angel—I rushed down the steps and toward the green space near the parking lot.

"There's more going on here than the attorney letting you go, isn't there? Has there been any developments with the Spider character?"

I gave my head a shake. "A lot is going on. I was just at my parents' house, and I swear, Mel, Mother was a wreck. Now she's here and saving Harper." I gave her the play by play of what transpired, including my visit with Mrs. Ross.

"Lyla!" We turned to see Piper marching toward me. *Terrific.* I had to get it together.

"What the hell? We pinky swore." She glanced toward Mel. "How are you doing, Melanie? Seen the consummate ass lately?" Mel and Piper had an interesting relationship since Piper shared the title as the ex-Mrs. Tim Howard.

"God, no! His royal ass can take a long hike off a short bridge."

They both had a little chuckle.

"Can you give us a sec, Mel?"

"Sure. No problem."

I tossed Melanie the keys to my car. She gave Piper a little wave, still snickering to herself. I had to smile despite my troubles.

"What gives?" Piper cocked her head, keeping her voice low.

I rubbed my forehead and then lifted my chin to meet her gaze, and she furrowed her brow. "I'm as blindsided as you are."

"You seriously had no clue your mother involved herself in this case?"

I shook my head. A thought occurred to me, and before I could overthink it, I made a decision. I no longer worked for anyone involved in this case. And now, more than ever, I wanted this case to go away but not without the responsible party being held accountable. "I've been blindsided more than once today."

She cocked her head to one side. "What do you mean?"

I glanced around conspiratorially. "Off the record, but," I held up my finger, "if you call and get corroborating evidence, I'll consider going on record."

Now I had her attention. "Okay," she said slowly.

"A little bird told me that the night of the murder, LJ Richardson was out on a call at my parents' neighbor's house. And at the scene of the crime, the backdoor was wide open." I raised my brows for effect. "I feel sure if you contact Hewitt Electric and ask for Farrah, she will confirm that even though Julio Gonzalez's name is on the work order, both Julio and LJ worked that job."

"Very interesting. Now with Harper cut out of the will because of criminal charges, that leaves the younger Richardson to inherit."

"Yes. It's fascinating. Equally fascinating is that a car has been following me for days. I caught a partial plate and had it checked. Guess who the car is registered to?"

"Intimidation tactics?" Upon my nod, she leaned even closer, her eyes wide. "LJ Richardson?"

"No. It's registered to Leonard but—"

"He's not driving it."

"My thoughts exactly." I bit my lip and appeared to be battling with what I was about to say. "And there's also a rumor, and I use the word rumor because I have no solid evidence to support the claim that LJ may have seduced Harper while his father still lived." I couldn't divulge that Harper had confirmed the rumor. That would be too far.

A grin began to spread across her lips. "I heard something similar and already have feelers out there. And with this new tidbit about LJ's whereabouts, I'll have a front-page story."

"Good for you." I smiled.

Piper held up her pinky and winked at me.

We parted, and I hustled toward my car—score for the good guys.

As I slid into the driver's seat of my idling car, Mel asked, "What was that about?"

I filled Melanie in, and she gaped. "You're going to let Piper spread the rumors about Harper and LJ having an affair? Won't that make her look even more guilty?"

"Not if the story runs with the slant that a jealous LJ couldn't share Harper any longer and well, you know. They can place him at the scene of the crime. Then it looks like he took advantage of a damaged and vulnerable woman to set her up to take the fall of his father's murder. That'll create reasonable doubt."

Melanie chewed on the side of her index finger. "Okay, yeah, I can see that. Anything to get her off a murder charge."

"Give me two secs, and we'll go," I called my father. He answered on the second ring. "How could you not tell me?" I said without preamble. I couldn't hide the pain in my tone as my hands curled into fists. That's when I recalled the picture Charles had given me. I pulled it from my pocket.

Mel leaned over to get a better look. "What's that?" She mouthed, and I shrugged with wide eyes, unable to look at it just yet. She took the small square from my trembling hand.

"What are you talking about?"

"Don't play dumb. I sat right there in the courtroom and watched Mother stand up for Harper and offer up her house as lodging and posted bail for her!"

"What?" Daddy bellowed, and I felt the blood drain from my face. *How did he not know?* "Tell me everything."

I gave him the play by play about what transpired in the courthouse, beginning with Mr. Jenkins firing Calvin and me. As all the puzzle pieces seemed to start to click into place, chills spread across my body. For the first time in my life, I feared why my father didn't know everything about his wife and brother's past. Charles's words burned in my ears. And I had no clue who I could trust.

"She's not in her room. Your Grandmother said she told her she had an appointment and assured her she was fine." Daddy sounded unsure. "The cleaning service she called arrived a half-hour ago, and I just assumed Frances was here."

"That you didn't know makes me even more nervous."

Mel lifted her hands, and I hit mute. "Daddy didn't know Mother was going to do all this."

"Oh my God."

I nodded and unmuted the phone. "What's going on?"

"Stay calm. Your mother is obviously having some sort of emotional break."

"No," I said firmly. "She isn't. I just told you she's here at the courthouse. And she not only didn't she appear broken—she owned the courtroom. How after earlier? I haven't the foggiest. You should have heard her. Turn on the news, and you can."

Melanie reached out and squeezed my arm and held up a square photo. "Lyla. Look at this." It was an old sepia style picture.

I stared at a haunting image of men in old fashioned suits and hats. The women were dressed in drab, oversized dresses, their hair in long thick braids. A young man who looked a lot like LJ stood off the side, and the skinny young girl to his left caught my attention. She stood awkwardly and stared defiantly at the camera.

"Doesn't she look eerily like your mom?" Mel whispered and pointed to the woman standing behind the skinny girl. The woman had her on the slender girl's shoulder, almost as if she worried the girl would run away. The woman had her other hand on the lanky looking boy to her right's shoulder.

The woman's face. Those large eyes. I couldn't tell what color they were from the picture, but with the facial structure and the shape of those eyes, there was no mistaking the resemblance.

"God, Daddy, who is she?"

"What are you talking about? You know who your moth—" I heard the news in the background, and my father went silent.

I stared up at Mel, who had her fingers to her lips. "Could it be?"

"I've got to go." I let the phone drop into my lap.

"You think this is why Charles said you don't know who you are? Like maybe you come from Quakers or Amish people?"

My shoulder rose and fell as I studied the image in front of me. The woman standing behind the young girl looked an awful lot like my mother, though it couldn't be. That woman would be much older than my mother was today. I hadn't any picture of my maternal Grandmother to compare. Or if the dates could work out. They could be family. Were these the people my Grandmother fled from? I flipped the picture over. No date.

My heart raced. With every dig of the shovel, I unearthed something horrible. Though despite the horror, I had to keep digging.

"Does that guy," I pointed at the man that reminded me of LJ, "Look like the Richardson men?"

Mel tilted her head from side to side considering. "Maybe. You think that's the connection between your mom and Leonard?"

Mel and I were so in sync. I turned to my bestie. "What time do you need to be at work?"

Mel glanced at her watch. "I'm not on the schedule today but I have to run by and check in on the large catering order in about an hour and a half. Why?"

I pulled out of the space. "Because I'm going to have a word with the Richardsons' neighbors. I kept meaning to canvas the street, but there's always something getting in the way."

"Okay. I'm in."

Chapter
Twenty-Seven

Mel and I were knocking on the door of the house next door to the Richardsons' fifteen minutes later. An elderly woman about Gran's age answered the door. She was a slip of a woman with a pointy nose and wiry silver hair. She wore one of those old-fashioned house coats with pockets in the front.

I smiled. "Hello. I'm so sorry to disturb you. I wondered if I could ask you a few questions about your neighbors, the Richardsons."

"You the police? I already spoke to the police."

"No, ma'am. I'm a private investigator, and this is my assistant, Melanie." Mel beamed and I dug through my bag, searching for a card.

Mel noticed my struggle and took the bag, holding it open so I could dig out my wallet. I smiled sheepishly up at the woman, who watched us with intense curiosity. Finally, I had it. I held it up.

The woman squinted at it from behind the screened door. "Hang on." She searched through one of her pockets and pulled out a large magnifying glass, which she held up to the card.

Slowly she nodded. "This about the murder? I thought the police already got the wife. In fact, just saw it on the news there." She pointed behind her.

I smiled. "I just wondered if you'd noticed anything unusual about the family."

"What's that?" She cupped her ear. "You'll need to speak up. I'm hard of hearing."

I asked the question again, louder this time.

"Unusual?" She gave a cackle of laughter. "Those folks are nuts. All those people living in one house. Coming and going at all hours of the night. The girl over there, the young one, she blares her music too loud and shouted at her daddy right out in the front yard for everyone under the sun to hear." She shook her head. "No pride at all. None." I understood that she meant "pride" in a positive way. Like having family pride and not wanting to devalue the family's good name.

"That's sounds just dreadful." Mel shook her head sympathetically.

She nodded. "It is, and she throws herself at the young man that comes around all the time."

"What young man?" I said, louder than I felt comfortable speaking.

"The writer fella." She smiled a little. "He's a charmer, that one. He came by and we had tea and pound cake. He wanted to know about all the dirty gossip in the town." The ringing of a phone blared. The woman must've had some enhancements put on her phone. "That's my phone. I need to get it. I'm waiting for a call from the pharmacist."

"Thank you," Melanie and I said in unison as she closed the door.

I let out a sigh, "Well, that was a bust."

A black sedan slowly rolled past the house and pulled into the driveway next door.

Mel gripped my forearm. "Is that the car?"

"Yep." I felt my jaw clench. I'd had enough. "I'm beyond sick of not having answers. Well, by God, I'm getting some answers right now." I hustled down the wooden porch steps and power-walked after the sedan.

"Wait up," I heard Mel call from behind me.

I couldn't. I watched with narrowed eyes when the brake lights lit up. LJ hadn't turned off the ignition. *He better not even consider backing over me.* I increased my pace as the wind whipped my hair about my face. I went around the driver's side door and pounded on the window.

"What do you want, LJ? Why are you following me?"

The window slowly rolled down, and inside sat Beatrice Richardson. The girl was dressed in this era's attire today, with faded denim skinny jeans and an oversize tunic. She still wore that glittery headband with the feather sticking out the side, though, and must have waited until she got to her car to put it on because she hadn't been wearing it in the courtroom. Beatrice blew a puff of smoke at me. I coughed and waved the smoke from my face, then blinked at her, stunned.

"I'm here. I'm here. Don't you mess with her!" Mel caught up, ready to have my back if needed. She glared at Beatrice just as Beatrice noticed her. "It's you."

"It's me," Bea said brightly.

"Girl, what are you doing?," I asked. "Is this some joke? You've been following me for days! Did you have something to do with my attack?" I jabbed my finger into her face. "Tell me the truth! I've had it up to my eyeballs with people today, and I'm not about to mess around with some petulant teenager with daddy issues."

"We don't deal with bratty kids. And where is the rest of your crazy family, anyway?" Mel whirled around, surveying the area, and I noticed she had my purse over her shoulder, and she knew I was packing heat.

Thank God for good friends. I glanced around, half expecting to see one of Beatrice's other family members lying in wait to ambush me.

"No, I didn't have anything to do with your attack. Sheesh! You crazy old ladies."

"Crazy?" I said with wide eyes. At the same time, Mel said, "Old?"

Bea rolled her eyes in typical teenage fashion. "Look, Lyla, you came by my house and left voicemails for me to get in touch with you. I went to your house a couple of times." *A couple?* I only knew of one. "Then when you wigged out, I attempted to make contact at other places. I'm trying to help you."

I studied her. "Why not show yourself then? Why be so secretive with the flashing lights and not stopping when I spotted you?"

"I got scared, okay!" She wiped the sweat that had beaded up on her forehead. I believed her. She sounded and looked scared. "I tried to get your attention the second time, but you went in and got your phone to take pictures of me. And I can't be linked to this." She tossed her cigarette out the window. "What's she doing?" She nodded toward Melanie, who still kept watch for more Richardsons.

"'She,'" Melanie began, "is keeping her eyes peeled for your freaky-ass family members. And I'm here to tell you, they'll be sorry they messed with us." She patted my tote at her side. "Very sorry."

Bea seemed to take the warning seriously as her brows rose in an appraising type of way. "They all rode in Kenneth's van. They're on the way to the attorney's office. Chill."

I rooted through my bag and extracted the picture. "Do you know who this is?"

Bea glanced down at the picture and nodded slowly. "Where'd you get that? Did *he* give it to you?" Bea's eyes were wide. "Because if he did, you are in more danger than you know. I have to show you something. She opened the door and got out. Come inside with me." My God. All these strangers wanted to *help* me. And there was no way I was going inside a house with a nineteen-year-old girl who might have had a hand in poisoning Harper.

"Not a chance."

Mel folded her arms and shook her head in agreement.

"Tell me whatever it is you have to say and what you know about this picture, or I'll report you to the police."

Bea rolled her eyes again. "It's not me you have to worry about!" Her voice rose, and people were beginning to step outside their houses and notice us. *Well shit.*

After one last appraising look around, I took my bag from Mel, and waved toward the walkway. "Lead the way."

Mel kept up her bad cop routine as she leaned closer to Beatrice. "Then you better tell us. And if you're setting us up, I swear, little girl, we'll make you regret ever coming after us."

"Sheesh, bitchy aren't ya?" Bea was unfazed, looking quite transfixed by the picture I gave her.

Mel and I exchanged a worried, wide-eyed glance.

"This is dad," Beatrice said after she unlocked the door and we stepped inside the familiar eerie foyer. She traced the face of the tall, thin guy that I thought bore a resemblance to LJ, and nodded. "We have a large framed print of this hanging in the second-floor hallway of this house. I'll show you."

"Okay." I put my hand on the banister as she mounted the steps. Once she was out of eyesight, I pointed for Mel to do a quick recon and have a sneak peak in the adjacent rooms. The house did sound quiet, and I started to believe Beatrice had told the truth that her family was out.

"What do you know about the picture? When and where was it taken? Do you know the people in the picture?" I shot rapid-fire questions her way as I reached the top of the stairs. Mel cleared her throat a few steps below and made the okay gesture with her index finger and thumb. I let out a little sigh of relief.

"Here it is. All I know is that someone took the picture at some retreat my dad went to years ago." She rubbed her finger-tips softly over the image of her late father. "He and his first wife lived there for a time."

A huge painted portrait hung at the end of the dark pan-eled hallway. We all three stood in awe of the oversize painting. The enlargement made the images of the stern-looking men in old fashioned suits and hats, and the drably dressed, solemn, and sad-looking women, with their hair in long thick braids, all the more haunting. The resemblances I'd originally noticed were undeniable now.

"So he was married before your mom?" Mel asked, sounding more like herself. Seeing the type of man Beatrice's father had been gave us more compassion for the girl.

"Yes," Bea said in a faraway voice. "He was young here. Seventeen, I think." She touched the image of a young man with his hands folded in front of him. "He wasn't always so horrible."

The question I'd yet to ask took form as the lump in my throat. I swallowed. "Um, Beatrice. Do you know which of these young ladies was married to your dad?" I touched the edge of the ornate bronze frame.

"Yes. It's this girl, here." Bea leaned closer to the painting, raising her hand higher.

Melanie understood my question and squeezed my hand while I held my breath. Bea placed her fingers on a pale-haired woman who looked nothing like my mother or grandmother. I let out the breath I'd been holding.

"They weren't married very long."

"Were they Amish or something?" Melanie asked.

Bea shook her head. "Nope. They were some sort of minimalist movement. When he married my mom, he wasn't into it any longer. Not that she would have stood for it if he'd wanted to be. She adored fashion and nice things. The picture never saw the light of day while she was alive." She touched the edge of the picture and seemed to be working on composing herself.

Harper had told us that in the last days of Leonard's life, he talked about some sort of movement. She'd believed it only existed in his mind. With this painting hanging here, that just didn't make sense.

"What did Harper think of this painting?"

"Harper didn't care. She never said a word about it." Bea sighed, looking so very young. "Harper didn't love my dad. Not really. But my mother loved him dearly. When she passed away from cancer, my dad sort of got lost for a while. That's when Aunt Edna came to live with us. She took care of us kids." She turned away with a shrug. "Only after he decided to marry again did his weird shit resurface."

"Weird?" Mel pressed. "Weird how? Like all the family moving in and pooling funds?"

Bea nodded. "Yeah. I think he wanted to start this backup or something. Can you imagine?" She snorted, but her eyes were watery, and she looked so vulnerable. Perhaps she'd come to me for help all those times, and I'd misconstrued the situation. Now I didn't think she had anything to do with the attack at the hospital at all.

"This freaky group took place about fifty years ago or so, and on a remote farm somewhere. That would never fly today." Bea wiped her face.

"You poor thing." Mel patted her shoulder.

She seemed to see Melanie for the first time. "You the owner of Smart Cookie?"

"Sure am."

"No, shit? I love that place." Beatrice smiled, and when she did, I could see how pretty she was under that mountain of makeup. It was almost as if she was trying to hide from the world. She probably had been for some time now. "Harper used to bring home boxes every week. Back when she and I were friends. Then she got weird too."

No wonder. If Leonard was attempting to force Harper into the life. I shuddered at the thought.

"You didn't poison Harper, did you?" Melanie asked straight out.

Bea flinched and genuinely looked shocked by the allegation. "No! Why would I do something like that? I have my whole life ahead of me, and that certainly would cut it short, going to jail." She made the universal sign for crazy. "Is that what Harper's saying?" She groaned. "Nothing surprises me in this family."

"You didn't bring her a cup of Valerian root tea?" I prodded gently. *With a hefty dose of Haldol in it?*

"Yes, but I didn't make that stinky tea. LJ did. He asked me to bring it to her." Melanie and I exchanged a glance. Either this girl was a brilliant liar, or we'd completely misjudged her.

"And *you* all brought that stinky tea over." Bea shook her head.

I softened my tone. "Well, the tea itself isn't a problem, but it does react badly with other medications."

"Oh. I guess Harper knew that."

I cocked my head to one side. "Why do you say that?"

"Because she must have requested it. Why else would LJ make a disgusting cup of tea like that? He does everything she says. Loves her." She'd made a stupid face when she'd said "loves."

"LJ went on and on about how bad it stunk." I cast a glance over to Mel as Bea continued. "We laughed, wondering why anyone would drink that stuff." Bea shook her head and seemed to be considering. "Can't believe she tried to kill herself and then blamed me. LJ should be standing up for his only sister."

"Is there anyone in the house that's taking the medication Haldol?"

"I don't know. Probably. The whole house is on blood pressure meds and a lot of other shit." She waved her hands around. "This house a geriatric doctor's paradise. I can't wait to get out."

She seemed confused as to the purpose of the medication. "Haldol is an antipsychotic medication," I said gently.

Bea burst out laughing. "Well, the whole family needs that drug." She shook her head as she lit up another cigarette. Her phone buzzed, and she pulled it out of her back pocket. Her face paled. "They're on their way back. I set a notification for Edna's phone to ping me when they left the address." The cadence of her voice had increased. "Okay. I'm not giving you what I'm about to give you. And if you say I did, I'll deny it." She stared me straight in the face before going across the hall to the room locked with a padlock from the outside.

Mel and I both gaped. Who did they have in that room? My hand went to my bag and moved slowly inside, to grip holster of my gun. I undid the snap. Bea pulled a necklace with a key on it out from inside her shirt, unlocked the door, and went inside.

Melanie glanced around again. She, like me, seemed to be concerned about a trap. I didn't discount the idea that the Richardson family could have possibly sent the most innocent of the group to entrap me.

Bea came out of the room, holding a laptop bag. "It's theft just so that you know what we're dealing with here. Once he knows you have it, watch out."

"He?" I asked slowly.

"Charles." She hefted the darker version of the same laptop bag Charles had been carrying at the courthouse. "He gave me a key."

By the way she tossed her hair, I feared he didn't give her a key just for her to help guard his things. I hadn't expected that. "Charles is staying with your family too?"

She nodded. "He and my dad were close. They were working on something together. Kenneth thinks he participated, but that's total bull. Kenneth is a total deadbeat."

I shivered and stared at the briefcase. "What's in it?"

"You'll see." She started rushing us toward the stairs. "Charles is driving his car, and he could be way ahead of the others." She passed by me and hurried down the stairs. Mel and I had to rush to keep up with her.

"I won't get caught doing this. And when Charles finds out it's missing—and I plan to be far away when that happens—watch out." Charles had gone with the family to the lawyer's office.

"Why didn't you go with the others? Didn't you want to hear you dad's will being read?" Melanie asked when we went out onto the front porch with Bea.

"He didn't leave me anything. He left it all to his favorite. But it doesn't matter. My mom left a trust for me. I get it on my birthday, at the end of the month." She held out the bag to me, her eyes deadly serious. "I swear I'm not trapping you. I swear I want to help you. You don't deserve what's coming for you."

Was this girl a mastermind of trickery? I gave myself an inward shake. Bea seemed to be honest, and God help me, I wanted to know what was on the laptop.

"Okay," I said, and took the bag while trying to wrap my head around everything. "Why are you doing any of this? Why share anything with us?"

Bea patted her face where a few tears had left tracks. "Because as foolhardy as my father was, he's the only father I had. And there were times he was a good dad. Whoever killed him should go away. Forever. Then and only then can I truly be free. Free from this whole family. Once this is done, I'm gone. I'm helping you guys, and in turn you can help me. Whoever is guilty should pay. Agreed?"

Whatever Bea planned to hand over must be a smoking gun in the evidence department. I could understand how she needed justice for her dad—and her need to break free from her twisted family. But as she readily admitted, she'd stolen the evidence, and stolen it from Charles Hammond, a man who was a wild card in the whole ordeal. And I no longer worked for the defense and didn't have the firm's security to back me. I suppose I could just say whatever it was had been anonymously delivered to me. Yes. This opportunity felt too important to pass over. And the truth belonged to me also.

"Agreed," I said.

She nodded and swallowed. "I'm going to tell you this, but I'll deny it if you have me questioned by the police. I overheard LJ on the phone with someone the morning the police took Harper to the hospital. He said, 'She'll be there. Remember, she's tall, reddish hair, and a pretty face.' He's awful. He's my brother, but he lacks empathy or whatever you call it." She shook her head.

I felt all the blood drain from my face. *LJ sent the attacker.*

Bea frowned and gave me an awkward pat on the arm. "This is where we part ways for good. Good luck."

Chapter
Twenty-Eight

Detective Battle was waiting for me when Mel and I got home. The dark clouds that rolled in overhead were an ominous sign of the weather to come. There were a lot of ominous signs happening these days, and I prayed they weren't a foreshadowing of what was to come. The detective propped his large frame against the door and crossed his arms. He didn't appear to be in any hurry to leave, and this made us both nervous.

"God. Do you think Bea set us up? Maybe she called the police the second we got out of the car." She glanced in the back seat, where Charles's computer bag sat.

My stomach swam with nerves, but I refused to show my emotions. "No." I swallowed. "No. Why would she do that?" *Lord, please don't let her have set us up.* "You heard her. She seemed sincere at wanting the person responsible to pay." I said this out loud to convince myself as much as Melanie. I usually felt more confident in my discernment. Now, with everything going on with my mother and finding out about LJ's involvement in my own attack, plus the confirmation that he'd been in close proximity when someone murdered his father, my head was all over the place.

"Okay. Yeah, you're right. Bea even told us about her rotten brother and what he did to you. Do you want me to hang around a bit? Be backup?" She glanced at her watch. I could tell she was already running late for work.

"No. I've got it. We'll sync up after your shift."

Mel smiled. "We have day one of pub crawl tonight. You still want to go? Probably not, right?"

I'd completely forgotten. The town's kick-off night started this evening and would continue the rest of this week, and the finale would be an all-day event on Saturday.

"I don't think so." I could see the detective staring in our direction out of my peripheral vision.

"I understand. I don't feel much like it either. I'll come by after work." We hugged, parted, and I watched Mel trudge to her car before I slung the computer bag over my shoulder, along with my purse. If this was some kind of sting, I didn't want Mel anywhere near it.

I began climbing up to my stoop as casually as I could manage—just a gal going inside with her bags. *Everything is fine.*

"Interesting morning," the detective said by way of a greeting, and he pushed off the door.

"Can I help you?" I hit the key fob. The car beeped a couple of times in succession. I turned back to the detective.

"I hope so." He didn't move from my door as I closed the distance between us. "Geraldo Morales woke up."

"That's good." I waited for him to elaborate. "I was beginning to think that wouldn't ever happen. Where's Quinn? I thought he was the liaison?"

"He's busy. And is it?"

"Is what?" I raised my brows.

"Good that he woke up."

I squinted at him. "Listen, Detective, I've had a long and disturbing morning." No point denying what happened today at the courthouse, not to mention at the Richardson house. I scratched my head. "And I still have a lot of work ahead of me before I can call it quits for the day. If we could speed this little tap dancing act along, I'd be appreciative."

"Your mother didn't check in with you before her performance in the courtroom?" He had a little smirk going on, and his audacity gave me precisely the grit I needed at this moment.

I pursed my lips and raised my brows as high as I possibly could. I'd seen that look from my mother an infinite number of times when I behaved childishly.

"Okay, okay. I get it. It's too soon to joke just yet." His smirk disappeared. "Morales gave us the name of the person who paid him to attack you." He studied me for several beats, and my patience waned.

I shifted my bag higher on my shoulder as the weight of the bag began to dig into my clavicle. "LJ Richardson?"

He cocked his head to one side. "No."

Huh? "Okay, well, whoever it is, arrest them. Or did you come here to tell me that you've already arrested them?"

"Well, that's where it gets interesting." Again he watched me.

"Okay. And?" I huffed. *My God, all these games!*

"He said *you* paid him. He claims you told him exactly where'd you'd be and at what time."

I blinked a couple of times. "Come again?"

"You hired Morales to attack you."

I let out a harsh laugh. "For the love of God." I glanced briefly heavenward. "You've got to be kidding me. You came over here to tell me that the man who attacked me in broad daylight, in front of countless witnesses, blames me? Wow. So, you're wasting both of our time."

He rolled his shoulders back and stared down his nose at me. "No, ma'am. He swears by it. Some guy came into the bar representing you. And later he received a call from the man with the exact location."

LJ called him. "And you checked phone records then?"

"We have. So far, it turns out to be a burner they used."

I blew out a frustrated breath. "Useless people. You'd have to be out of your mind to believe some cockeyed story like that." My free hand went to my hip, and I could feel my blood about to boil. Today had been a day from hell, and I barely had control over myself. "Why in the world would I want to be tasered by some lowlife?" My face heated. "Have you seen the video footage, Detective? It's flipping humiliating!"

"People do crazy things all the time."

"Yeah, like accuse someone of hiring their attacker." I tossed my hair back and blew out a deep breath.

"Or harbor murderers in their homes."

Ah, the real reason why he's here. He probably flew directly over here after leaving the courthouse, and lay in wait to pounce. I should have gone to the office. I certainly wasn't ready to go to my parents' house yet. If I couldn't control my temper with this guy, I would fail miserably with Mother.

I decided to evade. "Okay. What do you need from me to rule this asinine theory out?"

"Your bank records. Morales said you sent a man with a thousand dollars in cash and promised another thousand after he attacked you. He also said you were looking for a murder for hire for fifty thousand. A week prior."

"Oh, that's rich. For the Leonard Richardson hit. I see. In a misguided effort to help my poor friend get out of her marriage, you think I paid someone to kill her husband." I held up a finger. "No, wait. A murder that took place in my parents' house without care for their safety or mental well-being." I rolled my eyes in the same fashion Beatrice had. "If you want to look at my bank records and see that I did not draw out the money, nor would I have the funds to pay fifty thousand for a hitman, I'll grant you access. I have nothing to hide. Where do I sign?"

"I appreciate your cooperation. I'll have someone get in touch with you if it comes to that."

Oh please. "Sure. Excuse me." I motioned to my front door.

He stepped aside and started down the stoop. I struggled with my keys, ready to unlock the door.

"One more thing," he called from behind me.

Sighing, I turned around and faced him.

"Your mother isn't hurting for money, and she has a keen interest in Harper Richardson."

I narrowed my eyes. "You've already charged Harper for the crime. She was arraigned an hour ago. Now, because my mother extended a helping hand to her, you want to go after her as well?"

"I'll go after anyone and everyone involved in the murder. I go where the case takes me."

I sighed, giving him what I hoped looked like a bored expression. "Got ya. I guess I expected more from a detective of your caliber. Brad tells me that you are tough but always search for the truth and almost always get your man. I usually agree with Brad's assessments. But," I said, shaking my head, "I'll admit I'm struggling with the theory that my mother decided to risk her reputation and her family by having me attacked after she hired someone to murder Harper's husband. Makes real good sense, Detective. You must be proud." I turned back around and shoved the key into the lock, opening the door.

"Did Mrs. Richardson say how long she and her stepson have been sleeping together? Is that why you thought LJ was the one who hired Morales?"

A slow smile spread across my lips as I turned again and began to laugh. "You're not stupid, are you? Harper didn't give me specifics of her affair. And I don't have anything solid to suspect LJ, so call it a hunch."

He inclined his head. "Okay. Harper did tell you about her affair with LJ Richardson?"

I nodded. "Yes. After Leonard's murder, she did. Before that night in the hospital, I hadn't a clue." Not a real clue anyway.

"Your friend Amelia said Harper told her of trouble." He kept his face relaxed.

"Okay." I sighed.

"You seemed surprised when the defense fired your firm this morning."

I inhaled, put my heavy bags right inside the door, and turned back around. "Yes. Mainly because I'd just discovered a key piece of evidence for the defense."

He lifted a hand as if to say *"And?"* When I didn't respond, he said, "Because of this so-called evidence you produced and your mother's declaration in the courtroom, you were so surprised you were off the case?"

"Yes. I never said my dismissal had anything to do with my mother. Though, it's no secret that she's never approved of my career path and could use her influence in this case if she chose. That still doesn't make her the monster you paint her as. The way I see it, it makes her just like a ton of other mothers in this town."

"Must be rough."

I'd had enough. "Okay, Detective. I'm going in now. Get back to me when you find out who wanted to assault me in public."

"Not my case." He turned around and strolled toward the gray Lincoln Town car. "You are quite a surprise."

"Why, because I'm not stupid either?" I didn't wait for a response. I went inside, shutting the door behind me. I rested my back against it and took several deep breaths, allowing the bags to slide down my arm and rest on the floor. I wiped my palms on my slacks. My hands were shaking a bit now.

My phone buzzed in my bag, and I bent down to retrieve it. Still feeling a bit weak, I decided to sit on the floor. "Hey, Brad."

"Hey. Wow. I just caught the news." I could hear car noises.

"Yeah. It's been a day. Detective Battle was just here adding to it. The Spider guy woke up and is claiming I hired him to attack me." I fingered the zipper on the black computer bag.

"They won't buy that. It won't take anything to find evidence against that theory."

"I know. I think the detective is more interested in LJ than me, and maybe my mother. I hadn't quite worked that out yet. And Brad, something crazy is going on with her."

"Like?"

I took a deep breath and stared at my popcorn ceiling. I'd always planned to have it redone. "I'm still processing."

"Okay. Well, I'm about to give you more to process."

"Go on." I really needed to dust my ceiling. "The fresh bodies? The Janes?" I tried to show interest in the new dumping ground cases. Soon, once I wrapped my head around what I was currently dealing with, I'd be ready to dive into the recent cases with renewed vigor. Now, I'd have to scrounge up what I could manage.

"No. A buddy of mine happens to be working a case about a quarter mile from the usual dumping ground site. We were discussing our cases over a cup of coffee, and something about his murders clicked."

"Okay." My tone sounded weary even to my own ears. I usually eagerly listened to all the shop talk. I just didn't have the bandwidth right now.

"The deceased woman had identification on her. It seems Phyllis Johnson is no longer with us. She, along with an unidentified male, were found in her Ford Focus at the bottom of a pond. There were both shot in the head. Execution style." My face tingled as he continued setting the scene. "They probably would have stayed there if the county hadn't deemed the pond runoff waste from the power plant and had it drained."

"My God." My fingers went to my parted lips. "Are the local police planning on notifying Harper?"

"I think they're going to have the coroner go over dental records to be sure of identification before notification." I heard his turn signal.

Time to woman up! I had cases to solve.

"Right. Of course. Have to dot the 'i's and cross the 't's.'"

"You sound frazzled. Take a deep breath. Focus on one task at a time. Babe, you are stronger than you know."

God, he was so good for me. "I hear you." I rose off the floor and hefted the bag over to the breakfast table. Harper already had more to deal with than I had. No more feeling sorry for myself. There was absolutely nothing I could do to bring her aunt back, but I could do everything in my power to help her. If I found enough evidence, what could Mr. Jenkins do? Turn me away and not use it? Not a chance. Especially if I went through my mother, who had an invested interest in helping her new prodigy. I decided not to focus on her having me fired. I shoved it to the back of my mind for another time. One thing at a time. There might be something on Charles's computer to help Harper and me both. Perhaps LJ went on record, and I could use it against him. Because right now he was my sole focus. I would not let him ruin Harper.

"Two deep breaths, and then tell me how you are?"

In through the nose and out through the mouth. "Okay. I've got my big girl panties pulled up, and I'm determined to unearth everything. It's time for truth."

"That's my girl." I could hear the smile in his voice.

"Are you still planning to kick off the pub crawl tonight, or is that a no-go after the day you've had? Because if you need me, I can be back into Sweet Mountain if I check out of the hotel now and bypass the station. I'll have to leave first thing in the morning, though."

I had built my life by being my own hero. I wouldn't stop that now by asking him to reroute his life for me. When he worked on big cases, we'd go long stretches without seeing each other, in the same way he understood if I was busy with work.

"Don't. I'm going to work." I went over to the coffeepot and started it up. "We'll see each other on Saturday for the all-day crawl, as we planned."

"You're sure?"

I glanced over at the bag sitting on the table. "Definitely."

We said our goodbyes, and I checked the clock. I unzipped the bag. I hadn't told Brad about the stolen computer. He didn't need to be bloodied by my decisions. To me, the risk was not only worth it but advantageous. I'd take my chances.

Chapter
Twenty-Nine

In a matter of an hour, and with the help of some handy software, I'd managed to crack Charles's password. I accessed all his documents with ease, which included his attempt at a novel. I wouldn't even call it a story. Perhaps it was his initial research. He'd compiled a bunch of facts about the strange movement. There were all these weird laws I couldn't discern—things about what to eat on what day and who could lead which group. There were categories for each type of facet within the group. As interesting as all this was—and it might help Harper prove her husband's frame of mind—an overwhelming sense of disappointment overtook me. There wasn't anything specific I could use.

Everything seemed like nonsense to me, and not the smoking gun I'd hope for. When Beatrice had behaved the way she had, I'd thought I was going to find out that Charles had evidence that LJ killed his father and attacked me, and, dare I say, I also wished for an audio confession. There wasn't anything like that on this computer. However, I continued to search Charles's files.

I tapped on the document titled "The Legacy of Father Bingham. The picture he'd given me that matched the enlarged print in the Richardson home popped up on the screen. Someone had drawn a big circle around the tallest man's head. A line drawn out to the side read "Father Bingham Folsom." *Folsom?* Why was that name familiar? I took a sip of my Coke Zero. The next few people had names that didn't ring a bell. But then I spied Leonard Richardson's name, and though I'd suspected as much, it still shook me to read my mother's and grandmother's names. My grandmother had a massive X over her face, and my mother had what appeared to be an infinity symbol drawn next to her. Another girl, standing on the opposite side of Father Bingham, also had the same symbol.

Huh. I did a quick search on the computer. Yes! He had a document entitled "Symbols." I scrolled down the doc and read that the infinity symbol meant future mothers of the movement.

My stomach turned. Were these girls supposed to be breeders? These crazy people had tagged my mother like an animal, to further the populace of their insane lifestyle. No wonder my grandmother had fled in the night. I wished I'd known her better. Finally, I understood why I'd found it so difficult to locate my mother and uncle's past. I'd had their surname all wrong. *Folsom.* It clicked! The name Charles had freaked Uncle Calvin out by mentioning. He'd known all along who Calvin was and how he'd been adopted. How?

Going back to the image, I stared at the little face of my much younger teenage uncle. He had such a stern and angry appearance. Someone had drawn a line from Calvin's picture and printed under his name "a future enforcer."

Reading Between the Crimes

I sat back and gaped. "What did y'all live through?" I said aloud.

I grabbed my laptop and went into my data bases to search Calvin Folsom. Nothing. I searched Mother's name with the same result. I got a hit when I plugged in "Bingham Folsom." News reports and old newspaper images came up on the screen.

"Local Raid on a Commune" one headline read. The date at the top of the paper read 1964.

Before dawn on July 26, 1964, 100 Oklahoma officers of public safety and soldiers from the Oklahoma National Guard entered the Plains Commune. The community—composed of approximately 200 mini-malistic fundamentalists—had been tipped off about the planned raid after abuse reports were filed with the local police department by a previous member, and were packing up to leave. The group leader, known as Father Bingham Folsom, resisted arrest and incited violence by shouting orders to the elders within his movement, who attempted to attack arresting officers. The officers took the entire community into custody. Among those taken were 112 children. Seventy of the children who were taken into custody were not permitted to return to their parents. None of the children born in the commune were registered with the state of Oklahoma. Girls in the commune were forced to marry at 14, some to men as old as 70.

I couldn't read anymore.

"Oh, Mother." I felt ill.

My grandmother, the one with the massive X over her face, had reported the group and fled the commune in the middle of the night. I just knew it. She probably ran to save my mother, who would have become a child bride. No wonder my mother had struggled and wanted me to be so strong.

That man doesn't deserve our sympathy. My bones chilled once again. She knew Leonard, and if she believed he planned on starting up another commune to abuse children, then by God, she was right. If only she'd confided in me and explained why she needed her life to be the way it was. Things would have been different between us. When she had me, she'd probably envisioned the life she'd never had. And when I became interested in true crime and working in the field, she believed she'd failed. Now she was trying to save Harper as her mother had saved her. Bless her heart. I saw my mother in a completely different light now. And my uncle. We'd all have to sit down and clear the air, wouldn't we?

I wondered if Leonard had recruited Charles or if Charles had found Leonard. I felt confident that Charles planned to write about their past and tie it together in some mystery thriller. And it would be a *great* story—a story I could not let him write.

I sighed. Bea meant well, turning over the clues that would leave me to discover my family's past. Yet I knew that in turn she wanted my help in sending her father's murderer to jail. Which told me she didn't believe it was Harper. I'd hold up my end and disentangle us from contributing to Charles's story in the process. Or I'd try to.

My cell rang, and I glanced down and saw Mel's face come up on the screen. I slid the green phone icon over to answer. "Hey, Mel. You on your way?" I was eager to share what I'd learned with my best friend. I had to tell someone.

"Hey," Mel whispered, her face too close to the screen.

"Why are you whispering?" I closed the laptop and slid it back into the bag.

"Because I'm in my car. I finished up at the shop a while ago. Amelia called, and she and Ethan came down with the stomach bug."

"Oh no." Poor Amelia. I'd have to call and check in with her.

"Yes, but that's not why I'm calling. She asked me to drop some ginger ale and other supplies at their front door. On my way back through town, you'll never guess who I saw right in the middle of everything!"

"Who?" I picked up the phone.

"LJ Richardson and his band of weirdos."

"What?"

"Yep. I drove around the square and parked in the second lot behind the new brewery, where I can keep and eye on them. I'm watching them right now, yucking it up and enjoying *our* local craft beers after LJ hurt you and while poor Harper is on house arrest. The jerk!" I could almost see steam emanating from my friend's ears. She flipped the view around, and sure enough, I could see LJ dressed in a faded denim jacket and matching jeans, standing in a group of men laughing. "I'm just calling to say I'm going over there and mess him up. If something happens to me—"

"Melanie Smart! You stay put." I was on my feet, grabbing my purse and shoving my feet into my shoes. "I'm coming to meet you."

Chapter Thirty

I flew out the door and was there in less than fifteen minutes. I'd forced Melanie to stay on the phone with me the entire time. When she got worked up, you never could tell what she'd do. She cared deeply and would do anything for her friends. And while I admired and loved that about my best friend, I did not want her to end up in a jail cell tonight. Darkness had fallen by the time I parked, and I moved through the crowd toward the brewery.

"Where are you?" Mel hissed in my ear. I'd switched to my earbuds after I parked.

"Right behind you." I could see her standing with a beer in her hand by a large maple.

Mel turned around, so swiftly her ponytail slapped a lady in the face. "Sorry." Mel made an apologetic face at the scowling woman, whose presumed boyfriend laughed and winked at Mel—a gesture his girlfriend did not care for, and she gave his tummy a little slap to the midsection before stalking off.

I was shaking my head when Mel spotted me. "God. People. You'd think I asked that guy to wink at me." Mel gave me a side hug.

"Only you." I put my earbuds back into the case and zipped it up in my purse.

"I know. Want a beer?" She took a deep sip from her cup.

"Yes. I mean, I'm here, right? And after the day we've had"— I moved aside to allow a group of giggling college girls pass— "and what I found out about my family today, I need a beer."

"Good. Me too." Mel dropped her empty cup into the metal bin, and we went to get in line. "I lost LJ because of stupid Tim."

"Seriously? Tim?" Seeing her ex always riled her up.

"Yep. He's dating Patsy's cousin." She rolled her eyes.

"I bet Patsy loves that." Our friend Patsy used to belong to the Jane Doe Book Club. But after a disagreement last year, she'd decided it was no longer for her.

We got our beers and sat on one of the cement benches in the middle of the square. The amphitheater was lit up brightly, and the smell of smoke from the barbecue food truck filled the air. For a couple of minutes, I just let myself breathe. Then I told Mel everything.

"My God." Mel looked dumbfounded. "Your poor mom." She raised her brows. "And uncle."

I nodded and sipped from my cup.

"But how does that help Harper?" She turned, her eyes wide, and grabbed my arm. "I didn't mean that how it sounded. We can totally discuss your family issues first. I just meant when Bea gave it to—"

"It's fine, Mel. I knew what you meant. I assumed that what Bea gave us would help Harper too."

"So we got nothing." Mel finished her beer.

"Yep. From the computer anyway. We still can place LJ at the scene of the crime. And we have Bea's testimony that she overheard LJ talking to my attacker. Which now I believe is linked. He wanted to scare me away from helping her. I won't stop, though."

Mel pointed. "There he is!" She grabbed my arm and pulled me upright. My beer fell from my hand. I stooped and picked it up, dropping it in the next available trash bin as we stalked after the man Mel identified as LJ and his date.

"Are you sure that's him?" In the dark, it was tough to tell. When I'd seen him before, when Mel called, he had been wearing a faded denim jacket. This guy wore a dark denim coat, and the woman hanging on him wore a leopard leotard.

"Yes. It's him."

We were heading up the sidewalk toward Smart Cookie and Cousins Investigative Services. We were on the opposite side of the street from the businesses. LJ and his group must be leaving because this far up there was nothing but parking lots. Fatigue began to settle in my bones from the day, and I lost my desire to chase LJ down.

"Hey, Mel."

She turned around and paused. "What?"

"I think we need—"

The sound of glass exploding and a chorus of shouts and screams split the night air. Mel and I gripped each other. Our bodies quaked. It took me a minute to orient myself and understand what had taken place.

"Oh my God!" I spied flames licking out of the office building across the street and a few yards ahead. Cousins Investigative Services and Smart Cookie blazed. I ran up the road but didn't dare cross the street.

My face and hands tingled. Mel shouted into her cell phone. She probably wasn't the first to dial 911 with all these people here. Police sirens were blaring. The fluttering in my chest had me panting. I spied a couple of people on the ground by the office. I rushed over and went to my knees. They were the college kids I'd seen earlier. "Are y'all okay?"

Over the cacophony, I could hardly hear a response. One of the girls was crying, and her arm looked cut up. I ripped off my jacket and wrapped it around her arm. "Come on. It isn't safe to stay here." I managed to get the group of four on their feet and across the street. EMTs arrived, and I waved them over.

I heard Melanie shouting, and I got up, smiling at the young, dark-headed girl who was having her wound cleaned. "You're going to be okay."

"Thank you," she said in a small voice and through a watery smile.

"Teresa!" Melanie waved to her cousin, who came running up the street toward Mel. "Oh, thank God! Thank God! I thought you might still be inside."

"Teresa." My hands went to my face. I hadn't even thought about the possibility she might be inside.

Mel opened her arms to her cousin as Teresa stood there bawling. "No. I just got back from dropping off the catering order. I parked the van out back and got a bit distracted because some idiots spray-painted graffiti on the backside of Cousins."

"What?" I gaped.

"Yeah. I was on the phone with the police to report it while I was walking to my car, and I heard the explosion."

"You aren't hurt, are you?" I searched Teresa's face. She shook her head. The shorter woman kept mopping at her face with the bottom of her apron. "Everyone else left before you did?"

"Yes. No one else is inside. I locked up when I left."

"Good." I let out a little sigh of relief.

"Someone did this." Melanie waved her hand toward our buildings. "My shop, my beautiful shop!"

Teresa let out a huge sob, and Mel wrapped her arm more protectively around her shoulders. I took Mel's free hand, and the three of us stood there helplessly as firefighters pulled up and rushed into action.

The temperature had dropped, and my breath made small white puffs in the air. I stood there, dazed, staring at the flicker of fire while the firemen unrolled the hoses from the truck, and a second team ran into the building. I hardly registered the next few minutes. A young EMT wrapped a silver thermal blanket around my shoulders, and I started to tell the man I hadn't been in the building, but I couldn't form the words. My mind swarmed with a flurry of worries. The warmth of the blanket didn't make it to my weary bones.

The two front windows were nothing more than frames now, and the door was gone.

Both hands went to my head. I spied a couple of extra fire-fighters running into Smart Cookie. Black smoke billowed out of the windows of the business sweet Mel had worked so hard to build. My eyes still stung, and I had difficulty focusing as I searched for where the police or EMTs had taken Mel and Teresa.

"Lyla." Rosa was in my face. "Lyla!"

I shook my head, clearing it. "Oh, Rosa." I wrapped my arms around her neck, hugging her tight. She perfunctorily patted my back, but I could tell it felt awkward for her, and I let her go. "Sorry. I'm just . . ." I couldn't think of how to finish my statement.

"It's okay. Come on. The press'll be here any minute. You're in no condition to deal with them. Where'd you park?"

"Yeah," I said, my voice sounding croaky. I cleared it. "I parked behind the brewery." I nodded in that direction.

"Oh God! Uncle Calvin!" I started fumbling with my phone. "I have to call him."

Rosa's hands closed over mine. "We've called him. We'll let the firefighters handle this, and we'll go back to your place and have a conversation." I glanced over and noticed they'd manage to put out the flames and let out a little sigh.

"My place," I mumbled. Today had just been *too* much.

"Yes. Or we can go down to the police station. The chief thought it might be better if we go to your house. With all the media coverage of your family." The way Rosa looked at me now shook me out of my funk.

I nodded. "My house is fine." I moved out of her grasp. "I'm good."

"You're sure?" She sounded concerned.

"Yes. Where are Mel and Teresa?" I shot another glance over my shoulder and spied the two of them, speaking to someone who looked like the fire chief, and staring at the now extinguished fires. *Thank God!* As Rosa had predicted, several media vans had arrived on the scene.

Mel waved in my direction, and I stopped. "Rosa, thanks for checking on me. I'm good now. I'll see you or whoever is coming to my house to take statements."

Rosa furrowed her brow. "Are you mad at me?"

My shoulders slumped, and I closed my eyes. What a god-awful day. I was starting to question the motives of my friends. "No." I opened my eyes and gave her a small smile. "Just a terrible, horrible, no good, very bad day."

She grinned at my reference to her nephews' favorite book. She'd told us how every time she saw him, he made her read it no less than a dozen times, and if she skipped a page, he'd know it, even at bedtime when his eyes were closed. "Okay."

As I drove away with nothing but the sound of the tires on the asphalt to focus on, I couldn't get LJ out of my mind. He had to be behind this. *Had to.* He'd been at the scene of the murder. He'd been at the crawl tonight. He had the most to gain if Harper went away for good. Bea said she'd overheard the conversation, and now I was going to tell Quinn. I didn't care if, in the process, I got a slap on the wrist about the computer. Or exposed my family's past. This had gone too far. Someone could have died in that fire. *Enough.*

Chapter
Thirty-One

Uncle Calvin, Melanie, Rosa, and Quinn all sat in my living room.

Mel and Calvin were on the couch. Rosa sat in a dining chair, taking notes, next to her boss, who sat on the edge of the chaise lounge.

Quinn spoke evenly and calmly. "The preliminary report is that the fire began in the back of the office and appears to be electrical. Which doesn't exactly go alone with the graffiti we found on the back of the building."

"Any ideas on who the *artists* could be?" I leaned forward. Graffiti was the least of our worries. Unless it could be linked.

"I was just about to get to that. We had a call about a group of kids vandalizing buildings. We're taking a look at the security footage you forwarded Calvin and those from the surrounding businesses." Quinn glanced up and made eye contact with me. "And it looks like the same group of kids were caught, but the message is exactly the same as the one Morales said to you."

"Strike the shepherd?" I asked. *Linked.*

"Yes," Quinn said. "Except this time, they managed a complete thought. Strike the shepherd so the sheep may scatter."

I nodded. "LJ works as an electrician, and as I mentioned to Detective Battle, was at the Ross's on a call the night his father was murdered."

"What?" Calvin studied me.

"And," Melanie rushed to add, "he was at the crawl tonight. I saw him. And Bea said she heard him on the phone the morning of the attack, giving Lyla's description to someone."

"Do you have any evidence to back your claim?" Quinn asked.

"Yes," I replied. "I spoke with Mrs. Ross and had a look at the work order. It wasn't signed by LJ, but when I called his office, the scheduler confirmed he was the second electrician they sent out on the Ross job. Just take a picture of LJ and show it to Spider."

Calvin's eyes swung toward me. "He's awake?"

I nodded. "That's what Detective Battle told me this morning. And he said the guy was talking. Apparently blathering that someone representing me paid him to attack me and shout those exact words."

This got a reaction from Calvin. His eyes hardened. "Why am I just hearing about this?"

"Because it's being handled by the police." I waved a hand toward Quinn. "Obviously, I agreed for the police to check my bank records. Especially since Spider claims I also paid fifty thousand for a hit on Leonard Richardson as well. Detective Battle asked if Mother were involved too."

Calvin's jaw clenched.

"This is the first I've heard of this," Quinn told us both.

"I thought you were liaising or whatever." I gaped.

"I'll make some calls and make sure someone gets a photo of LJ in front of him. We'll certainly need to speak with him about this fire as well."

"Oh, now we all feel better." Melanie let out a snort.

"He might have other gang members making a buck even after he got picked up. There's no accounting for criminals," I added.

Rosa lifted her pen. "Chief, you also had calls from Piper Sanchez."

Quinn glanced over at Rosa. "What calls?"

"She left messages for you about this case." She lifted a brow. "The heads-up message?"

"What? Just spit it out, Landry." Quinn sounded irritated.

"Ms. Sanchez claimed LJ threatened her when she inquired about his whereabouts the night of the murder. And he mentioned that ending, um"—she cleared her throat—"bitches like Piper and Lyla would make his day."

Go Piper! She was growing on me more and more.

"Why am I just now hearing about this? Did she file a formal complaint?"

"The call came in right before we heard about the fire, sir."

"Get back to the fire, Daniels. It's getting late. What kind of damage are we looking at?" My uncle looked like he was ready to blow a gasket.

Quinn cleared his throat and got back on track; I guess he needed to feel in charge again. "Your office is completely destroyed."

I gave Rosa a little head nod. She seemed energized by fieldwork.

"What about my cookie shop?" Mel nibbled her bottom lip, and I reached out and took her hand.

"I'm afraid the kitchen sustained the most damage."

"Oh God! We just spent twenty grand on the new commercial ovens."

"The good news," Quinn said, softening his tone, "is that the rest of the store was mostly unscathed."

Mel wiped her pale face, which a couple of tears had streaked. "I know its dumb to be so emotional over a kitchen when this could have happened when the staff and customers were in the store. And you're dealing with the gang and LJ's bullshit. He should be hanged, by the way."

I wrapped my arm across her shoulders. "It isn't dumb. You worked hard to build your business. It's a loss, for sure."

"Not dumb at all." Rosa rose and sat on the other side of Melanie, patting her knee.

Mel rested her head on my shoulder and took Rosa's hand. "Thanks, y'all. But I feel so foolish."

We tried to soothe our friend, making noises about her reactions being completely normal and understood.

"Quinn, are we done here? I think everyone is exhausted." Calvin rose.

"Yes. I've recorded Melanie's statement, and I got Teresa's before she had to get home to her kids. I'll have my officers getting in contact with the company to check up on LJ Richardson. It's best if we cover our bases. And we'll do our best to round up the vandals from the surveillance footage. They should roll pretty quickly."

Calvin nodded. He kept flexing his hand, open and closed. He seemed to be staring at nothing. I rose and walked Melanie and Rosa to the door, hugged them both, and promised to speak to them later today. I was dead on my feet.

Quinn and Calvin exchanged quiet words while I stood propped up against the open door. Too tired to be annoyed by the secrecy of their communication, I closed my eyes and ignored them. I'd find out soon enough, and all the indignation over being excluded evaporated.

Quinn's footsteps alerted me that he'd reached the place where I stood. "Give me a second outside."

Nodding, I covered my mouth while I yawned and stepped out on the stoop with him.

His eyes searched mine. "You okay here alone?"

I nodded firmly. "Yes. I'm fine."

"I got word Harper has been released into your Mother's custody."

I closed my eyes and took a deep breath. "That was fast."

"It seems your mother can move mountains when she wants to." He sighed, his shoulders slumping slightly. Fatigue was written all over him too. "I didn't know Battle came by to rattle your cage. I would have put a stop to it if I had."

"He's just doing his job. I don't really believe he thought I was involved. He's just thrashing the bushes to see if any surprises come running out that might help the defense. Which tells me something. I'm too tired to formulate what yet. But I will."

"You're a smart lady."

I squeezed his arm and held his gaze. "Thank you for everything." I wanted him to have no questions about my sincerity.

He covered my hand with his. "I care. You know that." His eyes were downcast when he spoke next. "I know you aren't interested in me romantically. I understand that too much has transpired between us. I'll always be your friend, always be here if you need me."

"I appreciate it. I truly do." I dropped my hand and stepped back inside. I wasn't against having a friendship with Quinn, and it was refreshing to hear that he understood where we were.

He lifted a hand as I closed the door. I gave him a small smile through the crack.

Chapter Thirty-Two

"Tell me what the hell you were up to today," Calvin asked when I turned back toward the living room. "For a fact, I know Jenkins notified you that we are no longer working on the Richardson case. And I get a notification of your searches, just in case you're considering lying to me."

"Calvin, do we seriously have to do this now? It's after midnight. Emotions are running high. Yours and Mel's businesses just suffered serious fire damage, Mother is housing a murder suspect, and I believe LJ has some vendetta against me and quite possibly you. Please. *Please.*"

He kept his gaze trained on me, and he hadn't moved a muscle.

Fine. I blew out a breath and counted to five. I guess we were doing this now. "I know."

"What do you mean, you know?" He narrowed his eyes at me.

"It means what it sounds like exactly. Do I need to say it aloud?"

"Yes." The one word sounded loaded.

I threw my hands in the hair and let them drop and slap against my thighs. "Fine then. I know why mother has taken an interest in Harper Richardson. I know why she doesn't want me involved. What I don't know is why she never informed my father before running off and offering her place up as a jail cell for Harper, but hey, no one tells me anything."

"What?" Calvin looked blindsided. "She what?"

Was he serious right now?

"Calvin! It was all over the news. Mother marched into the courtroom not two hours after she had some major meltdown about her past." I swallowed. "And she announced to the judge that she would be putting up bail for Harper and offering her place as lodging while she submitted to house arrest. She followed that up by making a case to the press about the injustice of this case."

He really hadn't known this. I could scarcely believe it.

"I helped a buddy out after I spoke with Jenkins," he trailed off. Calvin's face turned purple. His eyes looked wild. I'd never seen him react to anything this way before, not even when Charles had thrown up the name Folsom. I started to rethink my idea to clear the air tonight.

"God, Calvin, you look insane." The cords of his neck were bulging and so were his eyes; he gritted his teeth. "I'm sorry if I upset you."

He took a step toward me, and I took an involuntary scoot away as he spat out, "How could your mother be so careless? What is she thinking?"

I shook my head. "I think she believes she is helping a young woman in need. A mentally abused woman."

He paced the floor, and when his eyes fell on the briefcase on the chair beside the table, he froze. I'd been so out of it that I'd not even considered having stolen property in my house while Quinn was here. I guess Charles didn't know I had his computer. Perhaps Bea had already fled, and he believed she took his property. I worried for the girl.

Slowly, Calvin bent and lifted the tag. He whirled around, his nostril flaring. "Can I not trust anyone in this family to listen to me? I forbade you from seeing Charles Hammond."

Something in me snapped. My fists balled at my side; my freshly manicured nails stung my palms. I couldn't control the tremor of rage that ran through my body. "You freaking forbade me! What a misogynistic, high-handed, egotistical load of bull! You can't forbid me from doing anything."

"I'm your damn boss." His eyes were hard, cold, and intimidating. I'd never seen this side of my uncle before and certainly had never expected it to be directed at me. He'd had a background in special ops and had survived in the roughest squads in the most dangerous areas of the world. And now I knew how he'd grown up: with a father as the leader of some crazy movement. I'd been aware he was a mean SOB when he needed to be. But never ever to me.

"Not anymore," I shot back—both of us heaving. Oh my God, if this is how he acted when I mentioned Harper and Charles, I couldn't even begin to fathom his reaction to me telling him about Charles's notes. *PTSD*, my inner voice screamed. He has exhibited symptoms, no doubt about it. I wished Daddy were here. I forced myself to be calm. I picked up my bottle of water, took a sip, and then fiddled with the lid. My mind was whirling with fears, worries, and a bit of guilt from bringing any of this up. He seemed to be struggling with his own emotions.

This private man felt exposed. His business had just burned and would not be a functional workspace for some time. All of his equipment was probably destroyed. I tried to be mindful of this.

He began to pace, pausing here and there to cast a glance my way, clearly struggling with his warring emotions. I thought of the picture of the young boy and nearly broke. He'd done so well. He was a warrior. A survivor. He and my mother both. I wouldn't lie to him or patronize him. He deserved the truth.

I kept my tone low and hopefully soothing. "Charles came to the courthouse today and told me that I had no idea who I was. He said neither you nor Mother is what you appear." I held out my hand as if to try and calm a wild animal. "And right now, I don't recognize you."

"I tend to become agitated when someone who is supposed to trust me implicitly hides valuable information. This isn't the way we work, Lyla Jane Moody."

I leaned over and picked up a napkin off my table, waving it in front of his face. "I made a mistake by not telling you. I've been in the dark for so long."

He scrubbed his face with his hand.

"I'm sorry. I had no idea when I started digging that I'd dig up a life you wanted to stay buried," I said softly.

He dropped his hand and made direct eye contact with me. An expression I couldn't read flashed across his face. He opened his mouth, and his phone rang. He reached into his pocket and pulled it out, and I sat my weary self on the sofa. "What's wrong, Franny."

My phone pinged with an incoming text and image. I glanced down, and my world ended.

I have your family. Come to the house. Bring Charles's computer. No cops, or they all die. We'll be watching.

Chapter
Thirty-Three

Calvin and I sat down the street from my parents' house. He hit the steering wheel three times in succession. "Damn you, Franny, and your bleeding heart."

I sat staring straight ahead. My nails were digging into the stupid briefcase I held. My emotions oscillated between rage and terror. If Detective Battle hadn't had tunnel vision on this case, he would have seen the glaring evidence against LJ Richardson, and my family wouldn't be held captive right now. If I'd done my job better, I would have produced evidence to force the detective to look at LJ with urgency.

Calvin blew out a breath. "You clear on what you need to do?"

I nodded. We'd been over it several times. "I'm not to anger LJ or attempt to goad him in any way. I'll play to Harper's sympathies if he still has feelings for her, and hope she can talk some sense into him by letting"—I cleared my throat—"letting them live. If I appear cooperative and scared"—no problem there—"he might not frisk me everywhere." I'd taped Calvin's boot gun, a Kahr Arms P380, into my bra that had the strongest underwire. I'd been surprised by the gun's tiny size. At just barely five inches, it still could pack a punch with the right ammo and had seven-chamber capacity. If I could get by LJ, it would be a miracle. A miracle we *needed*.

"Good girl. And the second you get a clear shot?"

I met his eyes and swallowed. "Take it."

"Come on." He had his hand on the door.

Before he got out of his truck, I leaned over and flung my arms around his neck. "I love you, Uncle Calvin. You are the best uncle in the world. I'm proud to be your niece."

He hugged me back, and his arms tightened around me. "Don't count me out yet, kiddo."

"Never." I kissed his cheek.

"Okay. Time to buck up."

I nodded.

We walked slowly up the driveway and went to the front door. Uncle Calvin said LJ would tie him up straight away if LJ had any sense, and he suspected LJ had plans for him. My heart ached and my hands violently shook, but I did my best to put my fears to the back of my mind. My parents and Gran needed me. And by the look on my uncle's face, he needed me too. Now more than ever. I didn't know if LJ would hurt Harper— somewhere deep down surely he felt something for her. But I fully believed he had no compunctions with ending the rest of us if we got in his way.

The door opened and Gran stood there, her bottom lip trembling. LJ had a gun to her side. All the fear was instantly replaced with anger. Calvin gripped my wrist, and I took a deep breath, arresting the impulse to launch myself at LJ.

We stepped inside the door without a word. He handed a pair of handcuffs over to Calvin. "Put them on behind your back."

Calvin went on point, just like a setter, and I wondered if he would comply. He did, his eyes never leaving LJ in the process.

"Harper get in here and frisk Calvin and Lyla. And Granny," LJ pulled a roll of duct tape out of the back of his pants. "Tape his mouth." He tore a strip off, cutting it with his teeth and handed it to Gran.

I met her gaze and tried with all my might to will courage her way. I would save her or go down fighting. I hoped she could see the determination in my expression.

Harper came into the hallway looking like a completely different woman from the one she had been this morning. Still pale, but she'd showered and was in a Kate Spade jogging suit that came out of one of the drawers in my old bedroom. She avoided my gaze while she frisked Calvin with accuracy and efficiency, and I began to worry she'd find my gun. Perhaps she wouldn't say anything.

"He's clean." She patted his face. "Good boy."

What? My nails dug into my palm. I glanced down briefly at the half-moon shapes, forcing my whipsawing moods to settle.

Harper took the computer bag from my shoulder and swallowed. "Don't worry. It's going to be okay. If you all cooperate, we'll be out of your hair in no time."

We? My jaw started to drop and then I clenched it back into place. The truth stomped over me in a pair of military boots, and I swayed on my feet.

LJ said, "In the family room. That's where the party is. You okay with Lyla, Harp?"

"Fine." She gripped my hand. "Don't go passing out on me." LJ took Gran and Calvin into the other room. Calvin cast a surreptitious glance my way in passing, and I steeled myself.

Harper tapped her nose as if she had my number. "She's not going to risk her precious Gran getting shot. Spread 'em." She began frisking my legs.

"What are you doing?" I hissed.

"I'm looking out for myself." She stared up at me, and for a brief second, I thought about kicking her right in the face. But she was right: I wouldn't risk my family.

She huffed. "You heard them in the courtroom today. They'll find me guilty for sure. I can't do real time. If you just chill, give him what he wants, we'll be out of your hair and you can go back to your life." She moved up to my waist.

Dread knotted in the pit of my stomach. I sniffed. "And I cared so much for you. My mother cared."

"Please. People don't really care." She moved to my sides.

"I do! We loved you—the club took you into our fold. We came when you were in need. And I bent over backward to help." I swallowed, seeing she wasn't swayed. I played the only card I had to play. "I was terrified about how I was going to tell you about your aunt."

She froze then and stopped frisking me. "You found her?"

I nodded and swallowed. Her eyes began to water, and I began to believe perhaps she could still be an ally. I needed her.

"Harper!" LJ bellowed.

She sniffed and waved her hand. "Go on." I thanked my lucky stars that my news had distracted her enough to avoid her finding my gun. It was something.

"She clean?" LJ asked when we entered the room. I took in the sight of my parents gagged and tied to dining chairs set up in the living room. Despite all the sensible things I kept telling myself—how I could talk some sense into the LJ, how Harper wouldn't let this go too far, and how I was strong enough to handle this—I became increasingly afraid. My hands began to shake, and I clenched my fists to force them still.

LJ steadily worked on securing a gagged Calvin to a chair. Tears streamed down Gran's and Mother's faces. Daddy looked both helpless and furious at me for coming. He would've wanted me to call the police and save myself. *How could I do that?* They were everything to me. My gun, cold and hard against my skin, reminded me we still had a chance. I glanced at the gun in the back of LJ's pants, and I moved my hand to the top of my high-waisted jeans. Calvin who watched me like a hawk, gave his head the tiniest shake.

"Go on." Harper nudged me to the vacant chair by the fireplace.

I sat down, and she grabbed the rope and began tying me up. "Did you really find her?" she whispered, and I felt the bite of the rope into the delicate place on my wrists.

"Yes." I glanced at Calvin, feeling like I should have taken that chance. When would I ever get another? We could all be dead in a matter of minutes.

"Find who?" LJ wanted to know.

"My aunt Phyllis."

He gave Harper a glare. "We agreed."

She rolled her eyes. "I know. The past is the past. We're starting over."

I had to do something. "She's dead," I blurted. "Your aunt. She was executed by a gunshot in the forehead, and someone sunk her car in a chemical waste pond."

Harper's eyes were wide, and she gasped. She moved around to face me. Big huge tears ran from her eyes. "Are you sure it's her?"

"Yes." I spoke with urgency. "It isn't too late, Harper. I found evidence that LJ was—" And the next thing I knew a hand slapped me hard, and I hit the floor.

Chapter Thirty-Four

My head spun and I tasted blood. I was still tied to the chair, in an awkward position on my side. I wriggled my wrists against the rope and felt a hot, burning sensation. LJ loomed over me and reared back to kick me. Mother and Gran screamed behind their gags. Daddy and Calvin roared against their restraints.

"What the hell is going on in here?" Charles bellowed, standing in the doorway between the family room and my father's office. I blinked through blurry vision to focus on his face.

Harper and LJ whirled around, and both seemed to cower. *Cower?*

Oh my God. Bea had tried to tell me. Charles *was* the ringleader. Something I would have discovered if I'd had more time to dig. When Charles saw me, half tied to the chair and, I was sure by the sting in my cheek, with a welt across my face, his face reddened. His eyes bulged, and he rushed into the room, grabbed Harper by the upper arms, and flung her against the couch.

"Hey!" LJ stood and came at Charles. Charles, ignoring the gun, reared back and punched LJ right in the face. The man fell to one knee and shook his head.

Charles knelt down in front of me and ran his fingers over my cheek and brandished a knife. I sucked in a breath.

He put a hand on my shoulder, and I flinched. "It's okay. I'm going to cut you lose."

LJ stood up, still shaking his head, and I gasped as blood streamed from his nose. I was afraid he'd start shooting. Instead, he said, "We didn't want her to do anything stupid. You said to make sure she was here when you arrived. We thought she might run."

"So you hit her, tied her to a chair, and were about to kick her? You're on dangerous ground." Charles's lip curled as he glared at LJ, who cast his gaze toward his shoes. Wow. Charles had these under some weird mind control. My heart sank to my feet before it began pounding. He'd fed Leonard's delusions.

Charles helped me to my feet. "Don't be frightened. You're in no danger. They won't hurt you anymore." He gazed at me as if I were a damsel in distress and in need of his rescue. And with something else I tried to place. Adoration? Obsession? *Dear God.* "Where's my computer?"

I glanced around.

"Here." Harper handed it over to him. "Oh, Lyla. I can literally see the wheels turning inside your head. Just like something out of those crazy novels you read." She put her finger to her chin and said in mock falsetto, "Someone poisoned my husband, and the killer is still in this house." She rubbed her arms where Charles had grabbed her but showed no discomfort. "Isn't it funny that all along the most crooked house was your own?"

"Stop it," Charles said firmly.

"Is that the Netflix movie with Glenn Close in it?" LJ asked and moved closer to Harper.

I couldn't believe my eyes or ears. Harper and LJ chatted as if everything transpiring—kidnapping, assault, and blackmail—was completely ordinary. LJ went on as if Charles had never slugged him. Almost like he was accustomed to such behaviors. I studied their faces. If they had any compunctions, their faces didn't belie or betray it.

"Yeah. It's stupid. I would have killed off more people. Made it like a horror flick." Harper rolled her eyes elaborately.

"I said, stop." Charles voice came out cold and menacing. He spoke to them as if they were subservient. And they shut up. I'd remember that.

Charles pointed at Harper. "You were honored to be a part of her group. Perhaps you should have paid attention, and you could have learned to be a woman of honor." Charles took my hand and led me over to the leather love seat. Harper stuck her tongue out at him when his back was turned. She made a gun with her fingers and acted like she was shooting everyone. I stared in gape-mouthed surprise, then forced my mouth closed. At any moment LJ could unload on everyone. I had to force myself not to look at my family anymore. I needed to focus. The simplest answer is usually the correct one.

"You looked through my files?" Charles pulled my attention to him. I noticed he didn't sound angry a bit. My mind spun, knowing everyone's life was riding on my ability to control this situation.

I struggled but managed to focus on his face, understanding now that Charles was brutal to uncooperative and disloyal people. "You wanted me to? You had Bea give it to me?" I couldn't believe how stupid I'd been.

"Not exactly. I just maneuvered a few things, knowing how Beatrice would react. It was the best way for you to discover the truth. I knew that you, with your clever mind, wouldn't stop. You need answers. All I needed to do was supply you with the pieces, and you'd put the puzzle together."

I closed my eyes. "Leonard didn't really want to restart the movement, did he?"

"No. Leonard had dementia. He wasn't reliable." He held out his hand. "LJ, bring it here."

LJ dragged a duffle bag from behind the couch out onto the rug. He put on a set of gloves and then pulled the missing candlestick out of the bag. It was bloody and had tissue stuck to it. *What monsters.*

He brought it over to Charles, who looked at me. "You saw who Frances was in the movement?"

I nodded, trying to keep my eyes off the object LJ held. "Um, I believe I read that she was a mother of the movement."

He smiled and an audible heart-wrenching sob left my mother's lips. When her eyes met mine, she deflated like a pricked balloon with all the helium swiftly escaping. I struggled to remain seated, taking in a deep, quavering breath.

Charles took my chin gently in his fingers and turned my face back to his. "Right. And I came from the other mother of the movement."

How had I not seen the wild, crazy glint in this man's eyes before? He actually believed that he and I were destined to be together. I could read that all over his face. Yet I could also read that he wasn't sure if he could trust me.

"Hold out your hands, please." And now he would black-mail me so that I could never leave. And if that were possible, that would mean he didn't plan to leave any other witnesses alive.

I did as he commanded. My mind raced with how I was going to get us all out of this mess. When LJ put the heavy object into my hands, hot tears ran down my cheeks. "'Strike the shepherd.' You were referencing the past—when my grandmother alerted the authorities to the group and the house was raided."

He wiped the tears away with his thumb. "Grip the candlestick, please."

I did. "You had me attacked." I tried to look hurt. It was difficult to behave this way with an audience, but for some reason Charles wanted them to see us interact. He made it a point to not even acknowledge that they were there, which to me screamed of his need to punish my mother and uncle.

He had LJ take the candlestick from my hand and took both my hands in his. I had to fight to remain still.

"That went horribly wrong." He glared over at LJ and frowned. "He wasn't supposed to attack you. Just someone near you. We had to improvise afterward." *By telling the police I'd been the one to hire Spider to attack me.*

"Hey, man, I told you that guy couldn't be trusted to follow directions." He shrugged his shoulders. "Gangbangers, whatcha gonna do."

I blinked, trying to maintain composure. "But LJ *is* responsible. Bea told me that she overhead LJ describing me to someone on the phone." I glared at LJ and did a little improvising myself. "And told them to go at me *hard.*"

"Bea lies!" LJ's face paled.

I allowed my gaze to flitter toward Calvin in my natural turn back to Charles. Calvin's head bobbed an infinitesimal amount. He was encouraging me. I was doing well.

Charles's glare promised LJ pain. He turned back to me. "Spider was supposed to tase someone else. Anyone else but you. And when you ran, I was going to be there for you. It was supposed to connect us and open the door. You'd want to know what 'Strike the shepherd' referred to, and I planned to enlighten you."

He released his hold on my hands when he pointed at my mother. "You're right. Frances and Calvin's evil beast of a mother took a strike at the shepherd when she reported the movement to the police and spread all those vile lies. We all scattered like sheep, and your grandfather went away to prison. Father Bingham died there." He turned to glare at my mother and Calvin. "Did you know that?"

Mother and Calvin both had the same air of defiance. Although I respected it, I wished they wouldn't goad him. I let out a little sigh of relief when he turned back to me. "What your uncle and mother didn't understand was how powerful the teachings are. That when you're destined for greatness, it happens no matter what. Despite all the evildoers' efforts to stomp us out." He smiled. "Here we are, you and I, together as we should be. I searched and searched for you once I came of age. My mother never let me forget my purpose. She helped me search, and on her death bed I swore I'd find you."

"And Leonard? You had to kill him?"

"Yes. When I saw he couldn't be depended on, I corrected his will first, and he signed the will in front of his lawyer. It's binding. All the money will go to us." He meant himself. There was no *us*. If he managed to get me away—and I'd rather die— he'd be determined to control me.

"Where'd the meds come from?" *I bet they were his.*

"Mine. All it took was a little google search to convince the stupid doctor that I needed them."

I'm sure it didn't take much convincing. This guy was a lunatic.

"I'd been on something similar in my early twenties. They wanted to alter my natural thought processes. That's around the time I found a message board and found Leonard. When he proved to be problematic, I had Harper dose him. Just a little here and there to build it up in his system. Then on the night of the event, she gave him the killing dose."

Oh. My. God. I stared at Harper.

"Don't give me that Goody-two-shoes look," Harper swore. "You hated him along with me when I told you how my life was. LJ and I needed his money. You heard Charles—Leonard was losing his mind. And Charles is the one who brained him, not me."

"Don't worry." Charles stroked my arm in what I think he believed was a soothing manner, when, in fact, it was creepy and made me feel ill. "You're not going to witness anything awful again."

I'm not going to witness. Meaning it's going to happen when I'm gone?

"Our enforcer needs to take the fall for the tragedy that will occur here tonight. He knows the rules for abandoning the cause." Charles shook his head. "You'll learn the ways. You'll be perfect." He stroked my hair, and I fought not to flinch. "I'm telling you all of this so you know that I will never lie to you again. We'll start over fresh."

Harper laughed. "Oh, Charles are you in for it." She stood up and stretched. "That one is not the humble little housewife and baby factory you thinks she is. You might as well give up like I told you in the beginning, when you came up with this plan."

Harper moved closer to me, and Charles did nothing to discourage her. Harper ran her finger along my shoulder. "I mean, my part was brilliant. I befriend Lyla and her book club while behaving pitifully, making everyone think that stupid old man controlled me. Then I reach out to the damaged matriarch of Lyla's family." She moved to dance around Mother, and my gun itched to be used. "Get her to offer help, and then the family will take the fall. And I go free."

LJ grinned at her and she beamed back, and I wanted to wipe those smiles right off their wicked faces. "How did your aunt factor in?"

Calvin swallowed. *Dangerous ground,* I read from him.

Harper froze and then frowned. "She didn't."

LJ's expression turned serious. "Okay. Look. If Harper and I are going to go underground for a while, we need to get out of here before daylight. And we won't have long after I cut the ankle monitor off her. We have a schedule to keep, Charles."

Harper turned to Charles, and her breath sped up. "Did you kill my aunt?"

Charles raised both his hands and smiled. "Not me."

Harper whirled on LJ and frowned. "Was it you?"

"Baby, what did we say?" He closed the distance between them and wrapped his arms around her. She shoved him away.

"Naughty, naughty." Charles shook his finger in my face. He could tell what I was doing. "There's no way to save your family. Like LJ said, the past must stay there."

I forced my lips up in a hesitant smile. "This is all so new to me. I'm going to need time."

He studied me, not buying my innocent act. I had to work fast.

I blew out a breath. "Look. I'll be honest. I'm angry that Harper took advantage of me. I tried to be a loving and kind friend to her. How can I trust *anyone* when those who were closest to me betrayed me? You recruited two people to hurt me."

He opened his mouth.

I held up a hand. "You say your intentions were different, but that's what happened." I put my hand to my chest and forced all the emotion I was feeling for my family into this one moment. Tears welled in my eyes, and I let them fall as my voice broke. "How can I trust you when you are planning to hurt those I love? They're my family. Let them go and I'll come willingly."

His brows drew together, and he seemed to be considering my words. "That makes sense to me. You have no way of knowing that I'm completely on your side and you can trust me with everything." He took my face in his hands. "I can fix this. I can prove myself."

Hope bloomed within me. Maybe we could get out of this without bloodshed. I could keep this up.

He stood and faced the group. "Change of plans." In a blur, he whipped a gun from the back of his pants and shot Harper.

I screamed as Harper fell against the wall, sliding down. He turned to LJ, who bellowed Harper's name, and Calvin, still tied to the chair, lunged.

Another shot went off, and Daddy fell to his side. He struggled, working to get free. I didn't dare look at Mother or Gran, or I would lose my nerve. Calvin's chair broke, but his hands were still cuffed and blood pooled around him.

I ripped my gun from under my shirt, tearing skin. I couldn't have cared less.

"You're dead, Charles!" LJ pulled his gun, but Charles lunged and knocked it free. Both men fought for purchase of the weapon, the blood causing a slippery struggle.

While they fought, I scanned the area, vacillating momentarily. I didn't have time to call for help. I spied the knife on the floor, the knife they'd used to cut the rope, and went for it. I used it to cut Harper's ankle monitor, which took a little doing. She was unconscious, and Charles and LJ were still grappling. I checked her neck and she still had a pulse. The bullet had struck her in the chest, but high up near the shoulder. She'd need an ambulance, but I thought she'd live. The cops should be here in minutes now. I knew how that worked: her severed monitor would be setting off alarm bells, and the police were not going to let a murderer get away. I glanced over at the most important women in my life and mouthed, "It's going to be okay," before I went into autopilot, acting on one impulse to the next.

The gun Charles had used was next to Calvin, and not sure if Calvin was conscious, I kicked it away. I didn't want either Charles or LJ lunging for it.

I fired two shots over their heads. *"Stop!"*

Both men froze. One head lifted and then the other as they got to their knees to face me. Hands raised. LJ looked murderously at me. "Bitch," he spat.

"Throw those cuff keys over here."

I thought I would have to do more threatening, but LJ dug them out of his pocked and threw them, hitting me square in the chest. Never taking my eyes off them, I kicked them over to my father, who jerked his hands free from the ropes as he lay on the floor.

Charles appeared shocked. "I wanted to show you that you could count on me. I wanted to erase the damage by getting rid of those who did you harm. I can still fix it." He started to rise.

"Don't." I warned, and he didn't.

"You're so magnificent. We have a destiny; can't you see that? You read my notes. Our life will be holy and amazing. We'll change the world."

"She doesn't love you. Look at her. She's just like her mother. The one you hate so much." LJ snatched the gun from between them, and I fired, winging him.

"Thank you." I moved toward Mother and Charles's lips curled. "We're tough as nails," I whispered, and to my surprise, she smiled, tears streaming down her cheek.

"Calvin, you better be alive." I kept my gun on the two men as I nudged his side gently with my foot, while my father released him from his cuffs.

Calvin came to and rolled onto his back with a groan. He wiped the blood from his face and surveyed his body. "Fine. Just a shot in the leg."

"Charles, take off your shirt and toss it to my uncle."

Charles did as I asked, looking defeated and pretty darn pissed off.

My father stooped down and helped Calvin tie the shirt around his leg.

When he rose to his full height, he placed a hand on my shoulder. "Give that gun to me now, honey."

Sirens blared and I smiled. "I got this. You untie Mother and Gran."

Chapter Thirty-Five

The Jane Doe Book Club meeting was in full swing when I slipped onto one of the padded folding chairs in the back of the library conference room. The chatter and laughter brought a smile to my face. Melanie stood at the front of the room and wildly gesticulated while discussing her thoughts about *A Stranger in the House* by Shari Lapena.

Amelia slid down the row next to me and put an arm across my shoulder, hugging me. "How'd the therapy session go?"

I smiled. "Tell you about it after."

"I'll get you a cup of coffee. I've got a couple of offers to present to your parents after this meeting."

"Oh, that's terrific!" I whispered.

Amelia smiled and hopped up, heading for the refreshment table.

After the police showed up at my parents' house that awful night and arrested Charles, Harper, and LJ, we all went to a hotel and just processed for a few nights. Amelia listed my childhood home a week later. Now my parents were living in an excellent rental while their new home was under construction. It would be a fresh start for everyone. There was no hiding the past any longer. Charles, who hadn't been technically insane, still touted the destiny he believed we shared. He told anyone and everyone who would listen. And last I heard, he was writing his novel from his jail cell, where he'd spend the rest of his life.

Harper and LJ were also serving similar sentences. Harper rolled on LJ and Charles for a lighter sentence. She'd probably be out on parole by the time she was forty. The paper ran front-page stories about my mother and uncle's past and how it was linked to the Richardson murder for weeks. Piper got the first headline, and now she'd been offered several jobs at much larger papers, plus local television had expressed interest. She'd earned the promotion, for sure.

All of us, including Mother, participated in weekly therapy sessions, and it was helping the family get over past hurts and move into the future stronger. Well, everyone but Uncle Calvin. He said it wasn't for him. He seemed to be managing, and we all respected his decision. It would be a long, arduous journey to healing, but we'd get there. I no longer harbored hard feelings toward my mother or uncle for keeping me in the dark. I had no idea how I would have reacted in their situation.

Things were improving, and that's all that mattered to me. Mother and I started a new charity explicitly funded to help those trapped in horrific relationships or lifestyles. We joined with another group who helped those in imminent life-threatening situations disappear for a while. It was one of the most rewarding ventures of my life. Like the Jane Doe cases I worked on, the women deserved to have their identities restored and to live meaningful lives; these people deserved a chance to live and be safe.

Amelia handed me my cup of coffee, and my Gran came hurrying into the room. Out of all of us, she was doing the best.

Gran could shift gears swiftly and was always living her best life. "Hey, my fellow Jane Does!" She waved as if everyone had been waiting for her to arrive.

"Daisy! Glad you made it!" some of the women called out, and several hopped up to hug her.

I laughed to myself. Maybe the Jane Does had been waiting for her. She took a seat next to me.

She took my coffee from me. "Thank you for this. I was craving a good cup of hot coffee."

"Sure." I shook my head. Her hair was all wild about her head. "What happened to your hair?"

"Helmet hair. My new honey drives a three-wheeler motorcycle. He gave me a ride."

Amelia let out a giggle, and the book conversation halted. Everyone was turning around, staring at Gran. She began to give them all the juicy gossip about the new love of her life—a man she'd picked up from the senior center.

My phone pinged, and I dug it from my bag. Brad had texted me.

Gran texted me. We're going on a double date with her and her new fella tonight?

"Gran?" I tapped her on the shoulder to draw her attention away from her adoring fans.

She leaned over and I showed her the message. "Oh yeah, I set it all up. I'll show you how to reel that man in." Gran winked at me, and the whole group roared into laughter.

I shook my head, marveling, at how life just goes on. And with Gran around, it was a hoot. I wouldn't have it any other way.

Acknowledgments

I'd like to thank all those who had a hand in bringing this book to publication. I'm incredibly grateful to my agent, Dawn Dowdle, for helping me find a home for this series at Crooked Lane Books.

Thanks to the people who work diligently to bring it all together. To the team at Crooked Lane Books: Melissa Rechter, who picked up the ball and made the transition to a new editor a smooth one. The illustrator, Mary Ann Lasher, for the gorgeous cover, Madeline Rathle for marketing, and the copyeditors and proofreaders who make the book shine.

To Jackie Shephard, who is always willing to beta read and is eager to get the word out on an upcoming release, you're a rock star! A big shout-out to my Jane Doe Book Club street team. Thanks for all the support.

Thanks to my children, extended family, and friends for being my personal cheering section. And last but not least, to my husband, John. For being my anchor. It's everything.